Dead to Rights

Brand of Justice
Book 8

Lisa Phillips

eBook ISBN: 979-8-88552-241-0

Paperback ISBN: 979-8-88552-242-7

Published by: Two Dogs Publishing, LLC. Idaho, USA

Cover Design by: Sasha Almazan and Gene Mollica, GS Cover Design Studio, LLC

Edited by: Christine Callahan, Professional Publishing Services

Dead to Rights

Chapter One

Kenna Banbury, private investigator, didn't feel "normal" often. Not like regular folks who stood in line at the bank on Friday at lunchtime. The chance to be one of them, even if it was only for a few minutes, gave her an anonymity she liked.

Seemed like everyone from the town was in this slow line for the teller counters. Not true, given the size of this town an hour outside of Vegas. It just felt that way with the crowd in here right now cashing their paychecks.

Not why Kenna was there.

Despite the fact she felt decidedly normal right now, she'd felt a nudge to put on a bulletproof vest before she came in here. She didn't often wear them, and not usually in daylight.

A baby started to cry. Kenna glanced over and saw a young mother, a teller over at the front of the line, start that steady push-pull with the stroller. The crying went down a notch, but not by much. Across the counter from her, the uniformed employee—with a lime-green starched shirt and hair that kind of exploded in curls on the top of his head— scrunched up his face.

Instinct walked with what felt like icy fingers down the back of her neck, continuing their descent along her spine.

Kenna peered under the bangs of the blonde wig she had secured over her dark hair. Her contact, the teller at the front of this line, hadn't noticed anything. Noelle Hieron hadn't seen the...what? A barely discernible shift in the air.

Something else?

She rolled the shoulders of the thin jacket, grateful they had the air-conditioning in here set to *arctic*. The cool air helped her disguise the fact that she had a bulletproof vest on. Skinny jeans, as always, though these were military green and had cargo pockets on the sides. Her feet were in black boots she'd only laced halfway up.

Why had she felt that nudge to wear the protective vest?

She was a new Christian and had often operated based on a "gut" instinct. Now, it could be something called "discernment" that she was supposed to have—or be able to ask for. She wasn't sure yet where the dividing line was between her instinct and God leading her.

She checked her watch.

"What is it?" Maizie asked. Her voice didn't detract from the murmurs around Kenna.

The teen was currently two states away in a trailer, but that didn't mean she couldn't see what was happening in the credit union. She'd probably hacked the whole network and downloaded everything on their servers. And now she was watching the lobby feed.

Kenna tilted her head, not loving the heat under the wig.

"Dunno." No one would think anything of Kenna, earbuds in, talking to someone while in line for the bank. Not these days.

"Yet," Maizie said.

A pop cracked over the open phone line. The unmistakable sound of Maizie smacking bubble gum. Her newest obsession. Given everything she had been through so far in her life, it seemed like a normal teenage thing and nothing to worry about. But Kenna had called Elizabeth anyway, and the counselor said they should let Maizie express herself.

Kenna didn't know if she'd ever been given permission to do that in *her* life. But it sounded good for a girl who'd been tightly controlled and abused emotionally and physically for years to feel as if she had the freedom to do a few things simply because she wanted to. Safely test some boundaries.

Elizabeth's husband, Stairns, Kenna's former boss at the FBI—and the reason she no longer worked there—had given her a long explanation about daughters and how it worked having one. He had three. However, his speech only led her to believe he had no clue, even if he made it sound like he knew what he was talking about. Both of them would give their lives to keep Maizie safe, making it the perfect place for her to heal.

"Speaking of," Maizie began, "a van just pulled up. Outside in the alley by the west door."

Kenna wouldn't get to the front of the line by the time the van's occupants came in.

"Four men got out. Thirties. Plain clothes," Maizie continued. "Running them through facial recognition now."

Kenna leaned to the side and looked at Noelle. The thirtysomething woman caught Kenna's gaze and blinked.

No kidding. It was called a disguise for a reason.

Noelle shifted, and dark hair swung on either side of her face. Her features had a strong Native American indication, giving her glowing clear skin and dark eyes that helped customers find her warm and welcoming.

The door into the bank swung open, and three men strode in, carrying rifles and duffels. Wearing tan stockings over their faces to disguise their features and make them look scary. It worked. Someone screamed. The baby started to cry louder again.

"Everyone on the ground over there!" The lead guy motioned with his shotgun. "This is a robbery!"

Everyone froze.

Where is the fourth guy?

A suited man ran for the door and got clocked on the head with the butt of a rifle. The crack of metal on bone made someone whimper. The man slumped to the ground in a heap.

The first two gunmen through the door swung AR-15s around while the other broke off to the side, brandishing a shotgun.

Kenna pressed her lips into a thin line, pretending she'd frozen with the others. She knew exactly what they had come for, and it wasn't money.

The guy in front of her swung around. She ducked behind his girth, knowing he wasn't tall enough to completely disguise her.

Maizie said, "Hold."

Kenna froze. Where was... Noelle had disappeared behind the counter. Hopefully.

The gunman said, "You come with me," and a woman yelped.

Another guy said, "Six minutes."

In her earbud, Kenna heard, "Okay, go."

She scurried through the crowd in the confusion and caught up in time to see two customers dart down the back hall along with three employees. Where was Noelle? Hopefully, someone behind the counter had hit the hidden button that would alert the police.

That meant they had minutes until the building would be surrounded by the local Quick Response Team, armed to the teeth. Snipers on the roof. Did this town have a unit like that? Kenna couldn't get what she had come here for and then run out the back way, or she'd wind up detained. Or taken out.

Noelle wasn't behind the counter. Had she already run down the hall?

One of the men who'd run shoved an older woman, an employee, against the wall in the hallway and sprinted for the EXIT door at the end.

A gunman appeared in the doorway, silhouetted from the bright noon sun outside. The two men stumbled to slow their sprint, realizing too late the threat ahead. Boxed in with nowhere to go and a gunman in front of them.

Kenna held the woman's arm, steadying her, and shoved open the closest door. "Come on." She tugged the woman into the tiny room, a closet by the look of it, while the gunman was distracted by the others.

In her ear, Maizie said, "Watch—"

Gunshots cracked down the hall. Kenna's shoulders tensed, bringing them up toward her ears while she winced and ducked her head. She slipped into the closet and pushed the door closed behind her.

Stacked shelves with reams of paper and toner for the printer. Cleaning supplies on the opposite wall, brushes and mops hanging off the floor. A bucket below them.

One tiny window lighting the room.

No exit.

"They're going to kill us." The woman had paled, dark circles visible under her eyes even with the makeup she had on. Dark gray dress pants and the credit union uniform shirt. She had a gold chain around her neck with a tiny cross. Short hair above her ears, curled and styled—now mussed. Pink nails and a smartwatch.

"Tell me what your name is." Kenna stood between the woman and the closed door, wondering if, at any moment, the door would swing open, and they'd both be shot. She needed an update from Maizie on the situation in the bank lobby—and with Noelle.

"Cassandra Myers."

"Okay. I'm Kenna," the PI replied, keeping her voice low. "We're going to stay in here and stay quiet." She was also going to pray. She wanted to ditch the wig, but she needed to stay disguised if these guys were here for what she thought they might be.

Cassandra started to speak.

Kenna cut her off, lifting a finger for her to hold up. But she moved hair back over her ear so Cassandra could see the earbud and turned away, giving the woman her profile. "What's going on in the lobby?"

"They cut the cameras," Maizie said.

"Pros?"

"I'd say yes. I'm going back over their entry, looking for markers I can use to try and identify them. Facial recognition has no hits so far." Maizie had spat out the gum from the sound of it, now completely focused on the situation unfolding in the bank.

"Copy that." Kenna needed to get to Noelle and find out what was going on.

She could hear...something in the hall. A grunt. She reached to the back of her belt and palmed a stun gun. She turned the handle as slow and quiet as she could and peered through the slit that opened between the door and the frame. Stun gun ready.

A man slammed into the door, shoving it open. The door clipped her shoulder before it knocked against the shelves and rattled the toner.

Kenna jabbed him with the stun gun, her thumb already on the button. *Crackle.*

His body stiffened, and he fell to the floor.

She looked out in both directions but saw no one. "Cassandra, run for the exit." Then she swiped up his gun and checked it. "I'll cover you if necessary."

The woman hadn't moved.

Kenna glanced at her to find even more shock on her face. Wide eyes, mouth open, staring. "Cassandra." She reached over and tugged the woman again. "Get out. Run."

The woman stopped before the open door.

"Go." Kenna shoved Cassandra and turned the corner, gun up. Facing the lobby end of the hall.

Cassandra's shoes shuffled and squeaked on the floor.

The exit bar on the door clicked, and Kenna heard the drone of traffic outside. A couple of seconds later, she heard it shut.

"Good?" Maizie asked.

"Clear." But Kenna didn't want to get caught in a gunfight. She needed ID on these guys as much as she needed to get to Noelle and get what she came for before they took it first.

She backed up into the closet, praying none of the guys in the lobby had heard the door close, and came to investigate the fate of their friend—or anyone in his path.

Two customers lay dead in the hall. Cassandra must have stepped over them to get out.

Kenna snapped a photo with her phone of the gunman's

face, then checked his pockets but found no ID and no phone. He would come around soon enough—hopefully in time for the police to find him. She used plastic ties to secure his feet together, and then his wrists.

Maizie said, "Got it."

"Find out who he is." Kenna closed the door, swinging the rifle over her shoulder so she could get to it if it came to that, but hoping it didn't. She had no intention of facing down multiple gunmen in the process of robbing a bank if she could help it.

Even wearing a vest.

"Gonna get the surveillance back up and running?" Maizie asked.

"Nope." Kenna stopped at the end of the hall and peered around. There wasn't time for that, even if she could somehow find the system and reboot the program.

Two of the bank robbers watched over the customers and staff, standing close together, which had them engaged in a whispered conversation. She watched for a couple seconds, surveying the tops of heads—glad no one noticed her peering into the room.

Noelle was nowhere to be seen.

Her eye in the sky said, "Next time, you should wear a bodycam, and I'll rig it to transmit to me live."

Kenna heard a noise in the direction of another hallway on the far end of the counter. The complete opposite corner than the one she'd run to. *Great.* The only way to get down there would be to crawl along the floor behind the counter down to the far end and then sneak into that hall.

Without being seen.

Who was down there?

Did they have Noelle in there, opening the safe deposit box? Excuse me. That was *her* stuff to steal. Noelle knew it belonged to Cecelia because she'd met the woman. The Special Agent in Charge of the Phoenix FBI office kept a safe deposit box hours away from her home and work in a random Nevada town at a tiny credit union.

Which had to mean there was something important in the box here.

Kenna had offered Noelle five grand to take a look and promised not to remove anything. Cecelia would never know she'd come here and looked at the safe deposit box. The teller, Noelle, was the same woman who was going to pass her evidence on Cecelia Warren—the dirty FBI agent Kenna had been trying to take down for six months now.

Kenna had her stun gun and the rifle. The three men who had come in the front door now made up the four who'd exited the van that Maizie had seen if she added the guy trussed up in the closet. That meant one out of sight right now, possibly hurting her informant.

The serial killer "Walker," known south of the border as *El Caminante*, had racked up more kills with no conceivable rhyme or reason to the victims he chose or the manner of death. It was becoming more and more impossible to attribute deaths to him. Even ones she believed he was responsible for. He seemed to have gone dark—even the FBI was spinning its wheels.

Meanwhile her search for evidence against Cecelia had led her to the middle of a bank robbery.

"Hey!"

Kenna heard the cry to her left, out of her field of vision. But she knew what it meant. She spun, bringing the rifle up.

The shot slammed into her vest, front and center.

Her body flinched. Pain exploded in her chest, and she cried out at the searing pain. The world around her washed into an odd darkness, and she got that falling sensation as if her mind sucked her down, back into the past.

The door slammed open. "FBI! Drop the gun! Drop it!" A gun exploded.

Kenna slumped to the ground.

Angeline Pacer also hit the floor in front of her. Dead.

Consciousness swam in and out like the tide. Each roll brought a wave of pain. Her chest was on fire.

"Kenna." He bit out a curse. "Yes, this is FBI Special Agent Jaxton. I need an ambulance. Now."

Chapter Two

"Jax." Kenna managed to gasp. Next up was figuring out how bad it was.

She slapped a hand on her front, hoping to put pressure on... Her fingers touched the hot round embedded in the vest.

She could hear Maizie yelling from somewhere. The earbud.

The gunman.

He stood over her still. She wasn't in her RV facing down Angeline Pacer, Bradley's mother. She hadn't been shot in the chest. *Again.* The past wasn't here, and now, it was over. Washed clean. The things she'd been through lived in her mind, but today was a new day. Every moment was a chance to make the right choice. Take a step.

Get shot in the vest.

Thank You, God.

Maybe it was instinct, and maybe it was some kind of spiritual discernment. Either way, the forethought to wear a vest today had saved her life.

"What the..." He stared down at her. "You're wearing a

vest? You some kind of cop, huh? I'll put a bullet in your head right now."

Kenna lifted her hands, splaying her fingers. "I'm not a cop."

Only how was she going to explain the vest?

She sucked in a breath, and it *hurt*.

"I'm losing patience."

"I'm a bodyguard. Protective detail. I'm on my lunch-break." She could tell him her client's identity was secret, and she'd signed a nondisclosure. Something like that.

The gunman leaned down. "I would've believed cop better."

Kenna moved before instinct, or the thought of whether this was a good idea or not, could germinate. She swung out with her legs, swiped them to the side, and slammed them into his knees. He hit the ground, and she pushed with the rubber soles of her boots, sliding her body away from him across the floor. Then she scrambled to her feet.

The rifle she'd grabbed off the other guy, the one she'd trussed up in the closet, lay too far away.

He got up as well and came toward her.

"Enough." A man stepped into the hall behind him. "She works for me, and she will not be harmed."

Ramon.

As far as partners went, she would much prefer to be working with Jax. However, her boyfriend worked out of the San Diego FBI office, so she saw him when she could. As often as they were able to meet up and spend time together. Dating. They'd been in a comfortable season of dinners, hiking, and doing normal couple stuff for six months now.

And thinking about it more than in passing was going to get her killed.

Ramon, on the other hand might be her partner, but she

usually had no idea he was even around. He showed up when he wanted and promptly disappeared. However, given that he lived on the run, she didn't blame him. Cecelia had destroyed his life. The only thing Kenna and Ramon had in common was the fact they were both trying to take her down. Expose her.

Thus far, Ramon hadn't tried to assassinate Cecelia, and Kenna didn't want to ask why not. It would solve some of his problems but not all of them.

"Is that right?" The gunman faced off with Ramon.

Her friend wore a suit, making him look like a banker who probably had a side job as an enforcer for a cartel. Even if that might be stereotyping, it had been his job when she met him, so likely he wouldn't mind.

"Four minutes."

The gunman snapped into action, swinging the gun to her and then waving it at Ramon. "Both of you over to the corner with the rest of the hostages. No more trouble, or you both die."

Ramon let her pass him and followed her. They sat on the floor with the group of customers and staff. *Four minutes.* Did they know how long local law enforcement response would be? They might be planning on leaving before they showed up.

As long as they didn't take what she'd come for with them.

Ramon shifted, clearly uncomfortable in his suit on the floor. Kenna took a deep breath and winced at the pain in her chest.

"Better than being shot."

She glanced at him. "I know that because I've *been* shot there."

He chuckled slightly. "Your wig is falling."

Kenna righted it, checking her ears for the earbuds. One

was lodged in tangled strands. She had no idea where the other had landed. She eased the one she had in her ear. "Maizie?"

"No talking!"

Kenna pressed her lips together and scanned the bank lobby. At least what she could see from the floor in the corner. Thankfully sort of clean. Gleaming counters. The center island where folks wrote out deposit slips. Cubicles along the wall to the right, between the hostages and that back hall. Across the room by the door was the hall to the vault, tucked away from sight behind the counter.

In her ear, Maizie said, "You freaked me out. I thought you'd been shot!"

I was.

The baby whimpered and started to cry again. Her mother rocked her, tears rolling down her face. An older man beyond them had blood on his temple like he'd been clocked with the butt of a gun. Kenna looked at the rest, making eye contact with anyone who offered it. Even though it hurt her chest, she needed to see them all. She needed to be here in this moment with them, whispering prayers in her mind that no one would lose their life today.

"Shut that baby up!"

"I can't." The mother whimpered. "She's upset."

If he moved to the woman, Kenna was ready to intercept. She doubted she'd be shot in the vest again, but if she was going to be killed, then doing it protecting a mother and her baby was one of the better ways it could happen.

Ramon grabbed her forearm. "Not your job."

"It should be," she said.

Kenna found a different kind of pain, not as prominent as her chest but more...historical. Deep-seated pain that went back further than being shot a couple of years ago. To a nightmare from another life. Or so it seemed sometimes. Other times, it felt as near as yesterday.

"This case isn't a distraction," he added. "It's about justice."

"Is that what you want?"

Ramon whispered, "If it wasn't, she would be dead already."

Someone behind them gasped. Kenna glanced back, unsure how to explain that they weren't talking about anyone here. They were talking about murdering a prominent FBI agent.

It would be a kind of justice, in a way. But so would uncovering the poison in the Bureau and bringing down the empire Cecelia had created, leading to her arrest and conviction.

Kenna said quietly, "You don't get your life back if she dies."

"I already got my life back." He looked at her with a note of...something in his expression. His eyes betraying a tiny bit of gratitude, maybe? As if she'd been instrumental in giving it back to him.

She didn't need him getting soft on her. That would get one or both of them killed. But the killer instinct she knew was in there? That might not be exactly what they needed either.

She hadn't spent enough time with him to know how to tackle this. Speaking of which... "How did you know I'd be here?"

Ramon glanced at her with one brow raised.

In her ear, Maizie said, "I told him." So matter-of-factly that maybe Kenna should've known.

There was a lot to say about that. Given she needed to know who had contacted who—with Ramon being a grown man and Maizie being a traumatized girl. If it wasn't so far above board, they could hear angels singing a hallelujah chorus, then Cecelia wasn't the one who would have to worry about a hit out on her.

"I'd hand you the gun to shoot me."

She eyed Ramon, wondering that her intention had been so clear on her face. "Just so we're straight."

"Problem!"

The gunman at the other end of the room, closest to the front door, said, "Switch."

Their guy watching them backed up so he could cover the door and the hostages. "Where is four?"

"Dead, or he'll wanna be." The guy by the door hopped over the counter, and a second later, the last man came out. They'd traded places.

"What's happening in there?" their guy said. "She won't give it up?" He barked an oily laugh.

"Shut up. We'll get it."

The fourth guy appeared from the vault. "Send another one in."

A hostage?

Kenna got to her feet as fast as she could, praying she held steady when every breath felt like fire in her chest. "I'll go."

The guy closest to her came over, pointing the gun directly at her forehead.

"A murder charge is a lot more jail time than robbery."

He grinned, flashing neat rows of teeth no doubt paid for by his parents' hard-earned money. "Not if you don't get caught." He grabbed her arm and swung her around into the center island.

Kenna's hip bone hit the counter edge, and she cried out, moving right away so she didn't get trapped there between him and a hard surface.

All too quickly, his body pressed against her back.

She winced. The gun pressed against the underside of her throat, and she heard an appreciative hum from his throat.

The other gunman watched them more than the door.

This wasn't a show.

Kenna held still, feeling his roaming hand pat her down. A couple of times he strayed way too close to danger areas. Ramon probably wanted to rip the guy's head off. Or someone else among the hostages would jump up and come to her rescue. There were plenty of good guys in the world.

"Get on with it," she said. "Only a couple minutes left. Ticktock."

He huffed.

Breaking the tension helped her squash down the urge to elbow him in the face. It also likely kept Ramon from stepping in.

He was a good guy. Life had sent him from the FBI and an undercover career that had been impressive even if it wasn't long off a path that left him high and dry as the right-hand man in a cartel. Until Kenna walked in the door and realized who he was. She'd been determined to help him since.

Most of the time it seemed like he wanted to get his real life back.

Maybe not as an agent, but at least as a free man not a guy who has to live on the run so the law didn't catch up to him.

She wasn't sure she'd have returned to the US even for the chance at justice after walking the road he had. She'd probably have disappeared and carved out a life somewhere else. What was in Ramon that kept him here on the path to getting justice? It couldn't just be that she'd offered him the thing he'd been robbed of—a chance for something different.

The choice to go another way.

He shoved her behind the counter. "Go."

Kenna walked down the space between the tellers' desks and the cabinets that lined the wall where someone had hung a huge poster about savings accounts.

The vault door had been swung open, and the robber stood just inside. Someone had pushed back a rack of bags, probably money. A place like this didn't have millions on hand. Then again, these guys weren't after money.

Unless that was what Cecelia had stashed here. Though, she doubted it was a nest egg for just in case.

Noelle lay on the floor, blood in her hair.

"What did you do to her?" Kenna spat.

"She's being...uncooperative." He waved the gun. "Inside."

"What do you want?" She thumbed over her shoulder. "The money is there. Unless you already got paid."

"Half up front. The other half when we deliver what's in the box. Which means Noelle over here needs to give me *the number*. Since it has been erased from the database, it turns out she's the only one who knows what number is being used this month."

"It changes?" Kenna hadn't meant to say that aloud but supposed it made sense that Cecelia had someone regularly move the contents to another open box. To avoid situations like this. "And Noelle is the only one who knows?"

"Curious, isn't it?"

"I'll pay you double what she did to leave right now," Kenna said. "No harm, no foul."

He grinned behind that stocking mask. "There she is."

Kenna shrugged. "You might not have a choice but to accept my offer. Time is running out."

He swung the gun down and pointed it at Noelle.

"No—"

One squeeze of his finger, and he fired a shot, hitting Noelle in the thigh. She screamed and grabbed her leg, blood blossoming between her fingertips.

Kenna blew out a breath. "What is she giving you? I'm serious. I have money. We can make a deal."

"There's nothing you could give me but that box number. So come on, Noelle. Cough it up with some blood, or this is going to start getting *really* painful."

Noelle wept, hunched over on the floor.

He turned to Kenna. "Explain to her that if she doesn't give it up, I shoot you next, and she gets to see what brains look like sprayed on a wall."

Kenna moved to the teller. *I'm sorry it happened like this.* "Noelle, give me the number."

She shook her head. "No."

"Two minutes. Chop-chop, ladies."

"Noelle." Kenna didn't get farther than that.

Out in the lobby, chaos erupted. Thuds and scrapes. A gunshot went off. Then the sound of people running. Almost as if Ramon had staged a coup and rescued the hostages from those two men. Another shot went off.

Someone screamed, a woman.

Kenna prayed for protection for every single innocent in that bank.

She turned to Noelle. "Tell me the number."

The teller stared at her. Kenna wondered what Cecelia had threatened her with that kept her mouth shut now. Maybe she'd never intended to give Kenna a look in the box. She'd planned to keep the money, and this was all a setup. After all, how else could Cecelia have known ahead of time to send these guys to intercept and fake a robbery just to retrieve what had been left here for safekeeping?

"Come on." One of the other robbers pounded down the short hall. "We've gotta—"

Kenna turned in time to see his body jerk. Blood erupted in the center of his chest, and he tripped over his feet on the way to the floor.

Ramon stood behind him, gun in hand.

The robber grabbed Kenna's arm, dragged her to him, and held her in front. Covering him. His gun under the edge of her chin. "Come any closer, and she dies."

Chapter Three

Twenty years ago

He was finishing his peanut butter and jelly sandwich when she came in through the patio door, soaking wet. Breathing like she'd run from the creek behind the big house all the way to their tiny cottage on the edge of the family's land.

Walter hopped off the stool, leaving the crust behind. A smear of grape jelly on his finger, which he sucked into his mouth while he tried to figure out what was wrong with her. "Where have you been? I thought you were playing with Sarah."

"Sarah is mean." Celeste didn't quite look at him, her dark hair wet and sticking to the sides of her face. "She deserved it." Water from her yellow dress, which the housekeeper sewed for her, dripped onto the floor. "She deserved it."

Strangle her. He was gonna strangle her good. "What did you do?"

"Don't yell at me."

He grabbed the front of her dress, and water squeezed out between his fingers. "*What* did you do?"

"She said my dress looked like Mama got it from a thrift store, so I pushed her."

"And?"

Celeste swallowed. Didn't look at him. "She fell. That's all. It wasn't my fault. She shouldn't have been mean."

Walter let her go so hard she stumbled back. He flung open the door and raced down the steps, across the grass in his bare feet. Shorts too small because Mama couldn't afford new ones and he'd grown four inches this summer. Hair too long it got in his eyes, and he had to slap it back. Breathing hard. Pumping his arms and legs.

He raced to the creek, trying to find the spot where Celeste would've played with Sarah, the two of them vicious little cats who took great delight in clawing at each other. Sarah, because she was the princess who would one day inherit the kingdom. Celeste—and Walter—were illegitimate. Mama had used a different word, but he wasn't supposed to say that.

Celeste said it all the time when Mama wasn't around.

Walter just wanted to get a job. Try out for football so he wouldn't have to come home right after school. And he would get to tackle the other guys. Trip them if he could get away with it.

He'd been kicked off the team in seventh grade because he broke another boy's arm, but they had a new coach now. Sarah's dad was going to donate some money and get him on the team. His sister, their mom, would make sure he did it.

Walter didn't know how. He only cared if it worked.

One day he was going to get out of this place.

Walter lifted a hand and covered his eyes, scanning the

creek bed until he saw Sarah's blonde hair. Perfectly curled. Now it was covered in mud, and blood.

She lay still. Pale. Soaked like Celeste.

He raced over, heart pounding. Trying to figure out how to explain what happened.

"No!"

Walter stumbled and nearly tripped.

The man's cry behind him came seconds before the old man shoved him out of the way. "What did you do?"

Walter stopped.

Kneeling by Sarah, he turned to Walter and screamed, "What did you do to her?"

Celeste.

He turned and saw her a few feet away, hidden in a bush. Smiling that nasty smile that was always on her face when she got her way. She'd told them *he* did this.

Walter turned back to where Sarah lay, desperate for an explanation.

"I'll kill you for this."

The heavy fist came out of nowhere. His back hit the ground, and everything went black.

Chapter Four

"So kill her." Ramon shrugged one shoulder. "I just want what's in that box." The one they didn't even know the number of.

"Thought she works for you."

Ramon looked at Kenna, a sneer on his lips. "She had her uses. Now I'm done."

Kenna wanted to roll her eyes, even if he had saved her life. Then put it in danger again immediately. The gun barrel pressed against the skin of her neck, hot since it had been recently fired. That was gonna leave a mark.

Ramon wouldn't really let this guy kill her, right?

At least he would try and stop it. Maybe he would fail, but then he'd grieve her. Right? For a second she actually wondered if he didn't care whether she lived or died. She might only be useful to him so far as she provided leads on taking down Cecelia, and then he'd move on believing she'd outlived her usefulness. Literally and figuratively.

Yeah, no thanks.

Kenna waited a second for him to look at her. Then she glanced left hard, which was actually kind of uncomfortable and distracted her for a second from the gunshot bruise in her chest.

He paused a fraction of a second.

Kenna took that as a yes, planted her foot, and used the other to slam her boot on his shin. She twisted her body to the left. Not exactly out of his grip. The barrel of the gun glanced off the side of her face. She bent at the same time she twisted, taking a step away from him. Pulling hard against his hold on her.

Ramon fired.

The gunman barely flinched. Kenna twisted back, elbow first, and slammed his nose.

He stumbled back, fell to one knee, and collapsed on his face.

"I was handling it," Kenna said.

"Sure." Ramon moved to the gunman and knelt, checking his pulse.

Outside the bank, sirens blared.

A familiar sound, and yet foreign. These days, it didn't mean backup to hear local law enforcement were close by. Sometimes, it meant she would wind up in trouble.

Ramon definitely would.

She knelt by Noelle and turned to him. "Go. I'll catch up."

Both of them knew full well if any cop ran his prints, the entire federal community would jump like they'd been hit by lightning, and he would be locked down faster than he could blink. No way they could risk Ramon being caught.

Not when he wasn't at fault.

Ramon rushed out the door and toward the back hall.

Cecelia was the one who needed to pay for what she'd done. To Ramon. To others. She was the one who could provide intel about *El Caminante* that would ensure his arrest

—a fact Kenna was counting on. Kenna was sure Cecelia was connected to the serial killer.

She just hadn't quite figured out how. It seemed like nothing but instinct. Or discernment.

Kenna touched her fingers to feel for the slow-going pulse on Noelle's neck. There was so much blood. "We're going to get you to a hospital."

"That guy was a friend of yours?" Noelle choked out the words, still clutching her leg.

Kenna helped her sit against the boxes. "The cops can get you an EMT to take care of you. But I want you to give me the box number right now. So that something good comes out of all this pain and death."

Noelle flinched. "It only happened because I agreed to help you."

And Kenna would always carry the weight of guilt for that. "I know."

"I'll tell her I'm the one who kept it safe."

"You don't know that will work. She might send someone to kill you anyway." Kenna didn't like it. She couldn't even guarantee she'd be able to keep Noelle safe. Not when she had the case to work. Hard to do when you were also on protection detail covering one small piece of the puzzle.

Behind her Kenna's awareness caught a shuffle. Not the cops, who hadn't even breached the bank yet. Probably talking to people outside and getting a situation report.

A gunshot exploded in the enclosed space. Noelle caught a bullet in her chest, over by her right shoulder.

Kenna had no weapon that would be useful here, against a gun. She swung around to see the next bullet—the one that would end her life. But the gunman Ramon hadn't killed slumped back, and the gun tumbled from his fingers.

He'd killed Noelle.

Kenna gasped. Survivor's guilt was a close friend, but this piled more on top. Tears gathered in her eyes, stinging her vision with hot moisture she had to sniff back.

Noelle made a noise in her throat.

Kenna swung back. Two shots, and she wasn't dead.

Yet.

"Noelle, I'll get you help." Kenna scrambled up.

The bank teller grabbed her hand. Kenna stilled. Noelle's lips moved, but barely any sound emerged. "Four."

What she said next was either twelve or twenty.

"Noelle."

Her head lolled to one side and Kenna saw a key on a chain around her neck. Noelle must've tugged it out when Kenna hadn't been looking. The key to the safety deposit box. Cops would be here any second, and not moving meant failure.

And all this death would be for nothing.

She grabbed the necklace from Noelle's neck and tried four-twenty, her fingers sliding on the key. The rectangular door opened, and she slid out the box, flipping the lid as she moved. It tumbled out of her hands onto the floor, spilling a pile of photos on the tile.

Pictures of a little girl.

"Sheriff's department!"

Kenna took one photo and slipped it into her back pocket. Had she even opened the right box? What sense did photos make? But the wrong box wouldn't have opened. The key Noelle had alongside her teller key wouldn't have worked in the wrong box.

The cops were going to find her prints over the key and a lot of other things.

She would have to explain why that guy was tied up in

the closet. Assuming he was still there. What a mess this had turned out to be.

"Sheriff's department!"

"Yeah!" Kenna's voice cracked. "In the vault."

She took a step back, leaned against the wall of safety deposit boxes, and lifted her hands. Just in case they were inclined to shoot first.

The deputy who came in first had a puffy face, pale lips, and dull dark hair. No vibrancy to his features. "Ma'am."

"She needs help." Kenna didn't want to contemplate the number of dead people this incident had resulted in. What she wanted was to wake up. But that would mean that the entire memory of being shot in the chest had been a dream. Those weren't the kind of dreams she was interested in.

He touched her elbow. "Step out into the hall with me."

She walked in a daze, adrenaline buzzing in her mind. Making her thoughts scatter like mice when a cat showed up.

The cop led her to the front doors and out into an ocean of chaos.

"...still with me?" Maizie's voice came through the one remaining earbud. "Please say you're still with me."

"I'm okay." Kenna figured they'd both respond to that statement.

The cop glanced at her. "We're going to sit in the car. I want you to come to the station and give a statement about what happened."

There was no way she'd get out of that, even begging to get checked out medically. It would only delay things, and she wasn't injured.

Cops directed traffic in front of the bank. Others interviewed hostages, customers, and employees answering questions. Describing the ordeal. How long would it take them to find the guy trussed up in the closet? Or Cassandra, who'd escaped out the back?

Someone would piece together the fact she wasn't some ordinary bystander.

She nodded to his comment about going to the station. This guy was only doing his job. But if she was too fine with it, they'd think it odd. "I'm not being arrested, am I?"

He opened the door to the front seat of the car. "No, ma'am. We simply need a full picture of what happened." He looked her over. "Do you have any injuries? I can ask an EMT to come over and check you out. Or drive you to the hospital to be seen."

He didn't appear to like that idea, even if it was his. This guy probably had to clock out soon and didn't want to spend hours at the hospital waiting for her to get seen. The staff would be inundated after something like this.

Kenna slid into the passenger seat.

"I'll be back in a few. Gotta check with the lieutenant."

She nodded, and he clicked the door closed. Then she took in a long inhale. "Maizie, you there?" She reached up and adjusted the wig to make sure it was secure on her head. Not in danger of falling off and letting everyone here know some subterfuge was at play.

"Kenna." The relief in her voice echoed across the connection.

"I don't know how far I am from my phone. I lost it in the bank. And if we leave here, the connection is going to cut off."

"I can call Ramon, see if he can grab it for you? Jax can't get away until tonight."

Kenna was going to come back to the Jax thing. "You and Ramon are friends now?"

"If I ask him to do something he says, 'Yes ma'am.'" Maizie sounded amused, though in a quiet way. "It's mostly texts with Ramon. It's not like I speak to him." She paused. "Jax just emailed me. What was in the safety deposit box?"

Kenna smiled to herself. No one in the crowd was really all that bothered about her. Not in a small town. If she'd been in the back of the cruiser, then maybe it was an indication she was a suspect—one of the robbers.

"If I got the right one," Kenna said, "then it was pictures of a little girl. I grabbed one before I was hauled out." She glanced toward the front doors of the bank where they wheeled out a stretcher with Noelle on it. EMTs moving fast. Everyone in a hurry. "Noelle is alive."

Kenna could pray she would pull through.

Not much else she could do, but it turned out that was plenty.

"I'll update Jax," Maizie said. "He is asking me what happened because he didn't want to call you if you were in the middle of something."

"Tell him there's a chance I'll need him to make a call and vouch for me."

"Do you have your ID?"

"I haven't decided if I'm gonna be me or not." Kenna shifted in the chair, wanting to stretch. But getting out of a squad car you were put into usually wasn't a great idea. "He'll be back soon."

"Cecelia will know it was you."

"She already did. That's why she sent those guys to intercept what was in the box so we couldn't get it." But photos of a child? That didn't make much sense. Cecelia had no dependents.

Were the pictures from surveillance and something she used to coerce a parent into doing what she wanted? Children she had actively threatened.

Or had all those photos been the same little brunette with long braids and a sweet Easter dress.

Kenna didn't draw the photo out, but she'd looked long enough at it. "She knew we were gonna be there. She sent those guys. In fact, I'm kind of surprised they didn't try to execute me."

"Too much press coverage. You murdered in a robbery and you're wearing a wig? Bradley's father would start a campaign in Congress to get to the bottom of what happened. What you were investigating."

"Is that right?" Apparently, the teen had been reading her case history on Kenna's computer and putting pieces together.

"He follows you. Bradley's father," Maizie said. "Everywhere you're online."

"The only way someone could follow me is by literally walking behind me."

"Unless you had an account on a social media site. Purely for research purposes. So you can check out victims and suspects on their profiles."

"So you're an online stalker now?"

"People are so interesting." Maizie paused. "I'm learning a lot."

Kenna groaned.

"I told everyone I'm your executive director of media so I get to post on your behalf."

She needed to talk to Jax about this. "We'll discuss it later."

"Ooh, that was a total 'mom' voice."

"Believe me, I know." She spotted the cop coming back. "Gotta go."

"Byeeee." Maizie's long, high-pitched goodbye cut off as the call ended.

The driver's door opened, and the cop slid in. "We're good to go."

"What was your name again?"

"Officer Paige, at your service. Here to escort you to the precinct where we'll need coffee, and we can order sandwiches if you're hungry."

"Right." Kenna nodded. "That actually sounds good."

He started the car and pulled out, flipping off his lights and sirens when they immediately started up. "Don't need those now." He held up a hand. "Don't tell me what happened. Keep it all fresh in your mind so you only have to say it all once."

"Thank you, Officer Paige."

"And your full name is?"

She should've taken off the wig. "Kenna Banbury."

No way did these cops need the full story of the dirty FBI agent embedded in the Bureau. That would only raise too many flags when Cecelia already knew things were heating up. Why else risk sending a team to intercept?

She needed to be no one special in this, here doing nothing in particular. Maybe even just Noelle's friend from out of town. That way she wouldn't sound like an old acquaintance of Cecelia's with a serious grudge trying to wreck her life.

Which of course was perfectly true.

The car turned a corner onto a busy street, and she spotted Ramon walking down the sidewalk on a leisurely stroll. He carried a paper coffee cup and sipped as he walked.

Whether he really was on her team remained to be seen. After today, she wasn't so sure, and that gray area he operated in seemed really murky. Kenna and Maizie needed to have a conference about giving him information or trusting him at all.

They drove across town for about fifteen minutes. Long enough she was about to ask him how much farther to the police station when he pulled onto an empty street flanked by warehouse-type buildings. One side had an empty lot in front of the flooring store, except for a single white truck.

Officer Paige pulled around behind the building across the street.

Out of sight.

He parked the car.

She cataloged what weapons she had in reach. "What's going on?"

Paige pulled his gun from its holster. "I think you know you resisted coming in. I feared for my life and was unfortunately forced to take life-ending measures to save myself."

She stared at him, assessing that he didn't want to do this necessarily. He liked his job. But he felt he had no choice but to comply. Whoever pulled the strings had made a compelling case.

"Now tell me what's *really* going on."

Chapter Five

Kenna pushed open the door to the flooring store.

The guy behind the counter shook his head. "Don't come in here drunk about to puke." He had thinning gray hair, a clean-shaven face, and a lumberjack shirt over his substantial midsection.

"I need to use your phone." She had pulled off the wig and tossed it in a dumpster on the way over.

The guy eyed her, including the phone in her hand.

"This isn't mine. It belongs to the guy who just tried to kill me." She'd lost the one earbud and now had to buy a new set.

"911?" He asked it like the answer would give him more clues about who she was and what she wanted.

"Yes. I could use some medical attention." And a cup of coffee.

Or, you know, five.

Everyone knew coffee solved most problems. The ones it didn't solve? At least you had a cup of coffee. That was already better than not having one.

She lifted her arm and looked at her elbow, wincing. An

abrasion. Not bleeding too badly, but it had gotten on her shirt down by her hip since her sleeve was shredded from falling out the car onto the asphalt after she took care of...

Kenna shut down those thoughts or she'd end up in a spiral that left her lightheaded.

The guy was talking. He lowered the phone. "Ambulance is on its way."

And cops depending on whether he'd passed on the information that someone had just tried to kill her. "Can I use your phone to make another call, a personal one?"

He lifted his chin and motioned to it, then got back on his computer. Typing slowly but faster than hunting and pecking.

"What's your name?" Kenna sniffed and rubbed her nose, which of course hurt enough that her eyes watered. She cleared her throat. "I'm Kenna."

"Bart."

"Nice to meet you. Thanks for helping me."

He shrugged a shoulder. "Dial 9 to get an outside line."

She got the digits in on the keypad. Each press sent pain shooting up her finger, but she refused to have a broken trigger finger. That wouldn't be good. Things were heating up.

Cecelia was coming at her hard, which had to mean they were close. The dirty FBI agent was getting worried enough that she was taking preemptive action to get rid of Kenna.

The other alternative was that Ramon had paid that guy to take her out, leaving him with a clear shot at revenge. However, they didn't know everything they needed to know about Cecelia, so the timing didn't make sense.

Or the serial killer "Walker" had come after her. Another idea that made no sense.

The call on Maizie's desk phone connected. "Banbury Investigations."

"I have a phone."

"Are you okay?" Maizie asked.

"No." Kenna blew out a breath. "The guy tried to kill me. Can you get something from a phone?"

"The one you're calling from? It's registered to a flooring company."

"Cell phone." She didn't want to say *hack* or even *remote access* in front of a guy who could testify against her.

After a few seconds, Maizie said, "I'll need the IP address for the phone."

Kenna had used his thumbprint to unlock it and changed the settings to keep it unlocked. "Tell me what to do."

Maizie had her go into the Wi-Fi settings and read off a series of numbers. "Got it."

"I need to know who hired him to kill me."

"Got it."

"Ambulance is here."

She looked up at Bart, and he motioned to the window. Then she said into the phone, "I'll call back," and hung up, leaving a grimy blood smear on the phone after she set it back in the cradle.

Kenna moved to a couple of waiting area chairs and sat beside a water dispenser. She leaned far enough to get a drink of water, enough she could rinse out her mouth. Two EMTs strode in, white shirts and radios, insignia. Bulky bags and the look of people who'd been on the go all day so far.

Kenna lifted her elbow to show the woman who led the way. "I should've had you stop for coffee on the way and bring me one."

She smirked and sat on the coffee table, which creaked under her weight. The guy behind her, stick thin but muscled, pulled out a clipboard. The female EMT said, "I don't think that's how it works, but coffee does sound good."

Bart disappeared from behind the counter into a back room.

"Wanna tell me what happened?"

Kenna wrinkled her nose, which hurt. She touched it with two fingers while the EMT palpated her elbow with gloved hands. The sensation of latex gloves on her skin was odd. "He had a gun. He tried to kill me."

"The police are on their way. They'll want a statement."

"They always do."

The EMT paused, giving her an odd look. "Where's the guy now?"

"I handcuffed him to his steering wheel," Kenna said.

Another pause.

Bart returned to the counter. "I put on a fresh pot. If y'all have time for a cup before you head out."

Kenna could've kissed him, but she was tied up. The EMT blobbed something cold on her abrasion, and she hissed. "Coffee."

Everyone chuckled.

"That wasn't supposed to be funny." She'd never cursed much, but these days it was good to have something on hand to express negative emotions. If the situation was bad enough, practically anyone would let a choice word slip out.

Kind of like a cop turning on her and trying to kill her.

Kenna made an O with her lips and blew out a long breath. Outside a squad car pulled up. She glanced at the clipboard guy. "Tell him he'll find the guy behind that warehouse across the street."

"The one who tried to kill you?" Bart looked over from his computer, an interesting expression on his face. A good guy, not afraid for anyone to know he had a protective nature when it came to people getting hurt.

"It was a cop."

All three of them reacted, stiffening. Turning slightly. The clipboard EMT headed for the door, pushed out, and went to speak to the cop. They had a short conversation, and the cop got back in his car and drove across the street.

As the EMT checked a few things, Kenna managed not to let on that she had chronic pain in her forearms, which would lead to questions she didn't want to get into with a person she would never see again. And the cop was back. Driving over to the flooring store, where he pulled up out front and slid out.

Big guy, white shirt. The lieutenant, a career guy who worked behind a desk now—whether by design or just as a function of his job these days. Maybe he relished the chance to get out in the field.

Hopefully, he relished rooting out corruption in his department as much as she did when it came to the FBI. Not a vendetta, but someone had to clean house and keep people accountable. She knew the FBI. She'd *been* the FBI—ate, slept, lived, and breathed the Bureau and everything it stood for.

The fact Cecelia Warren had been her roommate at Quantico might be making Kenna feel a little guilty for what the ASAC had done since then. Enough to give her a boost of motivation.

"We're done?" Kenna asked the EMT.

"I don't think you need to be seen by a doctor. Unless you hit your head or passed out at all?" She glanced at her colleague, who nodded and made a note on his clipboard.

The EMTs got out of the way as the cop came in.

He lifted his chin. Hispanic features. Younger than she'd thought. He had an easy way about him, not just in the way he walked but in how he stood, not getting in her space.

Bart said, "Coffee?"

She glanced at him, and he must've seen something in her expression because he strode off fast.

The cop said, "I'm Lieutenant Gallegos."

"Kenna Banbury." As always, she waited a second to see if recognition sparked. When it did, it was clear. When nothing happened, like with Gallegos now, she didn't presume he wouldn't put some pieces together later. "I'm a private investigator."

Did any of them even know she'd been in the bank earlier?

Gallegos looked up from making notes on his phone—or whatever he was doing with it. "Any idea why one of my cops tried to kill you?"

"Maybe he just doesn't like PIs." Bart handed her a steaming mug.

"You're my hero," Kenna said.

Bart's lips curled up. "I'll give you my ex-wife's number. You can tell her that."

She smiled back.

Gallegos accepted a mug from Bart and settled with an elbow on the counter. "Looks like you fought him off pretty good."

"I don't like it when people try to kill me."

He glanced at his phone again. "Kenna Banbury?"

"Bingo." Whatever he was looking at now, he had a rundown of who she was. The highlights were probably pages long. "I'd like to know why one of your cops drove me to an out-of-the-way spot and pulled a gun on me. He said I'd know why, and when I asked further, he told me he had no choice. That he had to make it look like I gave him so much trouble he was forced to defend his life."

Kenna took a sip of coffee that burned her tongue in a

good way and set the mug down so it didn't burn her fingers. Her arms ached. She stretched out her hands and rolled her shoulders.

"What happened after the conversation?" Gallegos asked.

She stared at the mug on the coffee table. "He swung out with the gun. I blocked his arm. The gun went off, and the bullet hit the windshield. Thankfully, no one was around to get hit by it."

Gallegos glanced at Bart. "Did you hear a shot?"

"Now that you mention it, maybe I did." Bart scratched his jaw. "Thought it was a car backfiring."

"Just one, or more than one?"

Bart shrugged. "Wasn't paying that much attention."

He turned back to Kenna. "What happened after the shot went off?"

"My ears rang. I had to figure out how to subdue him without him shooting me." And the cop's stun gun had been on the left side of his belt, out of reach. "He had a hot cup, a metal one, in the cup holder. I hit him in the head with it. When he was dazed, I grabbed his cuffs from the loop on his belt and cuffed him to the steering wheel." He'd nearly elbowed her in the face. She'd managed to pry the gun from his fingers, but now her arms hurt like she'd tried to lift ten-pound weights above her head.

Kenna rotated her wrist. Whatever the EMT had put on her elbow was doing its job because it didn't sting nearly as much as it had. She needed an ice pack for her face, though.

Gallegos looked up. "And the gun?"

"I ejected the magazine and pulled back the slide. The bullet from the chamber went under the seat, and I didn't have it in me to find it while he was screaming and cursing at me. So I left the gun and the magazine in the glove box and got out."

Officer Paige had kicked her in the process, having wedged his legs over the center console in time to slam them into her rear and her hip. She'd fallen on her elbow on the asphalt and nearly grabbed the gun to shoot him for that. But she tried not to be petty if she could help it.

"Came over here," she continued. "Called for help."

"Can you tell me the officer's name?"

Kenna frowned.

"Or the number on the car?"

She shifted. "Why would I need to do that when he's around the back of that warehouse cuffed to his steering wheel?"

Bart glanced at her. A muscle in his jaw flexed.

"He's gone," Gallegos said. "Took off before I got here."

Kenna clenched her teeth so she didn't say something that would get her in trouble. "I'll give you a description, but he was the officer in the vault first at the bank."

Gallegos blinked. "The bank?"

"During the robbery. After it, he was the first one in." She sipped her coffee again, giving him a moment to absorb that. "It's why I was in his car. He was supposed to drive me to the station so I could give a full statement about what happened at the bank."

"Because you were there." Apparently, he needed another moment.

"How is Noelle?" Kenna asked. "She was the teller in the vault. She got shot twice, but I guess she was alive since I saw medics rush her to an ambulance."

"How about we go to the police station? I can find out on the way."

Kenna figured this was coming. "Given what happened last time I got in a car with a cop, no offense, but I'd rather just meet you there."

"I'll give you a ride." Bart hit a key on his keyboard. "I'll just let the boss know I'm leaving."

"Thanks." She said it to his back as he retreated down a hall.

"I am going to get to the bottom of this."

Kenna looked at Gallegos. "But you don't really think he was going to try and kill me. You think there's a reasonable explanation. Like I got the wrong idea or something like that."

"What would you think if you were me?"

"I'd want to know why I got it so wrong about someone who works for me."

She heard Bart come back and stood, checking her pockets.

He stopped behind the counter. "You got shot in the chest?"

She looked down at the bullet hole at the front of her shirt, where the round had embedded in the vest underneath. "It's been a rough day."

Bart coughed a laugh.

"Thanks for the coffee." She slid the phone off the counter —the cop's phone—and tucked it in her back pocket, feeling the photo she'd lifted from the safety deposit box. Two odd leads that didn't seem to interconnect. The only person who might have information was Noelle.

He opened a drawer and pulled out a set of keys. "Let's go."

Gallegos downed the coffee Bart had given him and led them outside. "See you at the station."

Kenna nodded. Bart led her to a company truck and cleared the papers and fast-food wrappers off the seat for her. She slid in. "Thanks."

"Where to?" he asked.

She glanced at him.

"The police station...or somewhere else?"

"The bank. My car is still at the bank." Where she'd left it *three hours* ago. She buckled her seatbelt. "I appreciate the lift."

"Like you said, you've had a rough day."

Kenna shook her head. "I'm not calling your ex-wife."

Chapter Six

Kenna relaxed back into the front seat of her little Nissan. This one was green, whereas the last one had been blue. She still preferred the red one to either. The dials on the stereo on this one didn't work all the time. But right now that was fine—she didn't want to listen to music.

She just wanted to sit here with an ice pack on her face.

Had Gallegos followed her in Bart's truck all the way to the bank parking lot? She wouldn't put it past him to have tailed her, and remain out of sight the whole time. It's what she would've done if she was the cop and some woman she'd never met said one of her officers tried to murder her.

Kenna groaned against the cold. Her nose hurt, and touching it didn't feel good, but she wasn't interested in what it looked like. If she got bruises, she'd have to deal with an extra layer of cover-up under her foundation. She didn't wear much in the way of makeup, but she had what she needed.

On the passenger seat beside her, the phone she'd lifted from Officer Paige buzzed.

She moved the ice pack long enough to see Maizie's

number on the screen, then swiped her finger across and hit the Speaker button. "Hi."

"Feeling okay?"

Kenna sighed. "Yeah, just waiting for the painkillers to kick in."

"You should go to the hospital and get checked out. Just in case."

"Is that what Elizabeth told you? Or Stairns?"

"Jax." Maizie hesitated. "I gave him this number. He said he could get to you in four hours if needed but that you should call him."

"Thanks."

"He's doing witness interviews all afternoon. There was a bomb scare at one of the local high schools, so they've been pulled off their caseload to help out. It's the third one they've had this week." Maizie paused. "And I'm supposed to wonder if that's Cecelia, right? That she's distracting the FBI in San Diego so they don't work the El Caminante case."

"Yeah, you're supposed to wonder."

"If we had a whole team, we could work all these angles," Maizie said. "Find out where the bomb threat calls came from. Find a trail, see if it leads back to her."

"It might not, and that would be wasted time. There's a reason she's gone unchecked this long." Kenna set the ice pack in the cup holder and looked around. The bank parking lot was still full, caution tape over the door. Cops milling around. If Gallegos was here somewhere, it would be hard to spot him in a sea of people dressed like he was.

She twisted in her seat and looked up and down the street, trying to figure out where she would hide if she was tailing someone.

Traffic would pick up for rush hour soon enough. Though maybe school was out because there were more cars on the road than before. And a school bus passed, though it looked empty.

The bushes disguising the dumpster for this parking lot with a strip mall of stores and the bank on the corner didn't move with any indication of a breeze. Kenna dug a bottled water from the cooler on the back seat. She chugged the entire thing and loosened the straps on the vest so she could pull it over her head, groaning the whole time.

"Sounds like you're doing great."

Kenna chuckled, which of course also hurt. "I'm scared to look. There's probably a bruise the size of Texas on my front."

"I won't tell Jax that part, but he did ask for updates."

Kenna had to wait until after he was done with his shift. Or at least, she tried to. Otherwise, they'd want to talk for longer and both of them would be distracted. She wasn't going to be responsible for him getting into trouble at work.

Ruining his career with the FBI wasn't part of her relationship goals.

She let Maizie make the calls, passing on quick updates when Jax was at work so he wasn't out of the loop. Often too much happened during the course of one shift for any of them to wait until after he left work to fill him in. Especially with a case like this going on.

"I need to visit Noelle at the hospital," Kenna said. "Make sure she's all right."

"Interrogate her."

"If she's up to it." Kenna looked for the easiest way out of this crowded parking lot. She might have to use the drive-up window lane as an exit.

"The cops there have a BOLO out on Officer Paige," Maizie said. "What does that mean again?"

She could've looked it up online, but Kenna told her

anyway. "Be on the lookout. So it means they don't know where he is."

"Don't those squad cars cops drive have GPS?"

"He probably turned it off, or they'd have known where he took me." Kenna turned on her car and pulled out, weaving her way to the main road, where she bumped onto the blacktop and headed for the hospital. She half expected him to jump out of that bush and try to get in the car. Or tell all the cops she'd tried to kill *him*. "I'm surprised he didn't report that I attempted to murder him."

"What does it mean that he just disappeared?"

"Paige must believe they'd see through his story. Or he's on the run from Cecelia more than his colleagues because he failed to kill me."

"Well, be careful," Maizie said. "Jax isn't going to like this."

Kenna smiled to herself, finally seeing the medical center ahead. A compact hospital since this wasn't a big town. They probably had the full range of medical services, but on a smaller scale. People would have to travel to the nearest big city for more specialized treatment. "Anything from Ramon?"

"You need backup?" Maizie paused. "I can text him. See if he hits me back."

"You don't know where he is?"

"I tried his phone earlier, and I worked a little more on identifying it."

"Since it's unregistered." Kenna didn't want to babysit Ramon, or force him more onto the grid than he already was.

"It's weirder than that," Maizie said. Keys clacked in the background. "Every time I look it up, it says the number doesn't even exist. Now, it comes back to an eighty-year-old lady in New Mexico."

"He stole her phone?" Kenna found a space in the

hospital parking lot but circled a couple of times, keeping an eye out for Gallegos. If he was tailing her, he was good at remaining unseen.

"More like he cloned it. She comes up. GPS and all her history. Calls and texts, web searches. But he texts me from that number." Maizie's tone hardened with irritation coupled with a competitiveness Kenna didn't have, or maybe it was the need to best a challenge in front of her.

Kenna wanted to go to Colorado, spend time with the girl, and see what other inherent personality traits came out. It would probably take years for her to work through the abuse and find herself. Kenna wanted to be there to see it develop through the good and the bad.

She parked and shifted far enough to pull the photo from her back pocket. "I need my phone." It was probably in evidence after the bank robbery. She might never get it back. "Or a new one. I've got a photo to send you."

"I'll send a text," Maizie said. "Hit me back with it."

Kenna took a photo of the photo and sent it as a reply. "It's what was in the safety deposit box. Find out who she is and how she connects to Cecelia."

Maizie was quiet.

"I'll be praying that wherever she is, she's safe. And if she isn't, I'll get her and make sure she is from now on."

"I know." Maizie's voice sounded thick.

Kenna wanted to pull her in for a hug, which, considering she wasn't a hugger, said more than maybe it should. She also wanted to see Jax. At the same time, the need to walk in the door to her RV, collapse on the bed, and close her eyes for a second compelled her to ditch the case.

All of it meant coming home.

But none of it solved the problem of corruption. Not that deceptive law enforcement officers only in it for themselves was anything new. No one was perfect, and most wanted to do a good job. It was that Kenna knew about Cecelia. She felt a certain responsibility to solve this. Not just so Ramon could be vindicated.

But for herself.

"I'll call you later, Maze. But I'm leaving this phone in the car."

Kenna wasn't entirely sure why she said that—maybe the same instinct that had her putting on a vest. A self-fulfilling prophecy or a nudge from someone bigger than she could comprehend.

She grabbed a clean shirt from the duffel on her back seat, locked the car, pocketed the keys, and headed into the hospital to find the room where Noelle had been admitted. Apparently, she was out of surgery. Not something that had been covered by Kenna's gut. She'd thought Noelle was surely dead.

Which meant she couldn't rely on what she felt. At least not in a way that was guaranteed.

She changed her shirt in the restroom off the lobby and tossed the dirty one with the hole in the elbow into the trash. She didn't often wear short-sleeved shirts, but it was still warm out, and no one would think twice about scars in a hospital. Kind of like the way Kenna hadn't thought twice about the fact she should've grabbed the armbands she sometimes wore on her forearms to cover the scars.

Kenna took the stairs rather than the elevator so she didn't get boxed in a small space. She could use rest rather than exercise, but the need to control her surroundings wasn't something she argued with.

Kenna eased open the door to the floor where Noelle's room was. Would the bank teller even be awake?

Sound from the hall filtered into her awareness, along

with the lemon scent of cleaning products. Gleaming floors. People chattering. Machines that beeped in a steady rhythm. An announcement began over the speakers high on the wall.

"Doctor Carl to the emergency department."

Kenna stayed by the door, feeling that odd sense of knowing again. Instinct she'd had her whole life and had never before attributed to something other than training.

The door to a room down the hall, possibly Noelle's, opened. A slender woman stepped out, long blonde hair not too different from the wig Kenna had been wearing earlier.

She eased back slightly and watched through a slit between the door and the frame.

The woman walked toward her. Light overhead illuminated her face, features she knew.

Cecelia.

Kenna's whole body stiffened in a way that hurt. The bruise on her chest was going to cause her trouble the next couple of weeks—but the problem of this powerful Special Agent would be much worse.

Cecelia headed for the stairs, a smug look on her face.

Kenna let go of the door, then turned and darted up the stairs so she could round the landing between floors and be out of sight when—

The door clicked open.

She peered around the edge and saw Cecelia start to trot downstairs. The agent had done what she had come to do, and now she was out of here.

A place she wasn't supposed to be, considering she was the boss of a huge department in the FBI's Phoenix office.

Kenna should follow her down, but running after her would create an echo of noise in the stairwell. She needed the evidence to take Cecelia down, which meant finding out what she'd said to Noelle.

She strode down the hall as Cecelia had done, just without the smug look. Past the nurse's station, where she heard a snatch of conversation.

"...seriously hot and heavy. Then, afterward, they were in the cafeteria like nothing had happened. They were sitting across the room from each other like they weren't even friends."

Kenna ignored the conversation.

Missing the man she was in a relationship was part of the deal. They'd been careful not to make grandiose promises when neither knew what would happen in the course of bringing Cecelia Warren to justice.

But she missed Jax.

Noelle's room was quiet but brightly lit by the overhead fluorescent bulb. As if anyone could sleep with that above their head. Kenna spotted a pillow on the floor, but everything else was standard. The machines were switched off, but the leads still connected to Noelle.

Her head had lolled to one side, her eyes closed.

She was pale.

"Oh no." Kenna moved to her and touched two fingers to her neck. "I know I wanted information from you, but I also came to see how you were doing." She bit her lip. "I'm sorry, Noelle." Then she grabbed the rail on the side of the bed and hung her head.

A second later, the door swung open and a nurse rushed in. She pulled up short. "Who are you?"

Kenna cleared her throat. "A friend. I guess she didn't make it."

"A friend who happened to find her not breathing and didn't call for help?" The nurse stepped back, hitting a button on the wall and pointing to the corner. "Move over there. Let's hope for a miracle that we can still save her."

Kenna shifted to the corner, and the nurse lowered the head of the bed with a button, checking for Noelle's pulse the way Kenna had. She looked at the pillow on the floor. Cecelia in here...and now the bank teller was dead?

If the agent had seen Kenna in the stairwell, maybe she would be dead right now as well.

All of them were simply nuisances. Loose ends Cecelia needed to clear up.

She turned to the door just as a white-coat doctor rushed in, followed by two more nurses in scrubs. They spoke to each other over Noelle's body, pushing meds into the IV line and doing chest compressions.

They didn't need her.

She didn't have the training to help save Noelle. All she had was the ability to bring justice after the crime had been committed. Sometimes it seemed like her job was too little too late. Noelle was dead. Cecelia had won.

She stepped into the doorway and came face-to-face with a security guard, a squat man with wide shoulders and a crew cut.

"Not so fast."

Which was how Kenna wound up getting detained by the police.

Again.

Chapter Seven

"Why would you need a lawyer? This is just a friendly chat."

Kenna stared across the table at Gallegos, wanting to laugh but knowing that wouldn't earn her any points with the local PD.

"Kenna Banbury. Private investigator." He glanced up from the tablet in front of him. "Your license is valid in the state of Nevada at least. So you've got that going for you. Did you really kill the director of the FBI?"

Of course, he was going to ask that question. "He was a bad guy."

"And turning him over to the authorities so he could be brought to justice?"

It was subtle, but his gaze dropped to her bare forearms. Why hadn't she dragged out a long-sleeved shirt? She had plenty of sweat-wicking base layers she put under a T-shirt like this. Now her scars were on full display.

Kind of like her life on that tablet of his.

"Detaining the FBI director wasn't an option at the time." She shrugged. "You know how it is."

"Do I?" Gallegos just watched her.

"Maybe you don't. You could be one of those cops who has never fired their weapon. It happens. It's not a bad thing."

"But your life is more akin to an action movie?"

Kenna scoffed. "I didn't ask for it."

She wasn't even sure about the whole nature versus nurture argument, given the fact an investigator had raised her. She'd followed in her father's footsteps in a lot of ways—like losing the love of her life to a murderer.

Kenna had tried over the last few months to look into the things Stan Tilley had said. Find out some more about her mother's death.

All dead ends.

Meanwhile the investigation against Cecelia continued.

Kenna said, "Did you locate Officer Paige yet?"

"I'm glad you brought that up." Gallegos tapped the screen of his tablet. "Why don't we talk about it? You said he tried to kill you. Walk me through what happened."

She didn't want to rehash all that. Her elbow stung, and she was so far past tired—and the cup of coffee Bart had given her—that her thoughts were trying to escape the train they should be on. Still, she ran it all down for him, doubling back when she got things out of order.

"I'd love to know why he did that." But Maizie would tell her soon enough. There had to be something on his phone to indicate if he'd been hired. Or pressured into it. "I did nothing to him to make him want to kill me."

Gallegos said nothing. He just stared at her.

"Where is he?" she said.

"We're working to locate him."

Kenna's stomach cramped. "If you guys don't know where Officer Paige is, then I'll have to ensure I'm safe until he's detained."

She still thought Gallegos might've been following her, given he was the first on the scene at the hospital. And she'd been arrested for Noelle's murder? Sorry, "brought in for questioning." As if there was much of a difference when she ended up at this table either way.

"He might try again since he failed the first time," she added. "And I don't want a desperate murderous cop coming at me next." She paused. "Unless you catch him first."

"At which point it's your word against his on what happened."

"Good thing you have my account," Kenna said. "Innocent cops don't disable the GPS in their squad cars and disappear. They return to the station and file a report."

Except, sometimes, the guilty ones did that as well. That way, they could spin the story and cover up what they'd done.

Gallegos stared at her for a while, then glanced at the clock. "Let's take a break."

She wanted to ask for coffee and something to eat, but he didn't offer so she wasn't going to risk pushing it.

Hours later, he still hadn't returned.

Kenna's back ached, but she didn't have the energy to lift her head. The clock on the wall had indicated the time was not quite three in the morning when she first put her head down. Who knew what time it was now.

The door clicked open. That must've been what pulled her out of her doze, which couldn't really be considered sleeping. Not in an interrogation room.

Someone knocked on the open door. "Time to go, Ms. Banbury."

Jax.

She lifted her head and sat up, pushing back her hair and wishing she had a hair tie. "Hey. Are you my lawyer?"

He gave her a soft smile, standing there in the open doorway in a suit. She didn't see him out of one much, considering how they usually worked together. When she did catch him in jeans and a shirt or sweats and a T-shirt, it was a time she savored because he could let down his guard. That wasn't the man standing here.

This was Special Agent Oliver Jaxton.

A good man whose career she was determined she wasn't going to ruin.

"Let's go." He tipped his head to the hall. "I've informed the department here that you're on retainer, consulting with the FBI. It's all connected to a federal case."

As if any agent or cop would ask for the help of a private investigator. Even one with her knowledge. Kenna pushed back the chair and stood, rolling the kinks from her shoulders.

"What happened to your face?"

Great. Her boyfriend happened to show up when she looked like she'd crawled out of a garbage can. "Officer Paige elbowed me in the face. Before he kicked me." She lifted her elbow and showed him the abrasion.

"That should have a bandage on it."

"I'm airing it out." She stepped past him out of the interrogation room into an empty hallway. The clock on the wall out here said it was five in the morning. Where was Gallegos? Probably disgruntled, doing paperwork about how he was forced to let her go.

She frowned at the wall she hadn't seen on the way in, facing this way. Going out, she saw it. A huge decal on the wall. A long desert highway with cacti on either side. A mountain range in the distance. Pahrump Police Department across the top.

Jax touched the small of her back to lead her. She wanted to hug him, but that would have to come later—like outside—when they could be unprofessional for a second and say hi to each other. She also wanted to take a photo of that decal so she could look for something like it online.

The sky outside had a dark gray hue to it, the nascent day only beginning to lighten the sky. He walked behind her down the concrete steps to the sidewalk and then off the curb into the stillness that seemed a little unnatural, given this was a town PD.

Kenna glanced around, checking the shadows.

Paige was still out there. Lurking. Waiting to take a shot at her so Cecelia could go on unchecked.

Jax's hand slid up to the back of her neck. "Come on. Let's get to the car."

"Maizie called you?" She tried to sound like it was fine, pushing away the fear. Instead of getting a lead and moving them one step closer to finishing this, she'd forced him to come and save her butt from being arrested for murder.

Great way to protect his career. She could've slapped her forehead.

Jax beeped the locks on a small SUV that was in no way as cool as his personal vehicle—a Toyota 4Runner. He opened the passenger door for her, letting her slide in while he waited, and then clicked it shut. When he slid in, he said, "I know. Rental cars suck."

She glanced at him. "That's what you wanna talk about?"

He glanced at her. "Egg, bacon, and cheese breakfast sandwich?"

"Did Maizie call you or not?"

"Of course. She was worried. She saw the callout come over the wire and sent me the info. The cops here have been running your information all night." He pulled out.

Kenna shifted in her seat so she could watch him drive, finally allowing her eyes to drift shut. She wanted to keep them open because he was here. She didn't have to deal with Ramon, worry about Cecelia, figure out how to tackle Maizie's latest nightmare...

All on her own.

Jax reached over and squeezed her knee. "Rest for a little."

"I need my phone. And my car. And my laptop. And breakfast and a shower." None of it necessarily in that order. "You need to get back to work so you don't lose your job because of me."

"You're a vital part of this case. Not too long ago, the serial killer I was trying to catch was actively hunting you." He said it as if it had become rote, reciting those words. Still, there was a note she detected.

"And?"

"Fine." He sighed. "If I don't get a lead here with you, the case will be relegated to the 'cold' drawer, and I'm being directed to turn my attention to the other five open cases on my desk. Not to mention the bomb threats."

Of course it was. "We knew our favor would run out eventually."

"I think someone is leaning on my boss to push it aside. No one can attribute any recent kills to *El Caminante*."

"He changed his MO." Kenna would have if the FBI was looking for her. "But that's nothing new. Serial killers are supposed to do things in order. It's supposed to make sense."

And yet none of this did. She was about to give up, except everything in her said going after Cecelia would net them Walker at the same time.

"Did he kill Noelle?" Jax asked.

"It was Cecelia." She paused, taking a moment to absorb

the grief at the fact a life had been taken. "She went into Noelle's room in the hospital. Next thing, Noelle is dead."

"You didn't see it."

Kenna shook her head, opening her eyes. "I saw her come out. She went into the stairwell and hurried away. Didn't want anyone to know she was there. The cops said the security footage had been corrupted when I tried to explain I saw someone."

Jax nodded. "And no one has any idea Cecelia was here. Everything Maizie has indicates she never left Phoenix."

"So we can add to the things we know about her. She can get around without being found out. Which means she could crop up anywhere we aren't expecting her."

"Sounds like someone else we know." He squeezed her knee and pulled into a drive-through.

The coffee would be terrible, and she would regret the sandwich, but if they gave her a hot and greasy hashbrown, she wouldn't complain.

After he had given their orders, she said, "Problem is, we have no idea where Ramon is at any given time." The man came and went as he pleased. "Although apparently he and Maizie *text*."

Jax whipped around in the seat to face her. "They *what*?"

Mama bears were supposedly fiercer, but dads could not be overlooked as a potential threat. Anyone would have to admit he was a contender the second they saw this side of Oliver Jaxton. He'd met Maizie only a couple of times and the teen—given her ugly history—barely spoke to him in person. But they'd put that aside and now updated each other by phone. Not just passing information back and forth between her and Jax, with Maizie acting as the intermediary when Kenna wasn't able. They also had developed their own rapport.

He cared about her.

Kenna nodded. "That was my reaction."

He was forced to pull forward through the line and handed her the hot paper bag that smelled pretty good, actually. She savored the aroma of warm breakfast. Definitely better than being stuck in an interrogation room. Or formally charged with murder.

"It was a fishing expedition." While he parked, she dug in the bag for a single hashbrown in its paper wrapper and handed the rest to him to figure out what was there. She took a bite, wondering why it had been so long since the last time she had one of these.

"Did you eat yesterday?" he asked.

"I don't even remember," Kenna muttered. "It was a weird day, but at least I only got shot once. First, a cop tried to kill me. Then, another one arrested me. But a nice man named Bart gave me a cup of coffee." She sighed. "I should put him on my Christmas card list."

"So it wasn't all bad." He glanced at her.

"It's getting better every minute." She smiled, pretty sure she had hashbrown grease on her lips.

He leaned over and kissed her, then leaned back. "I can see why you like those." Then he leaned back in his seat like nothing just happened. Like he hadn't kissed her after an epically cheesy moment. And he handed her a wrapped breakfast sandwich.

"My hero."

He snorted. "Drink your coffee. You're in no shape to drive. I'll have to take you back to the RV park."

She groaned. "You're gonna get fired. Then we'll have no hope of taking down Cecelia officially—from inside the FBI."

Assuming he wanted to be the face of the ousting of entrenched corruption. Maybe he didn't want that spotlight—

or the reputation for turning on a fellow agent. Was he going to regret this?

"You need a nap," he said.

"I need eighteen hours of sleep. But what else is new?" Eighteen hours was a thing at this point. Anytime she'd been running ragged, working a case, she hit the pillow and it was bye-bye interruptions for almost a whole day. "Sleep is life."

"As long as you're safe while you're completely out of it."

"That's so sweet." She took a bite of her breakfast sandwich and nearly rolled her eyes. "Why does processed sausage and chemically altered cheese taste so good?"

"Because food industry scientists are experts at hacking your taste buds."

"But you're still eating it."

"Because I'm hungry as well as informed." He pulled out of the space. "Where is your car?" He tapped the maps icon on the dash screen. Kenna typed in the name of the local hospital where she'd left her car with a greasy fingertip.

Napkin wipe.

Coffee sip.

"Thanks for breakfast."

He smiled at her. "You're welcome."

Jax navigated through this tiny Nevada town that she was so ready to leave. Only a ten-minute journey, but she soaked up the chance to rest while he drove. He'd have to head back to the airport and fly home. "You need help getting back to San Diego?"

She wasn't above chartering a plane if it came to that. Why not use the money her father had left her for the cause of justice...and to help her boyfriend get back to the job he needed to keep?

He smiled. "I'm good. But thanks."

She heard it there in his tone. *I'd rather stay and help you with the case.*

Neither of them said it, or even acknowledged what was only an echo of a sentiment in the silence between them. Their lives were what they were, and they caught snatches of time with each other in the in-between.

Jax pulled into the hospital parking lot and handed over a clear plastic bag. Inside were her keys and the contents of her pockets when she'd been brought into the police station.

"I guess it's goodbye." Another unspoken rule, and she'd just broken it.

Jax shook his head. "You know it's never that."

Chapter Eight

R ubbing her wet hair with a towel, Kenna walked down the carpeted hallway in her RV from the bedroom to the kitchen. Past the full-size refrigerator on which she had magnetized a photo of a man she had seen in Mexico at Kart's compound, alongside the blog post they'd found about "the Walker."

She checked her phone. Jax had arrived back in San Diego and was headed for the FBI office. Below that was a notification for her exterior security sensors—the basic setup she connected every time she parked her RV somewhere, alerting her whenever someone approached her vehicle. It took some finesse for it to not be triggered by other RV park residents walking by, going about their life with no nefarious intent.

A man had approached the outside of her RV. Kenna backed up the camera feed and played the recording. After he knocked for a while, he slumped into one of her plastic chairs outside the door. This wasn't an off-leash dog or a guest ducking between two RVs instead of going around on the path.

She slid her finger across the screen and played the live feed.

He was still there. And by the look of it, he was asleep.

She hung the towel in the bathroom then brushed and braided her hair so it would dry with a wave to it. Not the usual odd kink since it didn't seem to want to just dry straight on its own.

There was work to do, but after the last couple of days and the night she'd had, Kenna wound up taking a nap and then showering. Now it was time for dinner.

Good thing she was accustomed to defrosting twice as much chicken as she needed, cooking it all and then providing herself leftovers for the next day.

She also put on a pot of coffee, given they likely could both use a cup.

Once it was gurgling down into the pot, she eased open the door. It creaked back on its hinges and let in the late afternoon warmth, which felt good compared to the pumping air-conditioning in the RV.

She said, "Psst."

No way was she going to touch him and wake him up. He likely come up swinging, or with a pistol in his hand already firing.

Thankfully, that one noise was enough to get him awake.

Ramon sucked in a breath, and his eyes flew open. He got halfway out of the chair before he realized where he was. He looked around and saw her in the open doorway.

"Dinner in ten minutes," Kenna said. Then she turned away from the door and let the screen snap closed against the frame, wondering belatedly why she would offer to feed dinner to a man who had told the bank robber to go ahead and kill her.

Maybe she should put some kind of poison in his food.

Not to kill him, just to make him uncomfortable for a while so he would know they were even. Then again, she didn't particularly like being vindictive. That wasn't who she was supposed to be now as a Christian, and she'd never been like that anyway.

But was she supposed to just let it go and say nothing?

The door eased open, and he ducked his head inside. "Is your boyfriend still here?"

"That's why you were outside?"

He shrugged.

"He dropped me at my car this morning and went back to work." Kenna sliced up the chicken and heated up her cast-iron skillet. One day, she would have a huge range and a massive skillet from which she would feed a whole family.

The dream had crept up on her, almost insidious in how she had been forced to realize there were things she wanted but hadn't ever admitted to herself. Now that she had a boyfriend who wasn't around enough to distract her with the present, she found herself daydreaming about things she shouldn't. After all, there were no guarantees in life.

They might have a future. And just as easily, something could happen that ended it all.

She had decided it was being realistic rather than being cynical. Especially with her history.

"He's a good guy, by the way."

Ramon eased onto the bench seat, folding his tall frame into the space between the seat and the RV table, which would only really comfortably seat two. Kenna didn't know how people got the whole family around it. She needed space for her elbows when she ate.

His dark features gave nothing away. But then, as with her, he had lived a life that careened off in a direction he never expected—none of it in his control.

He'd changed clothes. She had no idea where he was staying or where he got money for incidentals.

She'd chosen not to ask.

Ramon said, "He's FBI."

"So was I. So were you." They had been at Quantico at the same time.

Ramon shrugged.

"You were gonna let that guy kill me in the bank."

"If that's true, then why would I be here watching your back while there's a cop out there trying to kill you?"

"Is it a hit?" Kenna asked. Surely, Maizie would have told her if she found something online indicating a person had taken out a contract to end her life.

"Cecelia." Ramon shrugged, as if that was enough of an explanation.

Kenna figured that was true.

He reached over and lifted the photo she'd left on the table.

"Pictures in the safety deposit box," she said. In case he hadn't had a chance to find out what was in there. "I managed to take that one, but there were a lot more. I don't know if they were the same person or if all the pictures were of different kids. They were all girls. At least the ones that I saw."

"Any idea who she is?"

"Maizie is working on it." Kenna turned the chicken in the pan and pulled out a bag of salad from the fridge. She handed it to Ramon, along with the mixing bowl and a wooden spoon. "Make yourself useful."

He snorted. "I'll have some coffee as well, thanks."

She poured two cups and handed him one. "I'm out of milk." Then added a little cold water to hers, which some would consider blasphemy. Like she needed to burn her mouth just trying to drink it. "Where did you go after the bank?" Kenna wasn't entirely convinced he'd admit the truth.

He didn't like to be controlled, kind of like her. But with Ramon, that extended all the way to no one knowing where he was or what he was doing. Not even Kenna. Not completely.

"I followed the van and got pictures of their faces."

"So did we." Maizie had been running facial recognition. Kenna needed to call her for an update. "Any idea who they were?"

Ramon tore open a packet and dumped it in the bowl on top of the lettuce. "I guess military, but it was just a feeling."

Lot of that going around. People being military or former military. The serial killer she had been trying to catch, the man Kart had referred to as "Walk" was supposedly military like the rest of them. But they had found nothing in any military database about the guy. As if he'd been scrubbed from every record.

If Kart hadn't vouched for the guy, she would consider it to maybe have been an instance of stolen valor.

Kenna grabbed her phone, called Maizie's number, and hit the Speaker button.

After one ring the call connected. "Banbury Investigations."

"You're on speaker. Ramon is here."

"So don't say anything I'm not supposed to know," Ramon quipped.

"Are you all right?" Maizie asked. "Jax said you were good, but it looks like you nearly broke your nose."

Hearing that made her wrinkle her nose, trying to dismiss the idea. Which of course hurt. Her elbow had also stung in the shower. But that was what happened when soap ran over

an open wound. She had put more cream on it and reban-
daged it with the biggest tan color bandage she could find.

Moving her arms sent pain thrumming through the epic
bruise on her chest, but she was planning on sleeping it off. It
only hurt to breathe.

"She does."

Kenna glanced at Ramon, then said to Maizie, "It feels a
little swollen, but I'm good to go."

"Nap, shower, coffee?"

"Yep." Kenna smiled to herself. Maybe she was just a
simple person with simple routines, but it felt good to know
that Maizie was growing familiar. They cared about each
other, and they were getting close. Neither of them trusted
easily, and that wasn't a bad thing. They would never have a
hundred friends. But they would always have each other.

Kenna handed Ramon two bowls, he split the salad
between them, and she dished out the chicken on top of it.
She grabbed salad dressing from the fridge and a bag of chips
from the pantry, which she gave to him so he could have a
carbohydrate.

"Anything on the bank robbers?" Kenna shoved a bite of
chicken salad in her mouth.

"Military contractors," Maizie said. "About ten years ago,
there was chatter about them being vicious. They got a bad
reputation. Since then they've pretty much dropped off the
radar and gone dark."

"Mercenaries?" Ramon said.

He said the word with a note of interest, which
made her wonder if he was trying to get into a gig like
that. Maybe it sounded more interesting because he
wouldn't have to care about the job he was doing—he
wouldn't be spending every waking moment trying to get
recompense for what Cecelia had done to him. Leaving

him high and dry in Mexico. Burning him and destroying his career.

Kenna nodded. "Probably."

"The question is," Maizie said, "how does Cecelia know them?"

"That's something I've been wondering about." Kenna bounced her knee, then shifted it to avoid hitting Ramon's knee with hers. "Do we have any indication in Cecelia's background that she was ever in the US Army or served in any military branch?"

Cecelia hadn't mentioned it when they were at Quantico. But looking back, there were signs in the way she made her bed, among other things.

"I've done a deep dive into her background," Maizie said. "I didn't find anything like that, but there were periods of time when I couldn't account for what she was doing. It all looks very aboveboard on paper, and then when you dig below the surface, it's like it was yesterday. She left her house in Scottsdale in the morning and checked into the Phoenix office of the FBI. You saw her in Nevada in the afternoon."

Ramon grunted. "CIA? Maybe she's in the FBI but works for another agency, feeding information."

"Is that a thing?" Kenna said.

Ramon shrugged.

"We already knew she was keeping plenty of secrets." Kenna bit her lip. "Maybe we need to pay a visit to Noelle's apartment before the cops do."

"Are they even going to bother looking around?" Ramon said. "What did they list as the manner of death?"

"Nothing has been entered into the system yet," Maizie replied. "It could be murder or natural causes. Or her death was a result of injuries sustained during the bank robbery. At least, that might be what they report. Regardless of the truth."

At least Kenna wasn't still in custody, suspected of being the one who had shut down hospital surveillance and taking her life.

Maizie continued, "Keys to her place are probably in her purse, which will be at the bank."

Which the police would have shut down as a crime scene.

Ramon snorted. "We don't need keys."

"And I don't need to get arrested for breaking and entering," Kenna said.

"Then don't get caught."

She rolled her eyes.

"I have one other piece of information for you," Maizie said.

"Go ahead." Kenna finished her coffee. They could pour the rest into two travel mugs and take it with them. Do a little surveillance outside Noelle's place, wait for the right time, and pop the lock on the front door easily enough.

Breaking the law, technically. But for the greater good of taking down Cecelia? She would argue it was worth it, considering Noelle was another victim of the dirty FBI agent. Others might not agree. Kenna had to live in the in-between.

As long as she could look herself in the mirror and see someone with integrity.

She knew Ramon didn't have the same standards, but she was working on that as well. A combination of trying to control his more radical tactics—the ones that made him a great candidate for a mercenary, or hitman even—and getting him to see that two wrongs committed against each other didn't necessarily lead to the right outcome. Even if justice was the end result.

Maizie said, "I found something deep in Noelle's social media accounts, going back to when she was in college. She had a boyfriend who was in the army. Oh...they got married.

He was listed as killed in action two weeks before she turned nineteen."

"Any connection between the boyfriend and Walker or any of those guys in Mexico?" There hadn't been time for Maizie to do a thorough workup of Noelle before Kenna entered the bank. They had only gathered enough intel to know they could trust her. It had been a risk Kenna was willing to take.

"I'll see if I can connect to any of those dots."

Ramon took his bowl and fork to the sink, then washed, rinsed, and dried them. Perhaps there was hope for him to become civilized yet.

"We'll hit Noelle's place and see what we can come up with," Kenna said. "Maybe she has photos of her husband still tucked away somewhere that can tell us what unit he was with."

"Got it," Maizie said. "Call me later."

"Will do." Kenna ended the call and turned to Ramon. "I just need a minute to finish getting ready."

He was already halfway out the door. "I'll check the perimeter and your car," he called over his shoulder. "Make sure nobody planted a bomb under your seat."

Chapter Nine

At just after two in the morning, Kenna eased her car door closed quietly on the street about a quarter mile from the apartment complex where Noelle lived before her untimely death. They had taken turns walking the complex, checking out the neighborhood and making sure no one was loitering around Noelle's apartment.

On the other side of the car, Ramon said over the roof, "I'm just saying. Everyone knows Chicago pizza is better than New York."

"Then it's a good thing Wisconsin happened where it did. Or you'd have been forced to eat thin crust." She knew Ramon had grown up around the Chicago area, with family trips to Wisconsin. It was in large part the reason why Kenna had been up in Door County earlier this year—finding out what happened to his sister. "But you're going to want to be careful you don't start a civil war over pizza. People like what they like."

They set off toward Noelle's place.

Ramon glanced over at her as they walked. "How about you?"

She pictured Jax in his kitchen a couple of months ago, wearing sweatpants and a T-shirt while he rolled out dough to make pizza he'd topped with chicken and barbecue sauce. Lots of red onions and spices. "None of your business."

It was her good memory, and she was going to savor it.

Ramon let her go first up the steps to the second-floor apartment. She let him use his kit to pick the lock on the front door, which he eased open slowly.

Kenna heard the unmistakable scrabble of nails on a tile floor and knew what was coming. She stepped inside and shut the door in Ramon's face. A tiny Shih Tzu rushed into the entryway, realized that she wasn't Noelle and pulled up short to bark, both front paws lifting off the floor.

Kenna held out one hand in a fist so the dog could sniff her. "Hi, doggy. How are you?" She kept her tone soft and easy. "You've been cooped up all day, haven't you?"

If there wasn't somewhere for the dog to take care of emergency business in the apartment, then this animal desperately needed to go outside and take care of it—probably on a bush or a fire hydrant.

"We can do it fast, can't we?" A leash hung on a hook beside the door. She clipped it on the dog's collar and opened the front door. "Back up, the dog might not like men, since Noelle lives alone."

Noelle's pet trotted out the front door, sniffing around the carpet-like mat in front of it.

"Seriously?" Ramon scoffed.

"I'll be back in a couple of minutes," Kenna said. "There is no reason to force cruel and unusual punishment on an animal that just lost its owner."

"If you see Officer Paige, you'd better start hollering."

Despite saying that, Ramon remained at the top of the stairs, watching Kenna and the little Shih Tzu descend the steps to the patch of grass beside the bushes. It took all of three seconds for the dog to do what he needed to do and for Kenna to realize it was a boy dog. When he finished, he trotted in a circle on the grass and then returned to where she stood.

"All done, then." Kenna led the animal back upstairs, given that he was apparently content to go back inside.

Ramon said nothing, but the vibe coming off him was not unlike exasperation with the way he turned and went into the home. "Maybe Noelle has a crate or something we can put him in."

"So that someone can discover him starved to death a week from now when family shows up to collect her things?"

"Maybe they are already on their way to pick up Bunny Foo Foo, or whatever its name is."

Kenna was pretty sure that wasn't it. She lifted the dog into her arms, grateful it didn't weigh much. The dog licked the underside of her chin while she wrestled with the clip on the leash. She hung it back up on the hook and looked at the dog's collar. "Ozzy."

She gave him a good rubdown since he was probably missing human contact after his human never came home. Then she pulled out her cell phone and sent a quick text to Maizie.

> Find out if Noelle has any family that will
> want to take her dog.

She stowed her phone and lowered the dog to the floor. Ozzy trotted off into the kitchen and slurped water from his bowl. He would need food as well. And someone to take care of him until his new owner could be located.

"Can we actually search this place now?" Ramon said from the living room.

Kenna moved to the opening so she could see the comfy-looking space, big poofy couches, and lots of throw pillows. A bookshelf on one side crammed with paperbacks. Window blinds closed so Noelle had privacy and which kept down the heat in here.

"Maybe something was left behind that can help us nail Cecelia. After all, she wrecked our plan to get intel, which just turned out to be pictures of little girls." Ramon trailed through to the bedroom. "Which means she's a creep on top of everything else."

Kenna followed so they could split the bathroom and bedroom closet and the dresser drawers between them.

The dog followed her into the room and curled up on the bed in the corner, watching them look around the room.

Kenna pulled open the top drawer. "We already know we need to stop her. Finding out she's worse than we thought just makes it more important to keep going and do this right." She heard Ramon opening cabinets in the bathroom, using a dim flashlight to look in the drawers, careful not to shine it around. That way no one outside could potentially catch sight of intruders.

Ramon leaned back far enough that she could see his face for a second. Long enough to say, "Can't Maizie hack her computer? See if she's got kiddie porn on there or something?"

He didn't know Maizie's history. Otherwise, he probably would've never made that suggestion. If he did and still said it, then he obviously didn't care about forcing Maizie to relive some of her trauma. Kenna chose to give the guy the benefit of the doubt.

"I'd hire a private company first," she replied. "One who doesn't mind breaking the law. But it's a leap. Why keep it in a safety deposit box in a town where you don't live when the images can just be on your phone or your computer?"

The one she had on her table in the RV, the girl was wearing a Sunday dress. The kind of thing parents dressed their kids up in for Easter. Hardly porn. It was more like a family picture.

Ramon trailed back into the bedroom. "Maybe it belongs to Walker? Maybe he's the one that's a creep, as well as being a serial killer."

"We can't connect him and Cecelia." So far they had no indication that the serial killer Jax and his colleagues were chasing down, the one connected to Mexico, was also linked with Cecelia Warren.

"We can. It's just that the connection is you." Ramon tugged open the closet door and removed a shoe box from the shelf. He spilled the contents on the bed and started to rifle through photos and concert tickets. Random coins that looked like souvenirs. "High school yearbook. Maybe it has her and the husband together. It still doesn't tell us whether she did what she did because Cecelia blackmailed her or if she was a willing participant."

Kenna nodded. "I'll go look for a laptop or tablet."

The search might be futile if Noelle had taken her personal device to work yesterday morning. In the same way it was futile for Kenna to wish she could get into Noelle's phone. Which was, of course, still at the bank. Probably part of case evidence the police had collected.

Noelle had no office, not even a desk in the corner of a room. Ozzy trotted after her from room to room as she moved through the small one-bedroom apartment. Not many places to look—or hide something. Did Noelle have a storage unit?

She couldn't have even said what she was looking for, necessarily. The last time she searched a house, she had discovered a severed head in a suitcase under the bed. Thankfully, Noelle didn't seem to have murderous tendencies. She was the victim, not the perpetrator.

Kenna wandered back to the bedroom and pulled open drawers in the side table next to the bed while Ramon continued to rummage in the closet. Noelle had a fluffy white queen-size comforter with lots of matching pillows. She probably let the dog sleep next to her on the bed. A quiet life that she liked, characterized by grief over the loss of the man she loved.

Kenna could certainly understand that. She'd lived it.

He muttered, "You're going in circles."

"And you're moody when you're tired." Not to mention getting into random arguments about pizza.

"There's nothing here." Ramon let out a big sigh. "Let's go. Maybe we'll get lucky and Officer Paige will show up again to try and kill you."

He strode from the room, and Kenna turned to look at the dog. "What are we gonna do, Ozzy?"

The dog trotted to the small basket in the corner of the room, selected a toy, and brought it to Kenna, dropping it on the floor in front of her.

"You need some playtime." Kenna tugged out her phone and checked the screen while she tossed the toy at the dog bed.

Ozzy ran over and grabbed it, bringing it back to Kenna. The dog was probably hungry as well as in need of attention.

Maizie's reply text showed on her screen.

> Noelle doesn't have any living relatives.

Most likely, Cecelia had selected her precisely because Noelle lived a solitary life, even if there were no other connections—like the soldier Noelle had loved and lost. Had Noelle's death given them a connection between Walker and Cecelia? It was possible, but it would take time to prove it when they couldn't confirm Walker had even served in the military.

Maybe some kind of under-the-radar black ops team?

That was a terrifying thought.

Ramon came back to the bedroom door. "Are you playing with the dog, or are we leaving?"

Kenna straightened out of her crouch. "Go in the kitchen and find whatever Noelle uses for dog food. Ozzy is coming with me."

Kenna grabbed the basket of toys and the dog bed, depositing both by the front door. She clicked on the dog leash but let it drop to the floor while they finished getting ready. Ozzy trotted around, clearly excited to be going on an adventure.

No way was she going to leave the dog alone in the apartment for who-knew-how-long.

She went to the kitchen, finding nothing resembling a junk drawer. Did people even have those anymore?

Ramon went from the cupboards to the refrigerator. "No bags of dog food."

Kenna looked over his shoulder and spotted a brand she had seen online. "Those containers on the middle shelf."

"She feeds the dog people food?"

Kenna reached around him and grabbed the containers. "More like she buys real food for her dog so he's not eating processed junk."

"Pup cups, trips to the doggy spa, and as many toys as he wants?" He shook his head.

She found a collection of plastic grocery bags under the kitchen sink and put the containers in one. "It's Ozzy's world. We're all just living in it."

To mark the occasion, the dog did a couple of circles in the kitchen.

"You're hungry." Kenna crouched and picked up the leash. "Let's go to the RV and feed you."

If it wasn't two in the morning, she would be stopping somewhere to pick up treats and things to make the dog feel at home in her RV.

Ramon did that loud sigh thing again. Over at the front door, he swept up the dog bed, holding it in his arms. It sounded like crinkling paper. He frowned, and she waited while he felt around the dog bed. On the underside, he patted the material. "There's something in here."

"Let's get to the car before you see what it is."

Ramon led the way down the steps, scanning around them with the situational awareness of a man who lived his life on the run. Wondering if any moment might be his last.

Kenna beeped the locks on her car from ten feet away, and the lights flashed.

Ramon lay down in front of the hood and shined underneath the car with his phone camera flash, much brighter than his dim flashlight, checking for an explosive again. He did the same thing under the seats.

"You really think Cecelia will just blow us up?"

"I think the time I do find something, you'll thank me for saving your life."

Kenna figured that was probably true. She loaded Ozzy in the back seat, along with all his things. He sniffed around the bag with the containers of food in it and then lay down, his nose close to dinner.

Not exactly the kind of dog she would have gravitated toward, but a living being had come into her care and she was going to do what she could to ensure he thrived. The same way she did with everything and everyone else in her life. If she wasn't a benefit to the world, why was she here?

God directed her life for a reason in ways He knew were best. There was a comfort available to her when she contemplated the sovereign plan. But at two in the morning with a hungry dog in her back seat and a wanted man on the passenger side, she had to remember all the things she was thankful for.

Number one being that she was still alive.

Kenna pulled out, looking out for any other cars. If she was being watched—or Ramon was the one hunted—then she was also being followed, and with enough care and attention, she could figure out who was tailing her. "What's in the dog bed?"

Ramon dragged it out of the foot well between the back seat and hers. He unzipped the underside and pulled out a handful of papers. "Handwritten letters."

She glanced at him for a second, then returned her attention to the road. "Maybe love notes from the guy she lost."

But why put those where no one would ever find them if Noelle had a solitary life?

Unless she believed someone might search her home. That was a good enough reason to hide the letters somewhere Ozzy would be the one keeping them safe.

Kenna took a roundabout route back to the RV park, which would take them nearly double the amount of time to get there.

"They're addressed to someone called Esmeralda Juarez at a ranch in Arizona." Ramon opened one and scanned the handwriting. "Noelle is telling her about Cecelia."

"Take a picture on your phone and text it to Maizie," Kenna said. "Looks like we've got ourselves a new lead."

Chapter Ten

Kenna could take a trip to a ranch in Arizona. Right now, that sounded good, considering there was too much heat in this town. One officer intent on killing her was too many as far as she was concerned.

As she turned the corner onto the boulevard that ran down the center of town, Ramon shifted in his seat and tugged his phone from his pocket on the front of his jeans.

"What's that?" she asked. Maybe a reply from Maizie since he had taken a photo of one of the letters and sent it to Kenna's assistant.

Ramon scanned the screen. "It's a motion sensor I put inside Paige's place. In case he came back to get something."

"It's the middle of the night, but you don't think the cops have someone sitting on his house waiting for exactly the same thing?" He'd taken a risk breaking into the house to put a motion sensor inside. On the off chance Paige would be dumb enough to come home for a change of socks or whatever.

"This is his dad's cabin," Ramon said. "He shares it with his brothers. They hunt or fish even though there are no lakes around here. It's probably more about bringing women to the cabin, drinking, and getting high until their wives call and ask why they haven't come home yet."

There was a lot to unpack in that statement, even if it didn't surprise her that he was cynical. Once they had cleared his name, she and Ramon could talk about finding hope in the world. Maybe getting a girlfriend who could help him have a good life rather than joining up with some crew of mercenaries and generally causing terror on behalf of whoever wants to pay them.

He told her the address, and she typed it into her phone GPS so the device could lead her to a man trying to kill her. It probably made more sense to go completely in the other direction. But the chance to find out why he had been tasked with killing her and who paid him to do it made the question a no-brainer.

It took forty minutes to get up into the mountains to the west of town. There wasn't much in the way of trees, but the brush gave enough coverage for someone to hide behind if they felt the need to flee for their life across the rocky desert terrain to those hills.

She never knew what would happen on any given day.

"I see it." Kenna peered through the windshield, slipping off her headlights so she didn't alert the occupant of the cabin up ahead as to their presence. She eased down on the brakes, slowing them to a stop.

The structure had a couple of trees planted around it, but they weren't tall, which meant they hadn't been established for long. Someone had attempted to make the cabin look nice. Too bad the condition it was in now, with siding falling off and missing roof tiles, didn't make it a place she wanted to spend much time in.

Empty planter pots flanked the front door. The hose had been left on the ground under the front right window, which had grown cloudy over the years. Behind the pane, light was illuminated inside.

Someone was here.

Ramon reached for his door handle. Kenna started to do the same, but Ozzy let out a little yap.

"Feed the dog." He closed the door and left her in the car while he headed for the cabin, going around the side, probably trying to use a back door to surprise whoever was in there.

Kenna reached back and tugged out one of the containers of food, pulling back the lid. "You probably don't need all of this, but you are also probably really hungry." The container had two sides to it, so she held the lid over one side while the dog ate from the other. She'd never had a tiny dog before, but he probably weighed ten pounds at most. She knew because she could pick him up without causing her forearms a lot of pain. "I'm going to have to find out how much you're supposed to be eating."

The dog just made contented licking sounds.

"You're not going to chew anything or rip anything while I go inside the cabin and make sure Ramon doesn't kill a man, right?"

Ozzy got up and turned around a couple of times on the seat. She secured the lid on the food and sat back in her chair, turned so she could watch him. He planted both front paws on the center console, so she gave his chin a little scratch.

The letters on the passenger seat caught her attention. She grabbed the first one and opened it, discovering they were written in Spanish. Kenna took pictures of each one, removing them from their envelopes and then putting them back in once she had taken the photo. Just in case it was relevant which one was mailed when if they needed to understand the timeline later.

No gunshot sounds from inside. Yet.

She checked her phone and found Maizie had sent her a text saying that she would get on translating the letters with a website that could quickly change the text from one language to another. It wouldn't be perfect, but it was a good start if they wanted to know what Noelle had told the other woman.

She sent a text in reply.

> Any idea who this Esmeralda Juarez is? Or anything about the ranch where she lives?

The three dots popped up, indicating Maizie was typing. A second later, the message came through.

> I have a driver's license for her with an address that isn't current. The ranch is a tourist destination, and it's seriously pricey. Maybe she works there?

Kenna sent a reply instructing Maizie to keep digging and get some sleep. They generally worked and slept at all hours, but one of them should at least attempt to maintain a regular schedule. This time it wasn't Kenna. After the nap this afternoon and all the coffee she'd had, she was wide awake despite the fact it was almost four in the morning.

Ramon rapped his fist on the passenger window, leaving a smear of blood on the glass, and Kenna rolled down the window. "He says he'll only talk to you."

Ozzy barked.

Kenna picked up the dog, pocketed her keys, and followed Ramon to the cabin. Above their heads the expansive cloudless sky sparkled with a million stars. A sight she hadn't seen many times in her life, but one that felt familiar in the way a certain pair of boots would. Or a battered copy of *Mere Christianity* that her dad should have paid more attention to.

They entered through the front door, which stood open.

Inside, she was greeted by the smell of cigar smoke and burned cheese. An old lamp on an end table lit the living area, blending into the kitchen and its ancient refrigerator and laminate countertops. A formerly white curtain hung over a window and now had a hole in it with charred edges, indicating it had caught on fire at some point and had never been replaced. Dishes filled the sink. Multiple pizza boxes, open and empty, had been stacked on top of each other on the oven. Kind of like the mail on the table.

Officer Paige sat in a wooden chair, glaring at her, his hands tied behind his back. Probably also secured to the chair. His eyes flared at the sight of her.

Or maybe it was Ozzy.

"Keep that thing away from me," he warned. "I'm allergic to dogs."

Kenna stared at him, wondering precisely how much satisfaction she would get from waving Ozzy in front of his face. Then she turned and handed the dog to Ramon. "He needs to go outside anyway." It would give her a chance to talk to the cop without an audience.

Ramon spun on his boots and stomped to the front door.

She called after him, "Don't lose that dog."

Paige smirked. "Is it a material witness?"

"It's more valuable than you are."

She moved close enough to intimidate him a little by standing where he had to crane his neck to look up at her. But not close enough for him to kick out and manage contact. "You were either paid to kill me, or someone forced you to do it by means of blackmail. Which is it?"

"I wasn't going to tell your goon."

So he'd bought himself some time by telling Ramon that he would only talk to Kenna? Guess he didn't figure she was outside in the car. "You're on the run now. Whatever career you had was destroyed when you decided to break the law."

He scoffed, sweat running down the side of his forehead. "Because you're so innocent? Not exactly the kind of people the PD is tasked with protecting. You probably think you can protect yourself." He hadn't managed to kill her, but he got some good licks in the process. She had a nasty scrape on her elbow to show for it.

"Who approached you?"

Paige shrugged his shoulder. At least as much as he could with his hands secured behind his back. "Some guy."

"You just don't know who he is, or you've never seen him before?" She wondered if it was Walker. Now there was a sliver of possible connection between Cecelia and the serial killer—via the man she had lost and the fact he had been in the army—there could be a wider net to cast.

"What does it matter?" Paige said. "When they find me because I failed, they'll kill me."

So it wasn't his colleagues at the police department that he was necessarily worried about. More the consequences of not doing the job. "Tell me who they are, and I'll make sure they aren't able to come after you. That's about your only choice right now. Giving me the information you have and letting me take care of it."

As if she would simply let him walk away.

Thankfully, Ramon didn't hear that since he was outside, or he would likely have objected to the insinuation that Paige would be free to go.

It was only this cop who needed to believe the lie.

"You think you can stop them?"

"It doesn't matter if I believe I can." Kenna paused. "I *will*. Because that's my job."

Doggy nails scrambled across the floor. Ramon stepped

into the cabin a second later and eased the door shut behind him.

Ozzy sniffed her pant leg and the laces of her Converse and turned his attention to Paige.

He immediately kicked out at the dog. The animal yelped and flipped over on the floor. Kenna lifted him, petting the dog so he didn't retaliate. Even though she wouldn't have minded so much if he did, Ozzy also needed to be able to live with a nice family that would take care of him.

"Paige, why did you take the job?"

The officer gritted his teeth. Hissed out a breath between the clenched enamel. Still, he didn't give anything up.

"Let me guess." Ramon grabbed a chair from the table, spun around, and sat on it backward. "Gambling debts. Drug habit. Or a report was made, maybe a bunch of them. Something about how you act inappropriately with young girls on a regular basis. Wouldn't look too kindly on a promotion request, would it?"

Kenna would have waited him out. The problem was, that might have taken hours. Instead, she got to see the look on his face when Ramon mentioned young girls. The flare in his eyes. "I guess now we know."

Ramon glanced at Kenna. "The question is, does it have anything to do with what was in that safety deposit box?"

Paige shifted on the chair, almost jerking against his bonds. "I don't have anything to do with that box. Or what happened at the bank."

"Whose box did they rob?"

"I don't know," Paige said. "I just know you don't touch it, or Noelle."

The bank teller had been protected. But when Kenna looked into her life, she saw a woman who wanted to get out of her situation. That's what their meeting had been about.

The chance for a fresh start. Only, it was supposed to have happened after she showed Kenna that box.

Now, Noelle was dead.

"So Noelle had been connected and practically untouchable, but that didn't save her life. You don't have the same protection." Kenna gave a little shrug that indicated her thoughts about his life expectancy. "Your best chance is to trust us."

It seemed odd, indicating Ramon as well as herself. Meanwhile Ozzy had lain down beside Kenna's foot, his chin on her shoe.

"Who gives the orders around here?" Ramon asked.

"It doesn't matter. You just follow them whether you like it or not. Or you get fired. Your mortgage is suddenly due in full in thirty days. Your car is repossessed, and your bank account suddenly empty."

"The entire town?" Kenna had been places where it seemed like everyone who lived there was in a chokehold by somebody who thought they should have power over other people.

Paige shrugged. "It is what it is. Why would anywhere else be any better?"

"You've gotta give us something." Kenna stared at the guy, wondering if he ever had a chance. "Or we have nothing to go on but following you until somebody kills you and then we start following them. Eventually, we will work our way up the chain to the top. It would be faster if you just tell us who sits in those lofty heights."

"Why don't you start by checking who owns most of the property in this town? Buying up huge stretches of land, dumping one shipping container in the middle and nothing else? Look at who holds everyone's mortgages. Who runs the bank?"

Ramon snorted. "I'm guessing they have control over the police department as well."

"I'm telling you guys the truth."

Ramon crossed his arms. "And at the same time managing to give us nothing at all."

Kenna had a different point to make. "Why this town? Who cares about a stretch of desert in nowhere Nevada?"

"She's right." Ramon nodded. "If you wanted to go somewhere, you'd just hit Vegas. It's not far. Talk about valuable real estate worth investing in. What is this town so famous for that someone would want to kill for it?"

Paige's gaze darted around. He was losing control of himself and the situation. Sweating through his grimy T-shirt and jeans. Things weren't going well for him.

Kenna was just about to nudge him for a response when the kitchen window shattered, and that curtain blew out. Paige's body jerked in the seat. He slumped to the side, his head on his shoulder.

A bullet between his eyes.

Ramon let out a cry.

Kenna twisted on her way down to the floor, trying not to land on the dog. *He has to be right outside the window.* Ozzy yelped—hopefully only in surprise—and got out of the way. She landed shoulder first and scrambled around.

Ramon clutched his shoulder, breathing hard. He frowned. "I've been shot."

Chapter Eleven

Kenna hissed out a breath. "Walker."

She shifted around on the floor, caught the dog about to run off, and scooped him up by the belly. She handed Ozzy over to Ramon. "Keep an eye on him."

She drew her weapon from its holster at the small of her back. Got up and headed for the door. Where she would probably be shot just like Paige the second she stepped outside. What a senseless death, and a serious threat they now had to contend with. A sniper could take her out before she even realized she'd been hit. Or anyone else standing around her.

It was enough to make her hunker down and stay inside the cabin.

But if she did that, she would never find what she was looking for.

Ramon groaned. "It's probably just another one of those mercenaries from the bank tying up loose ends."

"I'll give them your number." Kenna stepped outside and headed for the west corner of the cabin, peering around. Apart from the barn and a few bushes, there wasn't much in the way of cover. Just the normal shadows of night hiding someone moving across the landscape.

A sniper would have to find a good place to wait out the scene, patiently looking for the perfect time to squeeze off a round.

She sprinted between the cabin and the barn, which was padlocked shut. All the way around, past trash cans that smelled like old Chinese food. Knocked over and rummaged through by some curious wildlife. Hopefully, there were no mountain lions or coyotes out here.

At the back corner of the barn, she spotted a couple of larger bushes growing close together in the middle of the rough terrain behind the property. Jagged hills with ruts of dirt between peppered the landscape, interspersed with craggy peaks. Plenty of places to hide.

But she spotted a flash of light in one spot and crept toward it, leaning against the dirt where it veered up in front of her. She lay with her shoulder to the earth and watched.

He was packing up his rifle.

She planted her hands on the top of the pointed ground, ignoring how it poked into her skin.

A rifle would've been better. Still, she lined up the sights, blew out a slow breath, and squeezed off a single shot. Then two more. She heard a yelp and then the scramble of feet as he took off running.

Interesting.

Kenna shoved off the ground and chased after him. It was slow going, or at least slower than a stretch of flat ground and the right shoes. At least she had decent footwear with the rubber soles, but the uneven earth rose and fell ready to break her ankle at any moment.

She wouldn't catch up to him at this rate, but she also didn't plan to give up.

She heard a vehicle engine start, a rough cough followed by the sound of a running motor with a distinct click in the cadence. He sped away in his vehicle, and she rounded a particularly nasty-looking cactus about seven feet tall just in time to see one brake light was out. Too dark to catch the license plate.

Kenna returned to where he had been packing up his rifle and flipped on her camera flashlight. All of his stuff was still here.

An open duffel bag with inserts for the pieces of his weapon lay partially open, the weapon somewhat disassembled beside it. She loaded it all in, then got her shoulder in the straps and hefted it up so that she carried it across her shoulders and not with the strength of her arms—which wouldn't have worked anyway.

Kenna deposited the duffel bag beside the trunk of her car so that it leaned against the wheel. Then she went back to the cabin.

Ramon and Ozzy were nowhere to be seen. In the grim yellow light of the kitchen, Paige looked like an omen of death from a nightmare. Even after all the times in her life she had seen a dead body, it still didn't get easier. Not when one moment you were talking to a living breathing human being and the next they were nothing but a hollow shell of something that used to be.

Ramon strode out of the bathroom, holding the dog in one arm and trying to put pressure on his other shoulder with a towel. He grimaced.

"He got away. But I have the weapon." So they had something. Weapons had serial numbers. Manufacturers. Merchant records of purchases—and the name of whoever bought it. That meant more leads. "Let's go before you leave more DNA at this scene."

She glanced at Paige one more time, realizing they'd have to anonymously alert the police department here to the fact one of their officers was dead.

Even if the guy was dirty and wanted for questioning, and even if the department was under some kind of stranglehold—if what Paige had said was true—they still needed to know. A body had to be disposed of and a report would need to be filed.

Ramon said, "He was going to kill you if he got the chance."

"Yeah, but going out like that?" Kenna winced.

"You're right." Ramon handed her Ozzy like he was a hot potato. "I'd rather see it coming."

They headed for the door, and she secured it shut so no animals got in before the police.

Ramon hung by the door, watching the shadows. "Thanks for having my back."

She nodded, finding solace in giving Ozzy pets as she walked to the car. "Can you get that loaded in the trunk?" She lifted her chin in the direction of the rifle bag.

Ramon popped the trunk. "I know a guy. I can find out everything you need to know about that weapon. You could take Esmeralda and the ranch."

Kenna did want to get out of town since things had heated up recently. Pack up her RV and put some distance between her and the Pahrump Police Department. But did she really want Ramon taking a key piece of evidence and going off on his own? She wouldn't be able to do damage control if he got in over his head. And if Cecelia somehow managed to find him and take him out like Paige, she wouldn't know anything had happened to him until much later.

Kenna slid in, depositing Ozzy on the back seat. As Ramon settled in and checked his phone—rather than buckling his seatbelt—she thought it over. They definitely would achieve more if they divided up tasks between them rather than working everything together and taking twice as long. "Where do you want me to drop you?"

"You could just loan me your car."

Kenna shot him a glance.

"What? You have to tow it anyway. It's not like you can drive the RV and your car at the same time."

She sighed and made the turn in the dirt out front of Paige's cabin. "Figure out how to leave an anonymous tip for the police department that informs them one of their officers is deceased and where to find him."

"Already done." Ramon lowered his phone. "I used the contact form on their website and the email address for a library in Alabama."

"How is your arm?" She turned her headlights to the bright setting and eased their way back to the asphalt highway.

"Feels great." He shifted in the seat and groaned. "So good."

She let him have his sarcastic moment and figured out the best way to get back to town. If it wasn't for her RV, she wouldn't even go back there, but no way was she going to leave her home unattended while she went to Arizona to follow up on a lead. "It's no coincidence that Esmeralda is at a ranch in Arizona, and Cecelia heads up the Phoenix office. It can't be."

"There are no coincidences. Anytime I even think there might be, it turns out to be a targeted series of events. And I'm usually the victim."

Kenna flipped her brights back to normal headlights on the highway now headed back to town. "How do you not fall into the trap of hopelessness if other people have made it so hard for you to just have a normal life?"

He didn't glance at her or open his eyes. And she couldn't see his face much in the dark. Ozzy, passed out in the back seat, started snoring.

Ramon said, "How did *you*?"

Kenna thought back to those days after she'd been involuntarily retired from the FBI. Dealing with her injuries and the aftermath of all that physical trauma had kept her focused simply on healing. Not on the innate need in any human being to exact revenge on the one who has wronged them.

"I didn't set out to put it all straight." Kenna gripped the wheel, feeling the pull of the damaged tissue in her forearms. "I was pretty much dragged back kicking and screaming to face it all. Might be a case of, 'If I knew then what I knew now' considering how much I've changed since."

She would hope that the fact she became a Christian a few months ago meant she would now do things differently, but sometimes the effects of the past were so strong it sort of eclipsed any ability to take a thought captive.

Let alone try to make a different choice.

"So why help me?" Ramon asked. "It's not like you get anything out of my reputation being restored. As if that's going to happen."

"Just make sure when Cecelia is taken down that you're in a position to be able to get your reputation back." He had to understand that. "You can't allow yourself to be so far gone that you can never walk back."

"And how do you know, with everything I've done since she destroyed my life, that I'm not already so far gone it isn't worth it?"

Kenna figured the answer to that one was simple.

"Because if you were, you'd have put a bullet in her head a long time ago."

Ramon made a small grunt.

She let him think about that in the dark in the quiet of her car. With the hum of the road and the still of the night all around them. She saw maybe one car, and when it didn't flip a U-turn in the middle of the highway in order to follow them, she figured they had no idea who she was. No need to worry about them.

Ramon's breathing evened out as he drifted into an uneasy slumber. How he could sleep with a gunshot wound was interesting to ponder, but Kenna kept her focus on making sure they weren't followed as she made her way back to the street where the RV park was.

She flipped her headlights off, just to ensure she didn't disturb any of the other residents and stopped just inside the entrance. She dug out her cell phone and checked the security in her RV. Everything remained undisturbed, so she proceeded over to the row where she had parked.

Definitely time to unhook everything and get out of Dodge.

As she pulled up beside her RV, Ramon sucked in a breath and sat up.

"Are you going to be okay to drive, or do you need to crash for a while first?"

He shook his head. "I'll hit the sack at my motel room before I go meet up with my contact. The guy who can run the serial number on that gun. Find out who shot Paige."

"Okay. I'll have Maizie pass along what we get when I talk to Esmeralda." She gathered Ozzy and his things, including the dog bed and all the letters.

Ramon rounded the car for the driver's side.

She glanced at him.

"You're gonna get all sappy on me now?"

"Just don't get yourself killed."

"Even if I do," he said, "you can still clear my name. I don't have to be alive for that."

"If you are, and I am as well, let's meet up somewhere and celebrate."

He grinned, a flash in the moonlight. "Deal." Then paused a second. "Thanks, Kenna."

She turned and walked backward for two steps. "Don't get all sappy on me now."

He laughed and slid into the seat.

Kenna went into her RV, realizing they might have a fresh lead, but it wasn't the time to text everyone and wake them up. That could wait a couple of hours until morning. She fired up her laptop and started a fresh pot of coffee.

There was work to do.

Half an hour later, she sat back in her chair, then got up to stretch and pace the length of her RV. Ozzy snoozed in his dog bed on the floor beside her queen bed at the far end of the rig.

"A dude ranch, resort, and spa—among other things. Willowbrooke." Kenna stopped by the kitchen sink. "Sounds pretentious. She works at a dude ranch for famous people, and the only way in is..."

She might need Ramon after all, given checking in as a couple would make it easier to have backup on hand. Which would be impossible to arrange otherwise. An undercover operation?

Given Cecelia's connection to everything so far and the implication of what Paige had told them about Pahrump... someone there might recognize him.

"Just call Jax and ask him to go undercover with you." Her phone buzzed on the table, and she wandered back to it, realizing she'd dialed Jax's number. "Huh."

When the call connected, he groaned a little. "Yeah, Jaxton."

"I woke you." She hadn't even meant to call him. "I'll call back."

"What time is it?" Before she could answer, he said, "My alarm is going off in a few minutes, anyway."

"Sorry," she said, hearing his movements.

"No need to apologize. It could be important." He was starting to sound more awake, but she liked the sleepy tenor of his voice. It sounded warm and made her miss being close to him.

Kenna poured herself more coffee and sat at the table. "Noelle was in contact with a woman we think works at a dude ranch in Arizona. The only way in is with a reservation, which means going undercover. And posing as a couple would be better than me going solo."

For a second, she realized how far she'd come that she would even think that. So many years going it alone, and now her instinct was to ask for help—for a partner?

"I can pull vacation," he added. "Go with you."

"Why not just have your boss sign off on it?"

"Unless you can tell me that's the last place *El Caminante* was sighted, it's a no-go. Otherwise, the case is cold."

Kenna winced. She could hear it in his voice—the pressure he was under, and the need to keep all this below Cecelia's radar.

If Walker was hiding, they'd just have to go after the dirty FBI agent.

Work on a case they *could* solve.

"Good news is, I might've shot him," she said. "After he killed the cop that tried to kill me."

"Paige?" Jax paused. "Wait, you shot Walker?"

"I have no idea." How did she find out, though? She glanced over at Ozzy. "I'll find out if they allow dogs at this fancy resort."

"Wait...what?"

She grinned. "There's someone you need to meet."

Chapter Twelve

Maizie had found an RV storage place for Kenna about twenty minutes' drive from the ranch. Two days after she and Ramon parted ways, Kenna stepped out of her rig and locked the door. Ozzy rustled around in a dog carrier she'd sat beside the door along with his things—including several new toys Maizie had shipped to her.

She checked her phone and the GPS app showing Jax's location. He'd already pulled into the RV park and now made his way around to her unit.

Why she was nervous to see him, Kenna didn't know. Maybe it was simply nerves over the task ahead of them.

The vehicle that pulled around the corner at the end of the lane was an extremely shiny black GMC truck. She blinked. *This* was his chosen vehicle? They were supposed to be undercover. Even if they were posing as upwardly mobile —dual income, no kids with a dog—that wasn't the ride she'd have chosen.

She lifted a hand to shield her eyes from the midday sun, realizing she should have purchased a pair of sunglasses along with that entirely new set of clothes and the suitcase to put them in. Along with all the accoutrements to transport Ozzy on their vacation.

The gold watch she'd bought slid down her arm under the long sleeve of the white blouse, which she'd paired with champagne-colored slacks and fancy-looking sandals. But she could run in them if necessary—at least without breaking her ankle.

Jax pulled up and left the engine running while he jumped out and came around the hood. He sported an open-collared dress shirt with and gray slacks. A belt he definitely didn't wear to work at the FBI and a pair of loafers with...no socks? He'd even gelled his hair.

She looked him up and down. "You look like the heir to an organized crime family."

"Good. Because that was what I was going for." He slid his arms around her waist just as Ozzy rustled in the dog carrier and let out a couple of barks. "I want to know what that is and how you got it. But first..."

He leaned in and touched his lips to hers, dragging it out until she rolled her eyes and shoved at his shoulder. "We have work to do." And as much as Kenna might want to, it didn't involve making out. At least not beyond what was necessary to maintain their cover as a married couple.

Otherwise, they would both end up distracted.

"It's good to see you," Kenna said.

Yeah, it really was.

He must've seen that written on her face because he grinned. "A dog?"

"It fits with the persona we're going for on this mission."

"Yeah, because that's the only reason you picked up another stray to add to your collection."

Kenna didn't know if he was talking about people, or animals. Probably both, although that meant he was one of them. They'd talked a little about the fact he felt he didn't quite fit in the FBI. Not just because he had been raised with money as part of an upper-class Californian family, which meant they had serious money. But also because he might want more from his life than punching the same clock for thirty years until he could apply for retirement.

There was no way she would tell him to quit now. He would only want to join her company and travel around solving cases with her. It was what she wanted. But that didn't mean it was also his dream—or anything close. Jax had to figure out for himself what the path ahead of him was going to be.

He set her fancy new gold-colored suitcase on the back seat and pushed it all the way behind the driver's side. As she picked up Ozzy's carrier, he bent down, running an index finger over the mesh. "Hi, doggy."

Ozzy barked and snarled at him.

Jax straightened, grinning. "He likes me."

Kenna wasn't exactly sure about that but figured she'd either manage it or they would work out some kind of truce. "Let's go. The reservation Maizie made for us has a check-in time of three."

He saw through it, but that wasn't the point.

Kenna climbed up into the truck. But before he shut the door for her, she said, "Whose truck is this?"

Jax grinned. "I always wanted one." He shut her door and climbed in the driver's side. Looking pretty comfortable in control of a huge black truck. "I borrowed this one from a friend of mine who works at the city council. Although, he made me swear I wouldn't get even a scratch on it."

How could he guarantee that? It wasn't a promise she would've made. "Ramon has my car. Who knows if I'll even get it back or what condition it will be in."

Then again, that was why she purchased only nondescript

older cars that zero people even noticed driving around. Not since having something flashy—like that sweet black Chevy Impala she'd put in storage for now—drew way too much attention. Still, maybe Maizie would want to drive it later.

She must have made that *huh* sound out loud because he glanced over and asked, "What is it?"

"Maizie hasn't said anything to me about learning to drive."

"It'll be scary for her to have that next level of freedom. Stairns said she doesn't leave their property and hasn't asked to do so. She feels safe there."

Kenna glanced back and checked on Ozzy, who seemed to be asleep again.

"So Noelle had a dog you found when you searched her apartment?"

Kenna huffed. "Can you believe Ramon thought we should just leave him there?"

Jax gasped, but it was pretty fake. And apparently, he thought that was amusing. Grinning, he glanced at her, scanning her outfit. "Please tell me you packed a dress as well as more outfits like that. Because you look amazing."

"Why would I need a dress?" The fact that she had actually bought more than one and they were in her suitcase didn't matter right now.

"Answer the question."

She smiled. "I guess you'll find out."

Jax shook his head. "For the record, I had a sudden family emergency and I have exactly one week off work to figure this out."

"Noted." She'd rather this was above board. But when the person they were going after was a connected FBI boss, that wasn't going to be possible.

"You said it's a dude ranch?"

"Seems more like a resort when you look at the website. *Willowbrooke*. A place for rich people to pretend they're living a Western-style life when it's actually somewhere new to get spa treatments, sit by the pool, and sip fancy drinks from tiny glasses."

"And Esmeralda works there?"

Kenna nodded. "When Maizie ran her information, we discovered that she also had a spouse in the army. He quit the service to come home and be with his family full-time. This was six years ago. He and Esmeralda were trying to get pregnant at the time, but before she did, he committed suicide."

"Did you look at the file?"

"Maizie sent me the information. It was pretty sparse, given how open and shut the case appeared on the surface. They never did an autopsy, and I don't have enough to request they exhume his body now and run the tests. Even if we did manage to do that, it might be pointless as anything in his system would be long gone."

The husband had supposedly shot himself. As far as Kenna had seen, it almost looked too neat. Life and death and all the in-betweens were a whole lot messier than that.

"I want to know what Esmeralda has to say about it," she continued. "And Noelle, and everything they talked about in their letters."

"Was any of it about Cecelia?" Jax said.

"They never specifically named her. But they talked about a 'she' and sounded scared of her and what she might do next."

"So naturally Cecelia gets wind of you coming to the bank, and Noelle possibly double-crossing her. So she hires mercenaries to rob the place and shoot Noelle in the process. Making it look like she was the victim of a dangerous crime. Just another statistic."

"There's more."

He glanced at her, and neither of them needed him to ask.

"We have a connection, though I didn't make the call so neither of them know it."

"Who?"

"Maizie went through everyone who works for the ranch, and the head of security is Antonio Ryson."

"Seriously?" He shook his head.

"They're cousins. I sent Ryson a text and asked him to call me back, but he hasn't yet. Hopefully, he will soon, and we can get some insight into how to approach the guy." She shrugged. "They might be friends, and they might've never really spoken." She explained everything Paige had said about the whole town being in a stranglehold from some corporation buying up land around Pahrump.

"Maizie hasn't managed to figure out who they are. It's just a lot of smoke and mirrors at this point, at least until she manages to tie them to a specific person—or even a bank account that isn't cryptocurrency."

Jax hit his turn signal and pulled under the archway for the ranch. "It's *always* cryptocurrency."

Kenna had to admit that was true.

He leaned forward, peering over the steering wheel at the red dirt around them. The series of buildings that stretched out in front of them in line with the horizon were all white adobe with red terra-cotta roofs. Tall palm trees lined the lane from the street to a circular driveway. Standing on both sides, each tree was about five feet from the next. It gave a kind of cordoned-off feeling—like a red carpet. Or so she could imagine.

The whole place sort of gleamed while at the same time managing to seem natural. As though it blended into the landscape of red dirt and a backdrop of sunburned mountains.

"I should have bought sunglasses." She shook her head.

"Why does this place seem familiar, like I've been here before?" He lifted his foot off the gas pedal, and the truck started to slow. With no one else on the lane behind them or in front, it didn't really matter what speed they approached the roundabout at the end.

A huge cherub fountain in the center looked like it had been torn out of the center of an Italian city. Squirting water in an arc that probably cooled the area around it. So much greenery, all kept alive with precipitous use of sprinklers on timers, and landscapers paid well to trim every leaf.

With parking for only a few visitors, no wonder there was a podium outside the pergola over the entryway. Behind it stood a white-waistcoat-wearing valet waiting for them. As if he had nothing more to do with his entire day than to stand there ready to help them as soon as they arrived.

"I think we came here when I was a kid." Jax frowned, still looking at the main building stretching above their heads as they drove to the valet stand. "I think my dad had a conference here."

"Hopefully, no one will remember little Oliver Jaxton running around." Kenna reached for the door handle. "Let's go find us a housekeeper."

Chapter Thirteen

Jax went into the room first, holding the door for her. "Looks like Maizie did all right by us."

"Can you believe this place has all those services for dogs? Ozzy will be so cute after he gets the full treatment at the spa today." She set her duffel by the entry table, upon which sat a huge vase with a profusion of flowers. She touched a petal. "These are real."

"Place like this? The clientele has serious money." Jax wandered across to the window. "I'll be fine on the couch even if it doesn't pull out into a bed."

The couch looked seriously comfy. Her RV had a couple of recliners. If she wanted to be horizontal, she'd lie on her bed. For the next week or so, however long they were here, she would enjoy having a living situation more like a regular house.

Once in a while she jonesed for a couch and a normal TV.

Or French doors like the ones Jax opened, leading out onto a balcony that overlooked the golf course and the man-made lake behind the main building.

He pointed. "There are tennis courts and horse stables out here."

The front desk attendant, a nice guy who was as tall as Jax but looked like he hadn't had an entire meal in six months, had explained all about the amenities. They could take out rowboats on the lake and hike trails up in the hills around the eighty-acre property. They had exclusive cabins in secluded areas of the rolling red hills. Plenty of manicured landscaping to ensure privacy. An expansive gym in the basement with a running track and an Olympic-size pool. A gigantic dining hall and ballroom.

Kenna pushed open the double doors to the bedroom and saw a giant king size on a platform. The bathroom was through the bedroom, so he'd have to disturb her at some point to use the facilities. She could share—Kenna wasn't worried about that.

Jax wandered up behind her. For a second, she wondered what he was going to do, and then his arms slid around her waist from behind and his front rested against her back.

She wasn't entirely accustomed to physical touch, with him living in another state from where she generally found herself. But when she got it, it was nice.

Maybe one day she'd be so used to his closeness that she'd take it for granted.

But that wouldn't be anytime soon.

She relaxed into his hold, leaning her head back on his shoulder. Thankfully, she didn't have to work this case alone —because having Ozzy with her didn't count as backup, even if he might alert her to danger.

"You know, we could've gone to the courthouse on the way over here," he said. "Then I wouldn't have to sleep on the couch."

Kenna bit the inside of her lip. *Danger zone.*

Still, it wasn't a bad thought. In fact, it was nice. *Very* nice. "And we wouldn't get any work done on the case because we'd be...busy."

He chuckled, sliding his arms from around her. "Yes, we would."

Kenna needed a cold shower now. "I'm sure you'll do just fine on the couch." She sent him a smile and grabbed her fancy suitcase—inside which was her duffel. "I'm going to get changed for dinner."

Her duffel unzipped to lay flat, and the clothes were on hangars in the bag. It didn't leave a lot of room for weapons, but she had a handgun with extra magazines and a couple of knives that she could put in a sheath on her thigh or ankle, or in a boot if she was wearing some. She closed the doors and hung up items that didn't need to be creased in the closet.

The dress was red with no sleeves and clung to her tight, the top high enough no one could see the bruise. And there was no risk it would fall far enough that she'd have a disaster on her hands. She zipped up knee-high black boots and tucked in the knife, added a choker to her neck, and fluffed her hair.

Poor guy usually only saw her in jeans and flats, lots of T-shirts, and sometimes blood and scratches—like the one on her elbow she couldn't hide. Not without the addition of the tiny cropped sweater that covered her shoulders and the long sleeves hooked over her thumbs, but it cut off high on her shoulder blades and at the front above the top hem of the dress. Just about the only hope she had of not showing off her scars.

Kenna stuck her head out the door, about to tell him to brace himself. And got a look at Jax in his slacks with no shirt on. She must've made a noise because he turned around, T-shirt over his elbows, about to put it on his head.

A knowing smile crept across his face. "Hey."

Oh boy. This entire case was going to be interesting. A series of near-misses and distracting moments they'd have to avoid. "This is why I'm better off three states away from you." Her voice came out sounding thick.

He didn't move to put his T-shirt on.

Two could play that game.

Kenna eased into view and leaned against the door frame.

His eyes flared. "I want to agree, but I also don't."

She grinned. "At least we don't have to fake being attracted to each other. One of those rich couples whose romance has gone cold and all that's left is awkward politeness between them."

No one would think it strange seeing them in hushed conversation or looking at each other like they wished they'd gone to the courthouse on the way here.

Did he really want to get married?

Just like that, no big deal. Sign a paper. Seemed like a flimsy reason if all they wanted it for was so they could share a bed without the guilt of knowing it wasn't the wise choice—the one that honored God. She'd been down that road before. Putting that cart before the particular horse. She'd been pregnant when Bradley died.

Who knew what her life would've been like. But she wouldn't have regretted it because at the time she didn't know better. She refused to feel guilty now. God wasn't going to hold it against her when He'd washed it all away anyway. That part of her was gone—forgotten.

She didn't have to carry the weight of guilt that had also been washed away.

Finally, he settled the shirt over his head. "We definitely don't have to fake that." He sat on the couch to put different shoes on right as her phone rang.

Kenna looked at the screen. "Finally." To Jax she said, "It's Ryson." She put the call on speaker. "Hey, it's me. Jax is here, too." Just so Ryson knew he wasn't talking to her alone.

"Good. Maybe I can talk some sense into him if I can't talk any into you."

"What?" This was one of her oldest friends. What did he need to talk sense into her about? "What did I do?"

"Going to that place." He hissed. "Antonio is bad news. Do *not* get mixed up with that guy. That whole place is something out of a conspiracy theory about government officials and private parties with trafficking victims. He sent me *pictures* once. Like he doesn't know I'm a cop? I have a daughter now. Why would I wanna see what happens there when I have no power to do something about it?"

Kenna slumped onto the couch beside Jax. "You're gonna have to give me some context on that one. What are you talking about?"

"Information I passed to the FBI's Crimes Against Children program."

"Good," Jax said. "So you did the right thing." Assuming it didn't simply land on Cecelia's desk and promptly get thrown in the trash, of course.

That might've been exactly why Antonio sent the images to his cousin. Because for whatever reason, he hadn't been able to risk sending them to the FBI himself.

"And now you two are eyeballs deep in it?" Ryson paused. "If Cecelia is connected to that ranch, you will need to get out fast. This thing will go sideways, and you'll end up in a situation you never wanted to be in."

Kenna said, "Maybe Antonio has had a change of heart, and now he wants to help us fix this. Shut these people down." She wanted to lift her legs and put them on Jax's lap but refrained. They would be on a slippery slope the entire time they were here, and the name of the game was *focus*. "Besides, that's a case for another day. This is about getting information on our target."

"Don't expect him to help you," Ryson said. "Proceed with caution. *Extreme* caution."

"Thanks for worrying about us."

"Watch each other's backs." He muttered something and hung up.

Jax stood, holding out his hand to help her up off the couch. She didn't let go of his hand all the way to the door, where she said, "Got the key card?"

He nodded.

"Ready for a recon dinner?"

He gestured. "After you, Mrs. Hawthorne."

The implication of what might happen if they stayed meant it was far better to head out into public. Not that she thought there was any danger of her needing to shove a chair under the handle on the bedroom door. They were capable of controlling themselves.

Kenna thought about it all the way down to the dining room, an expansive room with what looked like fabric wallpaper. Huge chandeliers turned down low enough they looked like twinkly lights. All the tables were covered with white linen and gleaming crystal, occupied with two or more people. She recognized a few of them in an abstract way.

She didn't keep up with who was currently famous, so she only felt as if she "should" know them.

Through the wall of glass at the end, she spotted a woman she did know on the patio. But she got up and moved from the wrought iron table outside the dining room out of sight too fast for Kenna to figure out if it was actually her.

Avery Masonridge.

Was it really her? They'd met for a few moments more

than a year ago. Avery probably wouldn't even remember Kenna and Jax—except that they'd saved her from a murder that would've looked as if she had overdosed on narcotics.

The last article Kenna had seen online was that Avery had run for the position of US senator for her home state of Florida as soon as she turned thirty. Had she won the race and moved to Washington?

Jax said something to a host behind the podium at the door, and the man nodded. "Of course. This way." He spoke in accented English and waved his arm, two rings on his left hand. Slicked hair, pressed slacks, and a shirt ironed with precision.

Jax walked with his hand on the small of her back. The host stepped aside, and Jax held her chair, easing it in as she did the shuffle of tucking her chair in and getting settled. Then in front of God and everyone in the room, he leaned down with one hand on the back of her chair and touched his lips to hers.

Just a second. Then he pulled back a fraction.

"You're making a statement," Kenna said. "And you know I can't object."

He sat with a knowing smile across the tiny round table from her. Close enough he could take her hand. "I've decided to change our backstory. I'm a rich playboy—naturally. You're my new sidepiece. An up-and-coming rock musician from Seattle."

She took a sip of the water on the table and discovered it was sparkling. She wasn't usually a fan of liquid hairspray, but she needed a moment. When she set the glass down, she turned to him. "Are we here so you can show me a good time?"

"I think I'm up for the challenge." He winked. Before she could think of a comeback, he said, "I sent my mom a text. She said we did come here when I was little." He shook his head. "Thankfully, they haven't been in years, considering what Ryson told us."

Kenna nodded, detecting something in his tone. "Everything okay at home?"

"I'm good as long as we don't run into anyone who could blow our cover."

"Okay, now answer the question."

He lifted a finger a second before the server appeared and ran down the specials for them—a Hispanic male in his early twenties with an earring in one ear that sparkled like it might actually be a diamond. Wearing the dining staff uniform of black slacks and crisp white shirt, shined shoes, and slicked-back hair.

Jax looked at her a second after the server mentioned cheese, and she nodded. He gave the server both their orders and asked for black coffee.

"Very good, sir." The server nodded at Jax, then at her, and was gone a second later.

Kenna said, "You were saying..."

"Was I?" He sipped his drink. "Why spoil our date with a conversation about how my mother holds my father's life in a stranglehold of dinner parties he abhors, and he retaliates by cutting up her credit cards. She just goes out and gets a new one, running up a bill for the next party. And around and around we go."

"Sorry." She wasn't sure having no parents was better than having frustrating ones.

"She wants to meet you." He set his glass down. "Probably because she wants another excuse to throw a big party. Tell all her rich and famous friends about my girlfriend, who is rich and famous."

Kenna frowned.

"I'm sure not all of them will believe you're pregnant by the end of the evening. But they'll all think we're at least engaged."

"The courthouse is looking more appealing."

Jax chuckled. "Good call. She'd take over everything, and our wedding would end up looking nothing like what either of us would want. My ex-wife..."

"What about her?"

"You probably don't want to hear about it." He scrunched up his nose.

"Tell me." Kenna tore off a piece of the bread on the table. Because hot fresh bread was always worth eating.

"Cayleigh was a force to be reckoned with. For six months they were at war over how it was all going to go down." He winced. "I pretended I had work even when I didn't."

"I'd have done the same," Kenna said.

"So you're going to leave me to plan our wedding and tell everyone you have an important case? Probably somewhere with no signal."

"There might be signal in specific spots. So I can call you. Other than that, I'll definitely be unreachable."

He chuckled. "You're terrible."

Kenna stared at her drink, her fingers going numb against the cold glass. Dampening from the condensation on the outside of the cup. "Why does even that feel like us in another lifetime?"

She wasn't scared over talk about weddings. She just didn't know how that fit into their lives. They lived in two separate parts of the country. Their jobs were like a military couple stationed apart all the time, finding snatches of leave to spend it together at random times and in out of the way places.

"I know what you mean." Jax touched the back of her

hand, and she turned it so he could lace his fingers in hers. "That's why we do what we can now. You're someone with an amazing capacity to just *be*. You live in the present in a way not many people do. That's not a bad thing."

The server placed their meals in front of them, and conversation around them swelled in her ears as she ate and thought about what he'd said.

Even if it had been born of trauma, she understood what he meant. Later, they could figure out what needed to change in their lives in order for their relationship to be different. But right now, they needed to focus on their top priority—taking down Cecelia. They had a housekeeper to find. Evidence to collect. Enough they could build a file no one at the Department of Justice would be able to ignore—and which Cecelia wouldn't be able to explain away.

She wasn't interested in a "normal" relationship with a picket fence, kids, and a dog. Though, she had the dog part down already. Still, sometimes in the quiet of the middle of the night, she wondered what that life would be like.

With Jax.

"Promise me something?"

Kenna lifted her gaze and saw the earnest look on his face, along with a whole lot of warmth. "What?"

"When Cecelia has faced justice, however that comes about, another bad guy is going to come along after her. Then another. Then another."

She knew where he was going with this. "I know I won't be doing this forever, but you have to know I'm not planning to give it up soon."

Jax twirled his fork in his fingers on the edge of his plate. "What if I wanted out of"—he looked around—"my job? What if I was ready for a change?"

"I don't want you wrecking your career for me."

"That isn't what would be happening."

Or so he thought. She started to argue with him, but commotion above the drone of conversation and clinking silverware in the room drew her attention to the door. Avery Masonridge strode in, her party speaking loudly to each other. Someone recorded the entrance on their phone. Half the group were young women who wore short dresses, and the males had suits on. They looked like a group of college friends and roommates who had remained close.

"So it was her," Kenna said. The party all seemed determined to enjoy their night. Loudly, which was likely why the host seated them in a smaller room off to the side.

"Avery Masonridge?" Jax asked.

Kenna nodded. "The one person in the room who knows we're not Mr. and Mrs. Hawthorne."

She looked around, wondering what other roadblocks they were going to run into. The quicker they could talk to Esmeralda, the quicker they could get out of here.

Kenna had a feeling it couldn't be soon enough.

Chapter Fourteen

A wave of fatigue rolled over Kenna. It had been a rollercoaster few days, and she was looking forward to a full night of sleep.

Actually, it had been a roller coaster few months. Driving, trying to keep one step ahead of Cecelia. Now, they had no idea where she was, since Kenna would have been positive the agent was in Phoenix at her office...right around the time she saw her in that Pahrump hospital.

She needed to widen the search parameters on kills they believed to have been committed by Walker. Assuming he was the one who had killed Officer Paige.

She had enough of a hunch to believe Walker was connected to Cecelia. But as with the rest of this case, there was next to no way to prove it. Had he been their sniper?

Kenna shivered.

Either she or Ramon could have lost their lives the other night. In a split second, gone forever. She wouldn't be here with Jax. Cecelia would go on unchecked.

God, we need a win on this. Or evil wins and justice never prevails.

Kenna put down the spoon for the dessert she hadn't needed and had no intention of finishing. Surprised to find the tension of playing a part wore on her more than she'd have thought it would. Even if she was here with Jax, the possibility they could be outed—and murdered—before they finished this sat like a bad taste in her mouth.

"This place is full of familiar faces." Jax set down his half-empty glass, somehow a signal to the nearby server that he needed a refill. As soon as the young man left again, he pointed. "Do you see who that is?"

A couple of tables away, two men sat together eating dinner and talking. One had short dark hair and tanned skin, wearing a faded tie-dye shirt and linen pants. If she peeked under the table, she wouldn't be surprised if he had Birkenstocks on. Across from him was a man as well-known as O.J. Simpson, or Robert Wagner.

Kenna nodded. "Preston Lightwood."

He looked over at her, but she was sure the man didn't hear her say his name. He wore a white shirt, open at the collar and a gold watch on one wrist. Styled dark-blond hair with a sweeping wave to it and plenty of gray, which also ran through his cropped beard.

"We've never talked about it," Jax said. "So what do you say, do you think he killed his wife?"

"He served nearly twenty years. I don't think it matters at this point whether I believe he did it or not. It's the stuff of internet conspiracy theories these days." She picked up her spoon, but didn't take another bite, already about to explode from all the food she'd eaten. It wouldn't look good if she wound up rolling around on the floor clutching her stomach in agony.

"Did they give you the case at Quantico?"

Kenna rolled her eyes. "I think everyone gets that one.

Even if only to see if they can find something new. Something all the investigators missed."

Lightwood had been convicted by a jury of his peers. So if evidence was overlooked, it didn't matter much after the fact, considering there had been enough to convict him. Still, Lightwood maintained his innocence through the entire trial, talking to anyone who would listen about the fact that someone else was in the house that night.

"I always took the missing girlfriend angle."

"An affair?" Kenna shook her head. "I wouldn't have pegged you for the salacious rookie looking for a juicy angle." She grinned at him, and the server swept away their dishes. No Styrofoam to-go boxes in a place like this. Though, she figured if she got peckish later tonight—which was next to impossible—room service was likely ready at all hours to bring a guest whatever they required.

Jax grinned. "Better than the clown angle."

Still, it was the one Kenna had leaned toward. "He didn't say it was a clown. He just said there was a guy in the house wearing a clown mask."

"With a blood alcohol level that high, mixed with everything he had taken? I'd be seeing killer clowns as well." Jax shook his head. "I've always been convinced he made the whole thing up to get the cops chasing their tails, looking for another suspect."

The server delivered china mugs on saucers in front of them, a dish with cubes of sugar, a tiny pourer containing what looked like cream, and two minuscule spoons. Hot black coffee tumbled into her mug from the carafe.

Definitely what she needed.

As soon as the server disappeared again, Jax said, "No one ever found evidence another person was in the house."

"Not according to the file given out at Quantico."

He stopped stirring his coffee. "What do you know?"

"More than what was in that file." Kenna dropped a cube of sugar into her black coffee. "My father is the one who arrested him."

"He was still an agent?"

She shook her head. "It was a few years later. I don't know what the deal was with him and Lightwood, but my father was the only person Preston was willing to turn himself in to. I guess he thought he was going to be shot by the police for what he did to his wife." Assuming, of course, that he'd been the perpetrator. Despite the fact Lightwood served twenty years for her death, Kenna's father was never actually convinced that he'd done the deed. "I was there when my dad walked him into the courthouse. Sitting outside in the car."

"Wow." Jax took a sip of his coffee. "Did your dad ever tell you anything about the case?"

"He absolutely would not say a thing," Kenna replied. "It was summer, I remember that. Given the date, I had to be six years old. We went to Wyoming and stayed in a cabin with a generator and no phone, but my dad bought me an entire book series about dragons in a magic kingdom, so I didn't really care. He taught me how to make burger patties from scratch—with all the seasonings." She hadn't thought about that time in a long stretch. "I should dig out that recipe. See if they're as good as I remember."

He had to have had a reason for them to be under total blackout. Off the grid. Maybe she needed his journal from that time in order to figure it out.

"If there is more to the story," she added, "then it's ancient history, and I have no idea what it was."

Jax had a look on his face, some kind of spark he likely felt every time he was handed a new case.

"Are you going to walk up to him and ask him what the

whole story was?" she asked. "I'm not aware he does interviews."

Jax grinned. "He's not alone. Maybe if I catch him in the elevator I'll ask him."

"Or you could read his book. I heard it's all about how he found Jesus in prison, so maybe not much in terms of juicy tidbits of leads the FBI refused to chase." She drank some more coffee, almost emptying her mug. Then they would have to make their way back through the dining hall without Avery, the wild child former president's daughter now a senator in Washington, seeing them close enough to recognize either Kenna or Jax.

"Any sign of the security guard, Ryson's cousin?" Jax looked around, but all the staff in here were for the dining guests.

"Maybe we should drop by his office later. Or tomorrow morning." Kenna paused. "As soon as Maizie is in the computer system, we will be able to find out when Esmeralda will be working."

Given Noelle was deceased now, Cecelia would have her attention on Esmeralda. Did she know about the letters? If she knew the connection, she'd have more mercenaries here. She would know if Kenna and Jax showed up at the woman's house. After what happened to Officer Paige, they needed to tread carefully to avoid another murder in cold blood.

Posing as a rich married couple had been the only way to get in the door.

And it was how they were going to find a quiet spot and see if Esmeralda was willing to tell them what they needed to know.

"Ready?" Jax asked.

Then something over her shoulder caught his attention.

Kenna nodded and stood. A man on approach stepped out

of her blind spot just as Jax moved in front of her. The two of them almost collided. Kenna moved around Jax to stand next to him in a flanking position.

Preston Lightwood held out his hand to her, mostly ignoring the fact Jax had intercepted him. "Makenna Banbury."

She accepted his hand just so they didn't make a scene and draw even more attention to themselves. "If you could not say that name around here, we would appreciate it."

He let go of her hand and offered his to Jax.

"Jackson Hawthorne." Jax shook his hand. "This is my wife, Kendra."

Preston's expression remained impassive. "A case?" After Kenna reluctantly nodded, he said, "Hopefully, nothing to do with me."

Kenna lifted her brows and slid her arm through Jax's elbow. "Hopefully."

Preston grinned. "You probably don't even remember me, but your dad was the best thing that ever happened to me. I just wanted to say that to you."

Not what she expected him to say. "Thank you."

"How long are the two of you here for?" Preston asked.

"Almost a week," Jax replied. "We think."

Preston looked at her. "I'd like to catch up with you at some point if that's okay? Your *husband* is welcome."

Hearing Jax referred to as her spouse, Kenna wouldn't admit this was more than just professional. "I'd like that."

Jax's arm flexed in her hold. She didn't think it was an objection. More likely, he was thinking she could ask the question the world wanted to know and pass some juicy tidbits back to this year's Quantico recruits. Give them a spin on the standard case everyone thought they could solve.

She didn't think Preston wanted to know that his life was a game mixed with an intellectual exercise.

"Thanks." Preston nodded. "My spiritual advisor—my rabbi, as it were—believes it would be beneficial for me to speak with you. A way to continue my healing." He motioned to the man he had been sitting with, who now waited for him by the host stand. Then turned back. "Have a good night."

They watched him walk away, and then Jax led her to a different door on the opposite side of the room, next to the wall of French doors that led out to the patio. A tiny side door led to a path that stretched into the grounds.

Once they were out of earshot of anyone else, Jax said, "I guess now we have to worry about Avery *and* Preston knowing who we really are."

"And the rabbi."

Jax squeezed her hand.

Kenna held on to his arm as they wandered slowly down the path, out for a romantic stroll in the evening on a gorgeous path flanked by bushes and flowers and with hanging bulbs giving the whole thing a yellow glow. "Let's have Maizie run them both and find out if there's any possible way they are connected to Cecelia. Though, I doubt in either case that they are."

"If they're not, they can still cause trouble for us."

She nodded. "It's a nice night. Feel like sneaking out and knocking on Esmeralda's front door?"

"After we agreed that wasn't a good idea?"

"Fine." Besides, given what she'd been up to with Ramon she might've had enough of breaking and entering for the week.

"You need sleep."

Kenna pressed her lips together. Of course, he knew that. Sometimes he had the eerie ability to read her, way more than most people. Maybe because he paid attention to her. More than acquaintances did. Or, around him, she let her guard down.

The path circled around, winding and curving.

"We're lost," she said.

Jax chuckled. "We're fine."

Until they weren't, and some mask-wearing clown guy jumped out and killed her, and he went to jail for it.

Kenna let out a long breath.

But the feeling didn't subside. And this wasn't just an irrational, overly tired, probably hormonal reaction based on nothing but the aforementioned.

"Someone is watching us," she whispered.

"I know. Keep going."

Did he know?

Maybe he was one of those guys who'd say he did, just for the sake of not being the only one who wasn't aware of what was going on. Then again, that was kinda petty, so probably not. She totally would if she felt like it. Lately, it seemed as if those old ways of dealing with stress and keeping the case going were becoming more like Ramon's way of doing things.

Not her style.

It almost felt like sanctification was a bit insidious. Or a word that meant the same, but with good connotations. She was different, but not from her own trying to be better or do better. More like God was changing her on the inside into a new person and every now and again something would happen, and she'd realize she wasn't the same.

When she wasn't so tired, she needed to ask Jax what he thought.

"He's to our left."

Kenna stiffened, not wanting to get hit with a sniper

bullet. Of course, Jax was between her and the gun—if there was one. Of *course*. "We need to run for it."

"I don't think it's someone out to harm us." Jax stopped, turning to the foliage on the left side of the path.

She couldn't make anything out between the big leafy bush, until someone stepped over to the illuminated spot by the trunk of a palm tree.

Definitely a Ryson. She'd have recognized him without even having seen a photo.

"Skulking around in the bushes?" she asked.

Antonio shrugged the shoulders of his suit jacket. "Had to make sure you weren't being followed. And that no one sees us together." A badge that read HEAD OF SECURITY hung from his breast pocket. "Otherwise, it'll blow your whole case."

Uh-oh. The way he said it, he didn't care. In fact, he might enjoy that.

Did this guy have a problem with her, with Jax, with the two of them here together, or just with the whole world and everyone in it in general? Doubtful he would be an ally.

Kenna huffed. "Seems like the only person we're being followed by...is you."

His teeth flashed in the dim light. "That's the way I like it."

Chapter Fifteen

"So why are you guys here? Did Javier finally decide to actually help instead of just ignoring me? I know what you do."

Kenna stared down Ryson's cousin, contemplating how different two people could be when they were from a similar gene pool. She didn't know what Javier had told Antonio. She hadn't given him specifics of the case because she never wanted to put his life in danger. Cecelia would absolutely come after him if she believed he and his family were Kenna's weakness.

The fact they *were* wasn't the point.

"Working a different case," Kenna said. "You know I'm a private investigator."

He didn't need to know the details of the case beyond what could be discovered from the news. After all, they had no idea if he was connected to Cecelia. On her payroll.

"I figured that's why you're here." He shrugged. "To bust up the resort."

They needed to talk about that. *After* Cecelia was taken

down. Antonio might prove trustworthy after all. "That's what you want?"

Antonio said, "Not much I can do without losing my job."

Kenna stared at him.

"We need to talk to Esmeralda," Jax said.

Kenna nodded. "She's friends with a woman I met recently, a bank teller killed in a robbery. Their spouses were both in the same military unit."

"And you think she has information?" Antonio seemed unaware of their surroundings. Or he was simply so used to every inch of this place he'd notice at once if something had changed.

"It's more of a courtesy." Kenna figured he'd consider her too soft to make it in serious police work, which fit with who she might want to be someday. She could try it on—see how it fit.

He'd write her off if he wasn't worried she might present a threat. And if he wasn't aware Jax was an FBI agent, all the better.

Antonio studied her. "And?"

Fine. He knew there was more. "Her life might be in danger," Kenna said, "but if we just roll up and knock on her door, *all* our lives might be in danger and our shot at this case is over."

"So you're covering your own butts." Antonio snorted.

Of course, he'd think that was her point. Not that there was a considerable threat out there. And on top of that, they might have a serial killer out there looking for them.

"I'll approach her." Before either of them could object, Antonio continued, "I make the connection. If she wants to talk, I'll introduce you."

Kenna shifted. *Nope. No way.* She started to say as much when Jax squeezed her hip.

"Thanks for the help. We'd appreciate it."

Antonio nodded. "She's one of mine. One of the employees here. I take care of them."

His tone sounded a little too oily for her taste. Which only meant she wanted to talk to Esmeralda even more now than she had before—and not with Antonio there.

"Kind of like you and my cousin." He looked her up and down. "I can see why Javier's so protective of you. Told me not to drag you into my thing. As if anyone else with influence is helping me. The sheriff isn't any further on it than I am."

"We're done here." Jax shifted her behind him.

Antonio lifted his hands and took a step back. "No sweat, bro." He wandered by them and headed back toward the main building.

Kenna rolled her eyes and muttered, "That guy is a piece of work," once Antonio was out of earshot.

"I'm thinking he's not as bad as he wants people to believe."

"Yeah?"

They started walking again. Jax snagged her hand and held it as they made their way back to their room, lacing his fingers with hers. "I think he needs to come across as if he operates in a gray area, or he'd never survive in a place like this."

"You're excusing it?"

"I guess time will tell if he's legit or not. If it's all talk or there's some substance underneath."

True enough. Kenna looked up at the whisps of cloud that seemed to want to obscure the stars, but their brightness didn't want to be shut out tonight. She checked her phone. No new messages.

Jax squeezed her hand. "We'll get something."

She didn't want to be all negative, and he also didn't know

how much she disliked this part of every case. Where she had more questions than answers, and the win seemed so far off that it might be impossible.

At least with this one, she didn't have to wrestle with it alone.

Having Jax here. Talking about what the future might hold. She barely recognized herself sometimes, and then at the same time it seemed so obvious that this was where life had brought her. To a good man who seemed to care deeply for her and a chance at the life she'd wanted before it was taken from her.

Risking it all on hope when she knew the pain of loss?

Also where life had brought her.

Assuming Kenna was strong enough to withstand that fire.

"Wanna talk about it?" he said.

"Nope," she said. "We should talk about whatever *you're* thinking about."

"It's fine."

Not when everything was about her and if she was all right. "Spill."

He chuckled. "We should pick up Ozzy from the spa."

"That's it?" She doubted that was all he had on his mind.

"I don't like that *El Caminante* has gone dark. We have nothing." His hand flexed around hers. "The trail is cold."

"Because he's stopped trying to draw me into something I'm not interested in being part of."

So he was...what? Planning?

That was a terrifying thought.

"Maybe he's still watching you," Jax said. "Which I don't like."

Even more so when they were states away from each other, but she figured it wasn't much help to point that out.

He continued, "I wish I could figure out what he's after."

Kenna squeezed his hand back. The serial killer was a man she'd met but hadn't talked to. She had no idea why he'd gotten fixated on her. Then he'd sent Stan Tilley to kill her.

And he'd told her that he killed her mother.

She shook her head. "Shame we can't wish he kills someone so we can get fresh leads."

Jax snorted. "Shame?"

"You know what I mean." She squeezed his hand again. "Any way you can pass me the file or get me signed on as a consultant? I could take a look."

"The FBI is currently not in need of assistance on this or any other case."

She grinned but wasn't going to let him know she wanted to laugh. "Of course. How silly of me." It wasn't just pride it was also a strong sense of professionalism. They weren't ever going to admit they couldn't do the work entrusted to them. And in that sense, the FBI was like a man who refused to ask for directions.

They lost something of public opinion if they admitted they needed help, and criminals had to respect their power to take down criminal strongholds and bring them to justice the same way the law-abiding public had to trust they were protected by federal law enforcement. Even if the average citizen never knew exactly *how* they'd been protected.

Kenna continued, "Do you think the bomb threats in San Diego were Cecelia, getting you all to chase your tails?"

Jax tipped his head a little. "That was my first thought. So I ran down the lead, even though my boss said it would turn out to be nothing. The calls came from a kid in Australia using a voice-over IP phone. An internet-based call."

"Local police there talked to the kid?"

"He said he was given five thousand Australian dollars

and specific instructions," Jax said. "I passed it to financials to track where the money came from."

She wasn't going to say *cybercurrency* again, but she was thinking it. "I wonder if they'll come back with something that connects to whoever is buying up land in Pahrump, Nevada."

"You really think Paige was telling the truth?"

"Sounds like Hatchet, doesn't it?" Kenna shuddered, even though the night air was barely chilly. "Who knows. Maybe criminals just aren't that creative. Or this isn't Cecelia—it's someone else. Maybe someone she works for?"

They stepped off the end of the path through the grounds to a wider patio area, people scattered around. Not a place to talk about criminals and investigations.

Jax led her to the side door, and up in the elevator to their room.

She appreciated the fact he didn't try to fill every quiet stretch with talk just for the sake of talking. She liked peace and quiet, and often spent hours alone not saying anything. Until the phone rang. Kenna needed time to think things through.

But he was here, and she was going to make the most of it.

So she wouldn't be doing her thinking alone.

He closed the door to their suite behind them and flipped the security latch. Kenna peeled off the cropped sweater she had over her arms and shoulders, unzipped her boots, and dropped them by the door. "One sec. I'll be back."

She tossed her phone on the bed and didn't have to rummage far to find a pair of comfy shorts and an oversize T-shirt, which she tugged on. She washed the makeup off her face before padding back to the living area where Jax sat on the edge of the couch. Looking at his phone, easing off his shoes with the other hand.

"Everything okay?" She settled on the other end of the

couch, curling her legs up in front of her and hugging a pillow.

He reached over and unlaced the other shoe. "Prayer requests from my Bible study group."

"Can I have a copy? I don't need their names or anything, but I could pray for them." She picked at the thread at the corner of the pillow.

"I'll forward them to you."

"Sorry you missed it."

Jax shrugged. "I didn't tell them I had a family emergency. I just told that to my boss. Honestly, he seemed relieved he wouldn't have to argue with me about it."

Kenna leaned the side of her head against the couch, shifting down so she could relax. Pain thrummed through her head, concentrating in her nose, and she closed her eyes.

A light touch, the softest stroke of a thumb across her cheek. "That looks like it hurts. But I'm equally impressed your makeup completely disguised it."

"At least my face isn't purple." She opened her eyes and saw he'd shifted closer. "So...Bible study."

Jax grinned. "Nice safe topic."

"Is it?"

He set his hand on her foot, then his fingers found the back of her ankle and he tugged her legs across his lap. "I like the group. But I can't tell them much about what's going on, given it's either part of an ongoing investigation or it could put people in danger."

She knew he valued the group, as he often sent her notes on what they'd talked about. Or if they had time, he would tell her over the phone and she'd read through the text so they could discuss it.

Not something she'd ever had as part of a relationship before. It left her off balance in a lot of ways, but not bad ones.

His phone buzzed, and he leaned forward to look at the screen without picking it up. "Maizie. She texted us both."

Kenna didn't move. "What is it?"

"A link to an article. The death of a police officer in Pahrump, Nevada."

"Paige."

"That's him," Jax said. "This says he was shot to death in his hunting cabin. They're having a parade to honor him."

Kenna kept herself from snorting out loud.

"And this morning they arrested Bartholomew Rault."

She opened her eyes. "Who?"

Jax turned the phone so she could see the screen.

"Bart?" Kenna nearly jumped off the couch.

"The guy who gave you a cup of coffee?"

Kenna frowned, even though it made her head hurt more. "What on earth? Does it say anything about him having a gunshot injury? Because I chased the shooter, and I shot him."

Jax shook his head, scrolling down the article. "We can find out."

"I already know he didn't do it. That's ridiculous." Heat swelled in her midsection, bringing her more awake than she had been all relaxed on the couch. "I can't believe them. Finding a good guy to be a scapegoat. I'm gonna prove they're all liars."

No way would she let this be.

Jax squeezed her ankle. "How about tomorrow?"

"Tell Maizie to get Stairns on it. I want Bart released."

"Yes, ma'am."

Kenna frowned. "What does that mean?"

"It means we're tired, and you'd make a great team leader."

"I do fine on my own."

Jax chuckled. "Yes, you do. Doesn't mean one day you

aren't going to wake up and find you have a whole company, a team who goes out taking the exact cases you love to work—need to work—and continuing your legacy."

"Hopefully, both my legs will be broken, because that's the only way I'll be staying home." She might be needed on the home front, but with him this close, she didn't need to start thinking about the future.

Right now, there was a case to solve.

And as far as she could see, they were in the middle of a complicated mess that made no sense.

His chuckle became an outright laugh. "Yes, ma'am."

"It's time to start pulling threads on this and see what comes loose."

"Sleep. Breakfast. Work."

"Sounds like a plan." Kenna yawned. "After we pick up Ozzy."

Chapter Sixteen

Kenna rounded the end of the running track at a gentle jog, holding Ozzy's leash. Halfway down the long stretch of the oval, Jax blew past her at what had to be close to a six-minute mile. Even if he left her in his dust, she had to admit the view wasn't half bad. Eventually, he would race back around to where she kept her steady pace.

After a good night of sleep, she felt much better. Not that it had reduced any of the swelling or achiness of her face. But the rest she got, knowing Jax was nearby, proved far more effective in making her feel safe and secure enough to really sleep. Way more than her security system, even if she paid for a top-of-the-line system.

Kenna slowed her pace to a brisk walk, although it seemed as if Ozzy wanted to keep running forever. "Whoa, doggy. Do you even know how to heel?"

Maybe Esmeralda knew if Noelle had trained her dog even a little bit.

Kenna slid her phone out of the pocket on the side of her leggings and called Maizie.

The teen answered the phone before the first ring even

stopped. "I don't have any updates, and Stairns is about to leave for Pahrump to go get what we need to clear Bart's name."

"Presuming he isn't the one I shot running away from the cabin."

An older lady with white sneakers and a dyed red pixie cut shot her an odd look but kept on power walking around the track.

"Actually," Kenna said, "I was just calling because I missed Cabot. How is she?"

"Slowing down a little. But I wonder if that's just because I spend so much time in the trailer."

"Have you thought about taking her out for some exercise?" Kenna suggested.

"I found a dog physical therapist online, and I've been emailing her back and forth, asking about exercises. There's only so much Cabot can do after her surgery. But moving is supposed to improve her mood."

Kenna had left the dog with Maizie for protection but also in order for her to be treated by a vet and continue care with the same doctor. Something that Kenna wouldn't have been able to provide for her given how much she moved around.

She didn't intend to train Ozzy as any kind of working dog, and she wasn't sure she planned to keep him long-term. If anything, she would leave the dog with Maizie, knowing that Ozzy would be cared for. That the girl would have more company she could relax with.

Jax slowed to a walk beside her, breathing hard. Sweat on the sides of his face and dampening his T-shirt.

"Keep me posted." Kenna hung up the phone. "Update on Cabot from Maizie. She's doing okay."

They walked another loop around the track and left it just as a young woman emerged from the gym building. Avery

Masonridge strode out in shorts and a tank top, a towel across her shoulders. Blond hair pulled back, the line around her face damp with sweat.

Busted.

Avery glanced between them, ponytail bobbing. "Kenna Banbury and Oliver Jaxton." Thankfully, she didn't say their names too loudly, announcing them to anyone within earshot.

They stopped facing each other, and Kenna winced. She leaned in a little so Avery would understand why she whispered, "We're on a case."

Ozzy wandered over and sniffed at Avery's shoes.

Hopefully, Avery wouldn't do or say anything that might land Jax in trouble with the FBI, considering he was supposed to be on vacation right now. "But it is good to see you," Kenna added. "You look a lot better than the last time."

Avery flushed under the sheen of workout warmth. "I've been working hard."

Kenna could see that in the tone of her muscles. No one got that much definition without some serious hard work over an extended period of time. Which meant she'd kicked any habit she may have struggled with in the past and turned her health around as well as her life.

Not that Avery had to prove to Kenna that her actions that day in the hotel in Albuquerque were to save the life of someone who proved to be worth it. Any life deserved saving, regardless of the life that person lived after.

"And you're a senator now?" Jax piped in. "Beating all the odds and getting elected despite how young you are? It's impressive. You should be really proud of yourself, Avery."

He sounded like a big brother. It almost made Kenna want to meet his family if he felt like this about his sister. His parents might not always do the right thing—who in the world did—but he obviously cared or he wouldn't be so wound up by them.

Avery gave him a soft smile that wasn't entirely sibling-esque. "Thanks."

"And you're here with your friends?" Kenna had seen her at dinner last night with the group. "Just hanging out, or celebrating something?"

Avery's smile tightened. "Hanging out. One of my girlfriends, her dad is one of the owners of this place. She's trying to persuade her boyfriend to have their wedding here."

"Sounds like fun. This is a beautiful location."

"I should go take a shower." Avery stepped slightly past them. "It was good to see both of you."

She wandered off, and Kenna glanced at Jax.

Ozzy found the end of the leash and ate the top off a flower.

Kenna hissed. "Ozzy, don't do that."

Apart from the issue of it possibly upsetting his stomach, the landscapers probably didn't want her dog eating the fruits of their hard work.

"That was weird, right?" Kenna blew out a breath.

Neither of them knew Avery very well. But she had seemed cagey. Keeping more of the story to herself and settling on simple answers rather than elaborating.

Jax nodded. "If I had to say either way, I'd guess she was totally lying." He swung one arm across her shoulders. One very sweaty arm. "Maybe when we don't have however many cases we have, we can worry about what she's up to."

Kenna frowned.

He tugged her forward. "Come on, Ozzy. It's breakfast time."

The dog trotted with them into the dining hall, which had been completely revamped for breakfast. Jax motioned to a server and then pointed outside. He led her to a patio table that was the only one empty in this busy area.

The dress code seemed to be business casual, with a serious nod toward high fashion. Certainly not sweaty gym clothes. Which made her glad she'd purchased some overly expensive ones that fit with the personas they were going for.

Of course, Jax didn't even seem to notice—completely comfortable with who he was. In a place like this, that was no surprise. This was somewhere he'd visited as a kid, part of his high society upbringing.

Maybe Kenna simply didn't relax anywhere other than in her RV.

Or on the couch in a hotel room beside Jax, where she promptly fell asleep and then he had to rouse her and nudge her off to bed. She'd lain there with her eyes closed listening to him moving around in the bathroom. Thinking how nice it was to be aware there was someone else in her space.

Ozzy put his front paws on her leg, so she lifted him onto her lap.

"Probably wants some sausage for breakfast," Jax said.

Kenna grinned, remembering the day she met Cabot. Another restaurant in another state, and she'd sat across the table from Jax. Not even knowing it would be the first of many to come. Or exactly how her life would change as a result of meeting him.

"And so do I," he said.

When the server came over, he listed off a host of things. Probably because he had burned so many calories running and needed the fuel now. What did he think they were going to be doing later that meant he needed to be in tip-top shape?

Kenna said, "I'd love a smoothie."

The server said, "We have pineapple mango or peanut butter banana today."

"Peanut butter banana, thank you." When Ozzy barked, she continued, "And a couple of sausage links for the little monster."

The server laughed. "He makes being a monster look good, though. Does he want a bowl of water?"

"Yes, thank you." Kenna grinned, taking a sip of the ice water on the table. On occasion she had to admit that she'd had plenty of coffee already. She rubbed Ozzy's fur on his chest while Jax put milk in his coffee. Then looked around and spotted Preston Lightwood a couple of tables away, sitting with his friend the spiritual hippie guy. His "rabbi."

Lightwood lifted his chin, and she waved with two fingers.

He said something to the man with him and then set his napkin on the table, pushing his chair in before he came over to them. "May I?"

Several people in the vicinity sitting at other tables glanced over at him as he made his way across the patio. At least one woman thought he was inclined to murder a person in broad daylight in public, given the expression on her face. A few men seemed more intent on keeping their valuables out of view, as if he might steal them.

Last night, Preston had told them that her father was the best thing that had ever happened to him. And that this was about healing.

Jax said, "Sure."

She caught his tone and agreed with him that Preston seemed determined to sit whether they allowed it or not. "What can we help you with?"

"I figured since you're here and I'm here, we might as well have our chat." Preston set his elbows on the arms of the chair and laced his fingers on his lap. The rolled-up sleeves of his white shirt pulled back a little to reveal tattoos on the inside of his forearms.

"What did you want to tell me?" Kenna asked.

Ozzy leaned over the arm of her chair toward Preston and sniffed in his direction.

Preston made a fist and held it out to the dog. Ozzy didn't seem to think there was anything to be worried about. Or Preston had just eaten sausage with his breakfast. "I know what the world thinks of me and the fact I never pled guilty. I wasn't going to lie even if it offered me the chance of a reduced sentence rather than a drawn-out trial."

"You served the time you were given, and you were released." Jax took a sip of his coffee. "Even if I believed you were guilty when you always claimed you were innocent, you cleared your debt. Who can argue with that?"

Just so long as he didn't ask Kenna to investigate that old case.

If her father hadn't found sufficient evidence to clear Preston's name, then that meant there was none to be found.

The server brought their food and asked Preston if he wanted more coffee.

Preston shook his head. When the server disappeared, he said, "Your dad talked me off the ledge of revenge."

"Did you know him before the warrant went out for your arrest?" Kenna took a sip of her smoothie, which was so thick it barely came up the straw.

Preston nodded. "My wife hired him about a year before she was killed to dig up information on her mother. She hadn't seen her mom for years, almost a decade. Your dad found her mom in a facility receiving treatment, and they were able to reunite because of him."

Kenna broke up the sausage links into little pieces and fed them to Ozzy one by one. As she did, she studied Preston, concluding this wasn't a man who had simply spoken the lies so many times it became ingrained as if it might be the truth.

He spoke about his wife as if he'd cared deeply for her. Enough to want revenge after she was murdered. On the person who killed her...

Or the police, who failed to investigate sufficiently enough to find the perpetrator?

That was the question.

Along with why her father had never produced the identity of the killer. Why Preston had gone to prison for years for a crime he hadn't committed, all the while allowing the world to believe he might actually have done it.

"When I realized I was going to be arrested for her death, I..." Preston cleared his throat. "I ran, and I called him from the first clean phone I could find. He convinced me the best thing for me to do was to turn myself in and not wind up in a shootout with law enforcement that would have left me as dead as she was."

There had to be more to the story. "This is some kind of conspiracy, or something else going on?"

It couldn't have anything to do with Cecelia. However, everything in her wanted to ask Preston if he'd ever met Cecelia—maybe show him her picture and see if he knew her.

"Let's just say I'm aware of the rumors about me, and they don't bear any resemblance to the truth." Preston rubbed his nose. "My wife was in the wrong place at the wrong time. Her death was a tragedy, and I lost more than just her that day."

"Someone else was killed?" Jax asked.

Preston replied, "I've asked God for forgiveness for the things I'm responsible for. And that list is between me and him." He pushed his chair back then, clearing his throat. "Thanks for listening." He didn't make eye contact with either of them. Just walked away quickly without pushing his chair back in.

"He's still grieving," Kenna remarked.

Jax chewed a bite of food. "Doesn't mean he didn't kill her."

Kenna thought maybe it was more that he had taken responsibility for the loss of her life. Not necessarily that he was actually the one who ended it. She closed her eyes. "I'm not going to take this case on. It isn't even a case."

Jax chuckled. "Maybe I'll email the training center at Quantico and provide them an update, something to add to the file. Give it a refresh for the new batch of FBI recruits."

Kenna shook her head. "Those days feel like fifty years ago, but also like everything has come full circle."

Jax nodded. "I know what you mean." He lifted his chin. "Heads up, Ryson's cousin is coming this way."

Kenna took a sip of her smoothie, wondering how Ozzy would react to a second strange man. How good would the dog's instincts be when presented with a threat?

"Mr. and Mrs. Hawthorne." The head of security stopped by the table. "Sorry to tell you this, but Esmeralda never showed up for work this morning. So you won't be able to talk to her."

Kenna frowned, the straw still between her lips.

He thought they were going to give up so easily?

Unlikely.

Chapter Seventeen

Kenna knocked on the front door of the townhouse, standing to one side the way they'd been trained. Jax on the other side. He remained a step back—off the concrete stoop. One in a row of slender houses sandwiched together. Garages at the back. Cute shutters and a rectangular flower box attached to the siding under each window. A profusion of all colors of blooms kept alive by a drip line.

She knocked again.

Jax moved over to the window and peered inside through what looked like a sheer curtain.

"What do you think about townhomes?" Kenna asked.

"Better than living in a subdivision."

She shuddered, and not because of that. *A subdivision?* "I think I might need acreage."

"Yeah, no kidding. I'm pretty sure I could've guessed that about you."

"I'm not saying I need a log cabin in the middle of nowhere, inaccessible by anything but a fire road. Not listed on any county records as being an actual residence. I'm just saying I don't like *neighborhoods*. Everyone is so artificially polite, and you *know* that the accountant's wife is having an affair with the teacher who lives across the street because in the summer you see them at the pool *looking at each other*."

"In case you're interested, in the middle of spinning this soap-opera-esque tale, there's someone inside." He backed up from the window. "Knock again."

She liked her story but did as he requested—ordered—and knocked on the door. "You know that upper-middle-class subdivision is exactly the kind of place Mr. and Mrs. Hawthorne live. They're probably trying to rekindle the romance."

No one answered the door.

"I'll check around the back," Jax said. "Make sure there isn't someone in there harming Esmeralda. They might try and make a run for it."

Of course, he had no authority to make an arrest, considering he was on vacation. They could call whoever the local police were. Probably a county sheriff since this was an upmarket small town, but still a small town. Maybe it was here to provide Willowbrooke with local staff who didn't have to commute far.

She thought her backstory was pretty good.

Kind of like her ability to break and enter, and she didn't need a lock pick kit like Ramon. As soon as Jax disappeared around the end of the row of townhouses, she tugged out her credit card. Kenna slid it between the door and the frame, wiggled, and bumped the lock open. She needed to explain to Esmeralda the beauty of a deadbolt.

The door swung open.

Kenna drew her gun and stepped into the foyer, closing the door behind her. Going from full Arizona sun to the nearly complete dark of the entryway pretty much killed her eyesight, but what bled through from the living room gave her enough light to see.

She listened first before she moved. Watching the stairs that steeply climbed to the second floor. Kenna liked the ones that had three floors, but that would've led her into a kill box—effectively. Getting sandwiched in a small space with nowhere to go and a gun on her.

Like the one she held as she stepped out of the side room.

"Esmeralda."

Dark hair, body tense—solid and muscled but not slender. This woman had strength in her. And she currently held a shotgun pointed at Kenna. "Who are you?"

"I can see how you wouldn't know if I'm friend or foe. But I'm not here to hurt you." Maybe she should've brought Ozzy instead of leaving him in his crate in the room so he could sleep after his long morning run. "My name is Kenna Banbury. I'm a private investigator."

Kenna lifted her free hand, sliding her gun into the holster. She didn't think this woman would shoot if Kenna presented no threat. But then again, being wrong meant it was over.

All of it.

Her whole life.

Now she had both hands raised. "Esmeralda? That is you, isn't it?"

She stayed where Kenna couldn't make out her features. Holding the gun steady—no wavering. Not scared. No, this wasn't the stance of someone who feared for their life. She was protecting someone.

"I found the letters you sent Noelle."

After a tiny intake of breath, Esme said, "What happened to Noelle?"

"I'm sorry." Kenna didn't have a good way to break it to

her if she hadn't heard about the bank robbery on the news. "I'm really sorry, but she died."

Esmeralda choked on a breath. "No. She isn't dead. She can't be."

"She was your best friend, wasn't she?" And it went deeper than that. They were sisters—wives of a brotherhood who deployed together and fought side by side. "She did the right thing. She fought to her last breath to die doing the right thing, and she was strong. So strong. She knew what she was up against, but she still did it even though she was afraid. She kept you safe."

Just like Esme was doing with whoever was in the house with her.

"Are you safe, Esmeralda? Do you need help?"

The other woman gasped but didn't lower the gun.

"Kenna!" Jax's call to her came from inside the house. Or so it sounded.

Esmeralda spun around. Kenna moved since the gun no longer pointed at her and moved quickly through the residence. From the sound of quick footsteps, the other woman followed her. Hopefully, not with the goal of shooting Kenna in the back.

Jax stood in the doorway to the bedroom. He took a step back and spotted the woman behind Kenna. "Ma'am, put the gun down." He said it with so much authority Kenna heard the shotgun clatter to the floor.

"Esme!" A man's cry rang out from inside the bedroom.

Kenna blocked the doorway. "She's fine." She spoke before she fully took him in, lying on the bed with no shirt on. Bloody bandages wrapped around his middle and his shoulder. Eyes glassy, sweat over every inch of exposed skin. Shorts and white tube socks. He'd made a sweaty, bloody mess of the sheets, but Esmeralda hadn't moved him to change them.

She couldn't remember the name of Esme's significant other, but she'd put money on this being him. A dead man who was somehow very much alive even with the injuries.

The only person she knew who'd been hurt recently... apart from her. *Paige.*

"You're the shooter from Nevada."

Behind her, Esmeralda let out a short cry and clapped her hand over her mouth. "Don't hurt him. He did the best he could, but he was chased from the scene."

Kenna assimilated that fast, concluding this woman thought they worked for Cecelia. "We aren't here to hurt either of you."

The guy on the bed stared at her, his chest rising and falling fast. If he made a move, he'd only wind up hurting himself more. "You expect us to believe that?"

Kenna told Esme, "Go in there and sit with him."

The other woman rushed past her. Jax strode down the hall and swiped up the shotgun. Kenna stepped into the room but stayed by the door with her back to the wall. Gun close, just in case. But they needed answers here—not to get in a gunfight.

Esme settled on the side of the bed, and her guy held her hand. In enough pain he couldn't quite focus. Couldn't pull his thoughts together. No one to call for help. No way to protect the woman he loved, and she was the only place he could go for aid.

"Noelle died for this." Kenna looked at him. "You nearly did as well."

"You're the one who shot me."

Esme gasped. "Carlos, is that true?"

He nodded.

Kenna held out her hands just in case Esme went for another sawed-off. "I mean neither of you harm. In fact, it's in my interest to keep the two of you alive as long as possible."

"Did you kill Noelle?" Desperation laced Esme's tone.

Kenna couldn't imagine what it was like. Doing the best she could, putting together a sparse life that amounted to waiting for the man she loved to come home. Wondering if he might not. "I knew I should've brought Ozzy."

"Where is he?!" Esme bounced on the bed, almost jumping up but seeming to catch herself.

"He's fine. I brought him with me to Willowbrooke." If she wanted the dog, maybe they could talk about it. But there needed to be a whole lot more exchange of information aside from that. Kenna asked Carlos, "Why did you shoot Paige?"

"Orders."

"Chain of command?" They couldn't operate on US soil, right? "Some kind of unsanctioned mission?"

"Doesn't matter," Carlos said. "I'm dead when they find me."

"Then I figure you have nothing to lose. Let me get you somewhere safe. Give you and Esme a shot at a future."

Carlos made a face, laughing until he groaned. He laid a hand on the bandage on his waist. The guy would be a force to be reckoned with on his feet, at full strength. She wouldn't want to meet him in a dark alley, or so the saying went.

"How about a doctor?" Kenna offered. "Then I promise Esme will be safe. I'll get her somewhere she will be protected, and no one will find her. I've done it before, successfully. I can do it again."

"Then I tell you everything?" He scoffed. "I might have a death wish, but I'm not insane."

"You came here because it's safe," Kenna said. "You didn't return to them."

"Because I failed to kill you."

Jax stepped into the room and directly in front of her. At the same time, everything in her tensed and came to attention.

She didn't have time to dwell on the fact their instincts seemed to be so in sync. Attuned to the danger around one another. Except now that he was between her and the injured but lethal man on the bed, it put Jax in danger.

Not a fan of that.

Would their lives be a constant battle of who was in danger and who was determined to protect them?

Probably.

She peered around Jax's shoulder but didn't see a weapon. Though, that didn't mean Carlos had no way to defend himself and Esmeralda.

"We only want to help you guys if you need it." Kenna patted the V-neck of her T-shirt. "That's what I do."

She moved into view next to Jax so she could look at Esmeralda. Maybe the woman could convince Carlos that they needed to let Kenna and Jax help them.

"We don't need help." Teeth gritted. Pain etched on his face.

Kenna just stared at him, daring him to double down on that. Out of pure stubbornness, he was refusing assistance that might leave him vulnerable. Or not in control of his own life.

Jax shifted and stuck his FBI badge on his belt. "You shot a cop. I should arrest you right now. You'll get medical attention, but you'll be cuffed to a hospital bed under guard. Maybe you should give me a good reason why I shouldn't do that."

Hmm. Kenna would've dug for the reason as well, but she had no authority to arrest someone. She often would turn a suspect over to the police. Usually along with the evidence of their guilt, or enough to dispel reasonable doubt.

Maybe this was an attempt at good cop, bad cop, meaning they'd be more inclined to trust Kenna because they didn't want to get mixed up with a fed.

Esmeralda paled. "You're FBI?"

Interesting reaction.

"Great. You found us." Carlos grunted, trying to sit up more on the bed. "If you're gonna kill me, just do it. I screwed up. I know that."

"That's not what this is," Jax said.

Kenna needed them to grasp the fact she and Jax were the good guys. "Like I said, we just wanna help you."

"If you weren't sent here to kill us," Carlos said, "or interrogate us and then kill us...then get out. We don't need your help." He glanced at Esme. "Pack our bags. We're getting out of here."

Kenna's stomach tightened. As much as she wanted to help them, she couldn't force assistance on them if they didn't want it. "Who ordered you to kill Paige?" She paused. "That's what it was, right? A hit. You were paid or forced to take that cop's life?"

And how did that make sense when she'd been convinced Officer Paige tried to kill her because Cecelia had ordered him to?

Did she then order him killed because he'd failed?

Or there were two sets of people ordering hits at work here. And wasn't that a terrifying thought?

"I don't ask questions," Carlos said. "I get orders, I fulfill them, or I'm the one with a bullet in my skull."

Esme stiffened. Her friend was dead, and her significant other was determined to face the reality of the situation. But that didn't mean this woman was prepared for it. Did she have any information that would help Kenna uncover evidence against Cecelia?

"Get out." Carlos glanced between them. "Both of you."

Jax lifted his hands. "We're leaving. But I have a card, so you can call if you need anything. Help, or what, it doesn't matter."

"We're gonna live on the run. Hunted for the rest of our lives," Carlos said. "That's bad enough but ratting out the person I work for will make it a thousand times worse. I'll be public enemy number one, with entire armies after me."

"All the more reason to take them down," Kenna suggested. "If they have that much power."

"You wanna go up against them?"

If it was Cecelia, that was the entire reason she was here. What started as setting Ramon's life and reputation back on track might've just become so much more.

Kenna simply said, "I want justice."

Carlos let out a huff. "I'm already dead, so what do I care what you do?"

Esme sniffed, and a tear slid down her cheek.

Chapter Eighteen

Kenna stepped off the front stoop of the townhouse, Jax ahead of her. He walked with his shoulders tense and arms tight, no doubt irritated that they'd gotten nowhere. No leads. No connection to Cecelia or confirmation of that. Nothing about Walker.

He turned at the end of the path onto the sidewalk, toward the spot down the street a little from where they'd parked. Traffic hummed on the other side of the hedges, which provided a barrier between the main road and the row of front doors.

A little alcove where people could pretend coming home was secluded.

Kenna preferred expansive spaces where she could plainly see no one was around rather than the illusion of privacy.

He spun to look at her, his gaze snagging on something behind her.

Kenna had shut the door. When she glanced back it was open, and Esme hurried out, her face lined with worry. Stress.

Fear. She left the door wide, and Carlos' voice echoed through the house. "Esme, get back here!"

The young woman winced. "I have to talk to you, but I need to get back in there."

Kenna nodded. "Do you need my help?"

"I think you need mine." Esme pushed out a quick breath and gasped. "You were there. When Noelle died. You saw it?"

Kenna softened her expression. This woman grieved her friend. "I'm sorry for your loss. If we're going to bring the person responsible to justice, then Jax and I could use your help."

"You don't work for her?"

Cecelia? Kenna shook her head. "No way."

She wasn't going to mention her personal connection. What she needed was to find out what Esme knew, not give her more reason to believe they might be lying and they actually *did* work for Cecelia.

"Noelle said her part was the most important." Esme winced. "At least, that was what the woman told her. That she was guarding the most valuable piece."

Kenna didn't have the photo of the child to show Esme, but she had other images on her phone. "We want her to pay for what she's done."

Esme flushed. "Noelle didn't have a choice. Just like I wouldn't have, but Carlos...he took extra assignments. Did things..." She swallowed. "He made it so I didn't have to live like Noelle."

"Doing favors for the boss?"

Esme nodded.

Kenna dug out her phone and pulled up the photo of Cecelia. "Have you ever seen the person who gives Carlos orders? The person who told Noelle to guard the safety deposit box at her bank?"

Esme said quietly, "I have."

"Is this her?" Kenna showed her the screen of the phone.

"Yes." Esme's eyes filled with tears. "Even Carlos seemed like he was scared of her."

"How did he come to work for her? He's army, right?" Kenna was only slightly aware of Jax behind her, watching out for them and listening but not getting so close that Esme retreated and shut down. His presence behind her, where she couldn't see him but knew he was there, had to be the reason the spot between her shoulder blades seemed to itch.

"His team worked together overseas, but it was all black ops. Super top secret stuff. Carlos could never tell me what they did, or where they went." Esme sucked in a quick breath. "He retired. I think they all did around the same time."

"And got himself listed as deceased?" There was no easy way to say that. And considering the same happened to Noelle's significant other, Kenna had to wonder if he was alive also.

How many of them were running around?

And were they connected to the men who had robbed that bank?

The thought that Cecelia had multiple teams out doing her bidding was more terrifying than going up against a serial killer alone with no weapons.

"They have to live like that. They would be in danger if they lived normal lives." Esme sniffed. "We do the best we can laying low and staying out of the spotlight."

Except when they started having children, and the kids wanted to know why their dad could never leave the house in daylight. Why he never came to any of their games, or performances.

"And they still work for Cecelia?" Kenna asked.

Esme frowned. "Her name is Sarah."

Kenna blinked at that new piece of this puzzle. "Do you know her last name or where she works?"

"I think maybe...Roseburg? Something like that. I don't know what she does, but she seems like she has power."

So Esme had been threatened.

"She has teams that work for her, and guys like Carlos," Esme added. "But then there's this other guy, and he's like the enforcer. The one who will carve you up if you don't do what Sarah ordered."

"Do you have a number for her, or a way to find her?" Kenna asked.

"Carlos has a website he checks. You can't find it on the internet just by searching. You have to have the right code to enter in the web address."

A dark web site. Unindexed so not even Maizie would be able to find it. "Can you send it to me? I can take her down. I can get you and Carlos, and all of his friends and their families, out from under her thumb. I *can* do this."

Esme bit her lip.

Kenna handed over a business card. "Please help me take her down. She'll never know you had anything to do with it."

Esme looked around, then took the card—apparently satisfied they weren't being watched. But the itch between Kenna's shoulders hadn't quit.

The door closed.

Kenna turned and found Jax had remained at the end of the front walk. "Now we have more than we did when we left."

"Did she say Sarah?"

Kenna nodded, walking beside him toward where they'd parked. "Sarah Roseburg. Why does it seem like I should know who she is?"

"We certainly should've heard that name before." He

stowed his phone and pulled out the keys to the truck, beeping the locks.

Kenna flinched but didn't slow. "Ramon checks for bombs every time."

"Probably why he's still alive."

She needed to call and find out if he had learned anything about the rifle. Right now, she didn't even know what state he was in, or what he was doing. Made it hard to keep track of the guy. Let alone watch his back.

Once they'd settled in their seats, he said, "Back to the resort?"

She did need to let Ozzy out. He'd be done with his morning nap and ready to do some business. "We should pray they get somewhere safe, and that they send us that web address."

"At least, he didn't try to kill you when he found out you were the one who shot him."

"I figure that's because Esme was the one with the shotgun."

"He was pretty surprised when I walked in from the back door." Jax shook his head, pulling onto the highway and hitting the gas pedal. "Who leaves their patio open?"

"Not me." Kenna knew people in states where not locking their cars or their houses was a normal thing. As far as she was concerned, that was asking for trouble, leaving your most precious things unprotected like that.

She called Maizie and listened to it ring, holding the phone up between her and Jax.

"Hey...hi."

Totally distracted.

"In the middle of something?" Kenna said.

"Just in a rabbit hole of military records," Maizie replied.

Jax turned his head slightly toward the phone but didn't

take his attention off the road. "Be careful. You don't want to get caught hacking classified files, or getting into secure servers you shouldn't even know exist."

Maizie said, "I could explain how they won't find me, and how I'm being careful, but I don't think you'd understand it."

Kenna figured that was true. "One day you're gonna dumb it down for us. Because I'd like reassurance."

"I want a webinar with slides," Jax quipped.

Kenna glanced at him, making a face. "She can just explain it."

"Sure, give us the quick version for non-hackers," he said. "More to follow. Don't forget to like and subscribe."

Maizie chuckled. "Fine. I've been going through the files of the men who robbed the bank and passing information on them to state police in Nevada. Local sheriffs in the areas where they've been seen. Basically trying to get someone to catch them for us."

"And Bart?" Kenna paused. "Is Stairns on the ground proving he's not the one who shot Paige?"

"Far as I know," Maizie said. "I'm waiting for a check-in."

His being gone from the acreage in Colorado where they all lived meant Elizabeth and Maizie were unprotected, except for an old dog. Maybe she needed to figure out better security for them. A team. An extensive system connected to local law enforcement dispatch...something.

Maizie continued, "Then I was looking at Noelle's significant other, and Esme's—"

"Carlos is alive," Kenna interjected. "I don't know about Noelle's."

"Whoa." Maizie paused a beat. "Okay, that changes the search parameters."

Kenna told her what Esme had said, reiterating it so Jax got all the information as well.

He said, "Did you show her a picture of Walker?"

"We still don't have evidence he's connected to any of this," Kenna said. "Even if it's becoming more and more evident Cecelia has all kinds of people working for her."

"Sarah Roseburg, or some other name similar to it," Jax said. "Look up that name, see what pops. Yeah, Maze?"

"On it. Who is she?"

Kenna said, "I showed Esmeralda a photo of Cecelia, and that's the name she gave me."

"Whoa."

"I know, right?" Kenna shook her head.

"No, I mean *whoa*." Maizie hammered keys on her end of the line. "Sarah Rosenberg? I mean, it might not be the same person. But if it is…"

"Run it down." She nearly added *Maze*, liking the shortened version she sometimes used—at least, the sound of Jax saying it.

"Sarah Rosenberg of the Massachusetts Rosenbergs died at twelve years old in an accidental drowning. She was buried on the family's expansive estate."

Kenna frowned.

"Parents are still alive but in their seventies now. The family, siblings and cousins, run a few charities that operate across the world, and a US-based foundation that lobbies for social reforms. Writing up those 'cookie cutter' bills that seem to be in state senates across the country, being argued at the same time. Like school reform, or book bans."

Kenna shifted in the seat. "So they sway the country by pushing stuff at the state level."

"They have a hand in federal policy also, funding a number of companies that do medical research. If you look under the surface they give a lot to hospitals who take patients with no money. Critical pediatric care. They look lily white, and holier-than-thou."

"And beneath that?" Jax pulled the truck through the gate at the Willowbrooke sign.

"They disappear into the ether," Maizie said. "Which means I need to dig."

"That might be riskier than hacking a military database."

"I'll step carefully."

Kenna planned to do her own research as well. "Why would Cecelia use the name of a dead preteen to inspire loyalty instead of death?"

Jax said, "Because she's sick."

"Or she wants to be associated with them so she co-opts their reputation."

Jax thought for a second. "Or she's illegitimate and can only claim to be one of them. She can't prove she belongs because she was the result of some kind of tawdry affair."

Kenna's mind spun with all kinds of possibilities. "Shame we can't find someone close to her and ask."

Jax slid the truck up in front of the valet. "Let's walk Ozzy and figure it out."

Maizie said, "I'll call if I get anything."

"Thanks." Kenna ended the call before she could say, *Be careful*, which Maizie would argue with. Kenna was trying not to micromanage her safety and didn't know if the teen would think she was overbearing or didn't trust her to be careful. "Teenagers are confusing."

Jax grinned. "You seem like you're doing just fine."

Kenna got out, thanking the valet for getting her door. Jax tossed him the keys and took her hand.

They retrieved Ozzy from the hotel room and went back outside, walking the same path behind the dining hall they had last night. Making small talk. Bleeding off the stress and adrenaline of that meeting. All the new information they'd gathered.

"I hope they're going to be safe." Kenna figured there wasn't much chance of getting a call from either of them, but she could pray.

"You didn't offer her Ozzy?"

Kenna hadn't even thought about it. "Maybe she knows about some relative of Noelle's and thinks we're finding them."

If Esme emailed her with that web address, she would ask about Ozzy and who might want him.

"You wanna keep him?" Jax eyed Kenna.

So what if she did. That didn't mean there couldn't be someone who would take better care of him. Give the dog a more stable life. "What about your sister? Do you think she and her family might want Ozzy?" She turned her attention to scanning their surroundings.

"Do you want me to offer?" he finally said. "Because you seem like you're getting mad at me for suggesting alternates."

"Don't you like dogs?" He was fine with Cabot when they saw each other. Why did it seem as if he had a problem now? She had loved every dog she ever took care of, though it did seem as if they came and went quicker than she'd have liked.

"I'm walking into a minefield with no idea where the explosions will come."

"You think I'm being irrational. Or *hormonal*."

He lifted both hands. "Nope. Not gonna touch that one." He huffed what sounded suspiciously like it might be a laugh. "Knowing you, someone will end up getting stabbed."

Kenna pressed her lips together. Why dignify that with a response? They needed to focus on what was going on, figure out what on earth was happening with Cecelia and a bunch of military guys.

At some point, they'd be able to resolve a piece of this puzzle. But right now, there were so many disparate pieces on the board she didn't know what to work on first.

"Are we back to square one?" she asked.

"If we are, then we should both take a nap after lunch. Because who knows what will happen next. We might need to be rested up for whatever it is."

"Lunch does sound good." The rest was back in that danger zone she was all too aware of standing close to him. Having him near for an extended period. She sighed. "Maybe we should've gone to the courthouse."

Jax chuckled and slung his arm around her shoulders, tugging her close and pressing a light kiss to her forehead.

They emerged from the secluded path—with Ozzy panting hard, sniffing everything and trying to pee on all the bushes—onto the area around the back patio. Despite the people hanging around, eating at tables, Kenna still had that itch in the middle of her back.

As if this idyllic scene was about to turn into a nightmare.

Chapter Nineteen

Jax was in the middle of a story about a case from a few months ago, telling her about how the suspect had climbed a tree and tried to hide, when Kenna's phone rang.

He paused laughing to say, "Who's calling?"

She didn't want his story interrupted. He loved his job, and it showed in the way he told the tale, even if the suspect that he'd been trying to arrest acted in a way that proved exasperating. She looked at her phone. "Oh, it's Ramon."

She would've put it on speaker, but there were too many people close by—including Preston and his friend. The guy hadn't done more than lift his chin thankfully. Kenna nearly answered, *Banbury* but caught herself. "Hey, buddy."

"Gun was a bust."

"What happened?" She caught Jax's glance but couldn't explain.

"Sent my guy some pictures. He texts me back, all 'Don't call this number. I don't know you anymore.' Who knows what that means. So I call another buddy to go over and do a duress check on the guy, make sure there's not someone over there holding a gun to his head, and he's packed up shop. Cleared out. Gone on an extended vacation. Forever."

Kenna winced. "Serial number?"

"That and the specs of the weapon are the only things he'd have had to go on. And he does this?"

In an odd way, it fit with a black ops military, ex-military, off-book—supposed to be dead, but very much alive—group. "I guess I shouldn't tell you over the phone."

"Good thing I'm in the area," Ramon said. "Nothing to do in Nevada, so I figured I'd hit the spot close by where you're at. Just in case anything kicks off."

"Thanks." But she had Jax for backup, and given his proximity, he would be pitching in a whole lot faster than Ramon could. Still, she could appreciate his willingness to help. "What about the package?"

Hopefully, he'd know she was talking about the gun.

"I—" The line crackled. His voice cut out after a couple syllables. But nothing else about the rifle Carlos left.

She wanted to know where it was now. And what exactly the cops had on Bart, who they had arrested for Paige's murder, if they didn't have the murder weapon.

The line went dead.

Kenna looked at the phone. "I guess he drove into a dead zone."

"Anything I need to worry about?" Jax said.

She took a bite of her chicken salad and shook her head. Ozzy had settled under her chair, curled up in the shade. Her thoughts rushed around each other like the beginning of a tornado, which would probably mean she was having some kind of seizure. Would she work a case one day that was so complicated she'd literally go crazy?

No doubt someone in the world wanted to see her locked up.

Talk about a nightmare.

She couldn't imagine anything worse than being trapped like that. So much she had to glance up at the sky and feel the warmth on her face. Look at the trees. Remember she was free, and alive. Things were good—even if she didn't have answers.

Thank You, Lord.

She wanted to take solace in the thought that whatever happened she wouldn't ever be alone. God had promised to go with her—even if she was in the grave, He would be there. She just didn't want to test the theory despite the fact that the Bible would turn out to be correct every time.

Some nightmares were too much to even imagine.

The snap caught in her ear sharp and fast, almost too fast to process. *Gun.*

Kenna's eyes snapped open. Jax fell on his chair, tipping back and toppling onto the ground, crashing into the guy behind. Preston Lightwood cried out and fell back, a spray of blood erupting from the side of his neck.

She ducked beside her table. "Everyone get down!"

People ran for their lives, which wasn't entirely wise considering a sniper in the area. Jax rolled over, groaned, and started to push up.

Kenna scrambled across the ground to where he was rising and laid on his back. She shoved him back down. "Don't get up. Stay down, or he might try again."

It could be a woman. She was usually an equal-opportunity gal, even with snipers. But in the heat of the moment, all she had in her heart and mind was the need to protect Jax.

"Are you hit?" Kenna asked.

"I'm okay," he replied. "Preston caught it, though."

She didn't want to get off Jax and go help the injured man,

but she did it anyway. Kenna squeezed his shoulder. "Find Antonio." Then crawled across the patio.

People were starting to get up. Maybe they thought the danger was over. Kenna passed their table, where the rabbi guy cowered against the adobe exterior, taking cover behind a fern in a clay pot. "Preston!"

He gasped, his chest rising and falling fast. Eyes glassy, wild, unable to focus.

She closed in. "I got you." She pried his hand away, and he grabbed her arm just above her elbow. She winced. "It's just a scratch, no need to be so dramatic."

He hissed out a breath between clenched teeth. "Liar."

She chuckled. "Don't worry, I won't let you die. But loosen up on my arm. Old scars." She pressed his neck to keep pressure on the wound and turned her head to yell, "We need help!"

An older couple with rumpled clothes and mussed hair turned away from the patio and entered the building. Looking at her and Preston like it was their fault this happened.

Jax crouched by her and handed over a napkin. "I think he's quit shooting."

"In and out just like Paige's death. One and done." And she'd shot him on the way out.

She pressed the napkin on the wound while a man lay bleeding on the ground in front of her. Last time, when she'd had blood on her hands and Jax had been there, she'd thoroughly freaked out. Right now, all she felt was the hot anger boiling in her stomach.

"This wasn't Carlos, though," Jax said. "And I don't think Preston was the intended victim."

Exactly what she hadn't wanted to hear. He'd been shoved off his chair by the shot, whether because he'd reacted or some kind of force propelled him. A reaction that sent him toppling back. Whatever it was might've saved his life.

"Hold this. And see if you can see where Ozzy went." She set his hands on Preston's neck, rocked back on her feet, and launched up, turning as she went. Antonio was rushing over with a staff person hauling a medical bag. He reached out for her, but she shook her head. "Move."

Kenna skirted around him and raced across the patio, jumping over a hurdle-like planter at the end like and landing on the grass. She only had a rough idea of where the shot had come from. Enough she could look around.

Tennis courts.

She couldn't go straight but spotted a three-story building past the courts. Maybe the roof of that, or an upper window. There was an open window on the top right row. Given the heat of the day, that was pretty suspect. Anyone in there would want to keep the heat out and the air-conditioned air inside the room.

"Slow down!"

Antonio.

She didn't even look over her shoulder. Just kept running. "You think he's going to wait for you to find him?"

She tore across the grass to the building. A van sped out from the back corner of the building, picking up speed as it headed right away from her. But she'd seen who sat in the front.

Kenna raced after it, gun raised.

She started to slow. No way would she be able to catch up to him before he was out the gate and away from here.

Antonio grabbed her arm and spun her around. "What are you playing at?"

She backed up. "Let go." Before he could come at her

again, she said, "A sniper hit Preston Lightwood. I was tracking him down."

"Who cares about that piece of garbage? He killed his wife."

Kenna blinked. "Do you want to see where he shot from or not?"

"Preston?"

"The shooter who just tried to kill him." And unlike Carlos, he had missed. Was it really Walker? Had she actually seen him come here and carry out a hit—or try to. Was he the one Carlos had mentioned, the person who came in when an operator in their group failed to complete a task?

So who had failed?

Kenna headed for the building and yanked on the handle.

"You need a pass." Antonio pretty much shoved her out of the way and went in first, heading up concrete steps to the upper floors.

Did the shooter fire a single shot, realize there was no way to complete the task, and then go? Or had he been waiting for another chance?

She didn't like the idea someone had her in their sights.

At least she wasn't the target. That meant she could do the work and keep safe whoever *was*. Preston. Jax. Someone else? Didn't matter.

She would be on guard now.

Antonio hit the landing at the top and looked around.

"Here." Kenna gestured. The door to the left, where the open window would be, remained slightly ajar. She pushed it all the way open and scanned the room before walking slowly through it, careful where she stepped. "Do you have an ambulance coming for Preston?"

"Of course." Antonio moved around, keeping his distance rather than straining to see what she was looking at. Which would only mean he got elbowed when she stopped. "This was an office. It's only empty because we had some damage to the roof a few months ago. I guess no one put the stuff back in here. We had some employee turnover."

She stopped and studied the floor. The ledge of the window.

Correct about the shooter using this window. She could see it in the scratches on the floor and a couple pencil markings on the window ledge. Didn't bother to disguise the fact they'd been here, which was interesting.

"Did you find Esmeralda?"

Kenna didn't react to that. "We went by her house." She shrugged.

If he dug, she wasn't sure she would lie. That was an interesting discussion for her and Jax—deliberately deceiving someone as a believer, whether it saved a life or simply preserved the details of the case. She wasn't bound by procedure, not as a PI. She made her own rules, and it was evidently time to think some of them through now she had fundamentally different beliefs.

Why did that have to come up now?

"He shot from here." She turned to Antonio. "And he's gone now."

The security guard's expression tightened. "I'll call the sheriff. She'll want to process the scene."

"Great, I'll go back and see if Preston is still alive." She took the stairs back down, passed the tennis courts, and found a crowd by the tables where a pool of blood would stain the stones until someone figured out how to get it out.

Might not be the first time it had happened.

Jax peeled off from the group and headed to her before she made her way to the group, which included several staff members and EMTs. The people standing there began to disburse, and she spotted Preston on a gurney being wheeled into the open doors, which was probably the fastest route to their ambulance.

He spotted her and lifted his chin, then winced. The EMT said something to him.

Preston barked something back at her that Kenna couldn't hear, his face turning red.

Kenna turned to Jax, who held Ozzy in his arms. "Want me to take the dog?"

"He's fine." Jax petted him with one hand and held Ozzy tucked against his chest with the other. "We forged a truce. Shooter?"

She shook off way-too-distracting thoughts about how he looked holding a small living being and the interior monologue of who she had become in the last two years since she met him. "Fled in a van. I didn't get a good enough look at his face to say definitively who it was."

"But you have an idea."

She scrunched up her nose. "Later."

A server Kenna had seen earlier headed for them. They turned as she approached, rolling her eyes. "Mr. Lightwood needs a word before the EMTs take him to the hospital."

"Thank you." Kenna nodded.

She headed inside, Jax coming with her. Through the dining hall, with a path between tables now cleared out for the stretcher. They found him in the lobby.

"Kenna!"

She winced. Did he have to use her real name? She sighed and made it close enough to say, "What is it, Preston?"

"I know why I was shot at." He spoke low, turning his phone so he could show her a video of a hotel room, not a suite like hers. Two queen beds but upmarket décor that seemed standard for this place. "Someone is in my room."

"So tell security."

He shook his head. "You take care of it." He handed her a key card. "Quietly."

Given the woman's build and the color of her features, Kenna figured she could do that. "Fine. Go get stitched up."

Preston motioned with two fingers. "Let's go."

The EMT broke off talking to a manager in a suit and gold name badge pinned to his breast pocket, and they pushed Preston out of the lobby.

The manager headed for them across the stone floor, passing a redwood table with a gold vase bigger than her duffel bag and a three-foot spray of flowers.

She turned to Jax. "I need to go upstairs."

He leaned down and kissed her, a quick touch of his lips to hers. "Go. I've got this."

Kenna went for the elevator, her head spinning again. The case. Jax being here reinforced how she could be perfectly comfortable being close to him. She barely knew what to do with any of it.

But she knew how to do *this*.

Kenna pulled her gun—just in case—but didn't think she'd need to use it. She used the key and heard it click. The light turned green. *Start panicking, girl.*

Kenna shoved it open and went in, gun first. She let the heavy door click behind her and looked around. Empty room. Or was it? "I know you're still here, Avery."

The senator sauntered out of the bathroom, her hair mussed like she'd flipped her head and fluffed it. Face flushed. Buttons askew, fastened one off so the shirt didn't fit her right —or maybe the supposed plan was to tear it off as soon as he came back.

Avery pretended to be surprised. "I was expecting Preston. Not you, with a gun."

Kenna didn't lower it. "We need to talk."

Chapter Twenty

"The honeymoon suite?" Avery entered the room ahead of Kenna, propelled in there by the nudge Kenna gave her. "Nice."

"Yeah, that's not what we're talking about." Kenna closed the door behind her.

Jax was already in the room. Ozzy hopped off the couch and came over to Avery, who crouched and petted the dog, then ended up cross-legged on the floor. So, not a powerplay despite the fact she'd been caught in Preston's room.

Kenna stuck by the corner of the wall, where the room opened from the entryway to the living area. "Start talking, Avery. Because I don't believe for one second you're having an affair with Preston. Not when he was on the patio for the last couple of hours."

"We can't let anyone see us together." She sounded almost sick saying it.

Kenna looked at Jax, silhouetted by the sheer curtains behind him. Maybe he should move away from the window, given her track record of people getting hit by sniper rounds when she was in proximity. She tipped her head to the side.

His expression shifted to look quizzical. She didn't want to speak her neurosis aloud, especially when it was only really based on fear that she should pray through. Get over. Worry every second if someone next to her would end up with a bullet in the head in the next moment.

"I don't buy it." Kenna folded her arms loosely, leaning the outside of her shoulder on the wall. She should take off her weapon and set the holster on the entry table, but she wasn't quite ready to relax.

Their cover here was effectively blown.

The question was, what would Cecelia do about it?

Avery huffed. "Doesn't matter if you do or not, it's true."

Jax said, "If you didn't look like you were going to be sick, I might believe you."

Ozzy wandered away from Avery to his bed and settled with his head on his front paws. She sat on the arm of the couch, trying to act all nonchalant. What she didn't know was that Preston had shown Kenna camera footage from inside his room of Avery accessing his safe.

"He wired up the room with cameras," Kenna said.

Avery flinched.

"He showed me. How do you think I knew you were in there?" They weren't so different in age, but in a lot of ways Kenna felt like an old soul or whatever people called it. She always had been in a way. Avery had partied her way through high school as the president's daughter, a motherless teen with drug and alcohol issues. Her early twenties, she hit a series of exclusive rehabs and got clean but never quite managed to repair her reputation.

Almost getting killed in Albuquerque—and the fact it would've been murder but looked like an overdose—had honestly done her public persona a favor. She'd played that card all the way to lobbying for reforms and running for

Florida senator on a stance of second chance values. Education reforms where kids saw firsthand what substance abuse did to them. Where youth drug offenses were taken seriously, and consequences were matched with help. Marrying facilities that aided sobriety with the old juvenile hall model, creating a more modern way to turn kids' lives around. Programs that gave them a helping hand but also realistic consequences for their offenses.

"Why are you here, Avery?" Kenna didn't for one second buy that this was some old college friends reunion trip. Or a way to blow off steam. It was far more likely Avery was here for a different reason.

The senator picked at an invisible fluff on her pant leg. She looked the part. Kenna would give her that. Sneaking around someone's hotel room in upmarket office attire—even if she still needed to fix the misfastened buttons on her shirt.

"It's *my* business." Avery lifted her chin, a blank expression on her face. "I don't need help, and I don't need to run it by you for permission."

"So you're the only one who takes a hit if things go sideways. None of your people know why you're really here." Kenna thought over that idea.

"They think I'm taking a nap."

Jax told her, "Since Preston was nearly assassinated half an hour ago, they're probably up in your room trying to tell you all about it."

Avery shook her head. "They don't bother me until I come out."

"So you have it all figured out." Flying solo. No one else was important enough to what she was doing that she needed to tell them—which meant it was personal. "What were you looking for in Preston's safe?"

Avery's gaze shifted to Kenna, some of the nonchalance slipping.

"Who is he to you?" Kenna asked. "The guy was in prison until six months ago. You can't have known him before."

Avery tucked a wayward strand of blond hair behind her ear. Finally, she said, "He knew my mother."

Kenna tugged her phone out of pocket and sent a quick text message, then dialed Maizie as a follow-up. She held the phone by her side and said to Avery, "Your mother was killed before your father became president. Is that right?"

Avery nodded.

Her father had used widowhood to propel him to the presidency, much like Avery had utilized her past and how she'd turned her life around as a role model for sobriety to land herself in the Senate in Washington, DC. Kenna hadn't thought they were much alike, but maybe Avery had learned her tactics from her father.

Something had always rubbed Kenna the wrong way about the former president. She had just never been able to put her finger on it. Her dad hadn't liked him, making her wonder if that was her whole reasoning.

Something she had learned from him, even if it was only an opinion she had taken on board.

"What were you expecting to find in Preston's safe?" Jax asked.

When Avery didn't answer, Kenna said, "So you wait until he's at lunch and you pay a guy with a rifle to take a shot at him and miss on purpose so there's no way he'll come back to the room and disturb you?"

"I..." Avery blanched. "What?"

"A sniper took a shot at Preston on the patio," Jax said, probably since it bared repeating.

"Risky move," Kenna said, swallowing against the sickness

that rose just thinking of the fact Jax could so easily have been killed in that moment—along with any number of other innocent victims. "Shooting at people in the middle of a crowd. Just so you can look around his room."

Avery's mouth dropped open. "I don't have anything to do with the sniper. What are you even talking about?"

"So you and whatever you're doing here have nothing to do with a hit out on Preston?" Kenna needed to find out if anyone had actually posted that to a marketplace where professional killers accepted contracts.

Another Maizie job to add to the stack of tasks on her plate right now.

The teen was probably listening to their conversation and freaking out over the fact someone had been shot at the resort.

"I don't want him *dead*." Avery gasped. "I want him to tell me the truth. I want him to pay for what he did."

Now they were getting somewhere.

"What did he do?" Kenna asked.

"He was dating my mother when he killed his wife," Avery replied. "He goes on the run, and she's killed eight days later."

"But you don't know why?"

The senator shrugged, looking every bit the grieving daughter and not a federal power player. "He has to know what happened to her. I don't buy for one second it was run-of-the-mill car accident, not when there are too many inconsistencies in the report. Things that were buried. Other pieces that were overlooked, and then the car is destroyed when that usually takes months to happen?"

Jax said, "Have you asked your father about the inconsistencies?"

Good question. Kenna figured if anyone knew about the death of Avery's mother, it would be her husband at the time.

And the fact Preston's wife and girlfriend had been killed in a matter of weeks added another layer to that whole case.

None of which had anything to do with Cecelia Warren—unless it did.

"Why don't you sit him down and ask him straight out if he was dating her?" Kenna pushed off the wall and retrieved bottled water from the fridge, a tiny semblance of a reward for Avery telling them the truth. Or at least starting to.

"I know he was dating her." Avery sniffed. "I have pictures."

"Sometimes asking a simple question will get you a straight answer." Kenna had experienced it many times over, when a remorseful person simply wanted to confess and be rid of a lifetime of guilt weighing them down like an anvil.

Avery twisted off the cap of her water and took a few sips. "I don't know what universe you're living in, but no one tells the truth in mine."

"Then how about this? I'm in the middle of a complicated case, but as soon as I'm done, I'll help you with yours."

"If all you're going to do is sit down with your new friend Preston and ask him if he killed my mother as well as his wife, then don't bother."

Kenna shrugged. She wasn't going to convince this woman if she didn't want any help to begin with. She lifted the phone to her ear. "Did you get all that?"

Maizie said, "Are you going to ask her if she knows Cecelia?"

"Yes."

"Call me back after and tell me what she says." The line went dead.

Kenna scrolled through to her gallery.

Jax said, "I'll need to go out to the lobby and meet with the local sheriff pretty soon. Is there more to talk about?"

She nodded. "I'm good, if you need to go."

"On second thought, I'll stay here, and then we'll go down together."

She shot him a look, thankful because her instinct was telling her the same thing. "Avery?" Kenna wandered over and showed her a picture of Cecelia. "Have you ever met this woman? Do you know her?"

Avery stared at the picture. Frowned. "I don't think so. Who is she?"

"The subject of my investigation. And if you don't know her, then I would steer clear, because she's the scorched-earth type."

Avery's brows lifted.

"Next question...," Kenna began. Given she had caught the girl and called her out on her lie about being in a relationship with Preston when this was all about finding the truth about her mother's death—something Kenna would need to tackle soon enough with her own history— she figured it was open season for information gathering.

"What do you know about the Rosenberg family?" Jax said.

Avery choked on a sip of water. "The Rosenbergs? Even my father steers clear of them. Everyone stays out of their way."

"So they're no good?" Kenna needed to send the information to Maizie—or start her own intensive search into these people. Figure out what she could about them. After she took down Cecelia, the Rosenbergs might be next on her list.

Avery nodded. "The Rosenbergs only care about their own ideas for the future and what public policy should be. My dad has his own intentions for the direction this country should go. So they were never going to agree in the first place."

Didn't seem like she had any love for these people.

"So the Rosenbergs want to steer the country?" Kenna paused. "One family can't do that."

Avery blinked. She glanced at Jax. "Maybe you need to explain some things to her about the way the world works?" She looked at Kenna. "What rock have you been living under for the last hundred years?"

"The quiet one, where I work cases one at a time and save lives."

"True." Avery tilted her water bottle in Jax's direction. "He knows what I'm talking about."

"Do I?" Jax stiffened.

"Your father tried to join the organization here at the Willowbrooke, didn't he?"

"That has nothing to do with the case Kenna and I are working on," Jax countered.

"We all have things we don't want to talk about. Family secrets that never see the light of day." Avery paused. "But my mother's death isn't one of those things. Even if it never goes public, I want to know the truth about how and why she died."

The ache in Kenna's chest wasn't only about this woman's need for the truth about her mother.

It was also about her own.

But there hadn't been any time to think about what Stan Tilley had told her in Wisconsin.

She pulled up a picture of Walker on her phone. A witness sketch the FBI had run through every known database and military record, coming up with absolutely nothing. She had seen him. He had lived at that compound in Mexico with Kart and his men.

He wasn't a ghost.

"How about this guy?" Kenna showed the picture to Avery.

"Isn't that the killer the FBI's looking for?" She glanced at Jax. "You guys didn't find him yet?"

A muscle flexed in his jaw.

His phone chimed. "Antonio says the sheriff is here."

"Great. I'll go back to my room and pretend I was sleeping this entire time." Avery got up from her perch on the arm of the couch, brushing off her pants. "It's been a lovely chat, thanks."

Kenna studied her, wondering if she ever told the truth about what was really going on. Which meant that most of what she'd just told to Kenna and Jax was likely a lie, or at least only partially the truth at best.

The question was, which parts should she trust?

Avery's reaction to Cecelia had seemed genuine. They could probably ascertain if she'd ever crossed paths with the woman, but it could be unlikely. Avery was here on a mission of her own.

Kenna said, "Given someone was shot earlier outside on the patio, my advice to you is to watch your back. Be careful." She felt the need to add one more thing. "Don't do anything stupid."

Avery grinned. "I'll try, but I'm just getting started."

She trailed out, letting the door shut behind her with a loud click.

"Talk about trouble." Jax shook his head. "She reminds me of my sister."

Kenna closed her eyes and gave herself a moment. "I don't need any more personal missions. At least not until I'm at a place where I don't have to worry that Ramon is going to snap and kill somebody."

Jax chuckled. She felt his presence close to her a second before he touched her cheek and pressed a kiss to her forehead. "Good plan. Let's go meet the sheriff."

Chapter Twenty-One

The local sheriff from the closest town was a stocky woman in her forties whose heritage was at least a portion indigenous. Her shiny dark hair would have been threaded with a lot more gray if not for her Native American ancestry. She had a long nose and deep-set dark brown eyes, but a smattering of freckles on her cheeks.

"I'm Sheriff Melinda Bracken." She held out a hand with stubby fingers. "Nice to meet you."

"Kenna Banbury. I'm a private investigator." She shook hands with the sheriff, then motioned to Jax. "FBI Special Agent Oliver Jaxton."

"Have a seat." Antonio settled into his chair behind the desk, wincing a little as if he needed to upgrade his lumbar support. The cheap metal desk and '90s-looking computer weren't a great sign as to this resort's level of surveillance tech.

Bracken leaned against the file cabinet and set one elbow on the top. "I don't suppose you're going to tell me what the two of you are working on here?" She glanced between Kenna and Jax.

Antonio smirked. He'd probably taken great pleasure in

explaining to the sheriff that they weren't who they claimed to be when they'd checked into the resort. Which probably said more about their security measures and the need to vet their guests than Kenna and Jax's ability to sell a cover story.

"I'm on vacation." Jax settled into one of the hard chairs that faced the desk. "Not working a case."

Antonio snorted aloud.

Kenna waved her finger between her and Jax as she took the other seat. "We're..." How much did she need to explain to the sheriff? "Taking some time out. Spending it together."

They had been called to this meeting in Antonio's office, which was barely bigger than the interior of her RV. It was crowded enough in here she wondered why the sheriff and Antonio intentionally stood so far apart, and neither even glanced at the other.

Bracken smirked. "And yet I am updating you on an investigation involving the place you just happened to be on vacation?"

Kenna wondered if she'd have a better read on this woman if Antonio wasn't here. Which considering he wasn't filling that coffee pot on the file cabinet made him pretty much superfluous. There were plenty of things she'd like to say to this local sheriff. But then, the fact people kept getting shot by sniper and one cop had already tried to kill her this week was no doubt going to keep her from explaining too much.

"I just want to know if you've heard anything locally about a threat against Special Agent Jaxton," Kenna stated. As if she might be convinced the shot had been intended for him.

Sheriff Bracken glanced at him. "You have reason to believe you might've been the target instead of Preston Lightwood?" She didn't give him a chance to answer before she added, "Haven't we all wanted to shoot that guy at least once in our lives?"

Kenna wasn't going to answer that. She glanced at Antonio. "Anything from the resort surveillance on the van that fled the scene right after the shooting?"

He stared at her. "You think the suspect was driving? He'd have left minutes before that."

"It takes time to pack up a rifle," Kenna countered. Not to mention the question of whether he'd been waiting around for another shot, seeing as he didn't manage to kill anyone. "Did you at least get a license plate, if not an image of the guy?"

Antonio shook his head. "That parking lot doesn't have any cameras. We have the van leaving the delivery gate, but the plates have something over them that isn't visible."

"But you have a log of the vehicle entering and exiting the property?" Kenna asked.

Antonio said, "The security guard didn't write it down. I'll be talking to him about that."

"Agent Jaxton, how about you?" The sheriff shot him a pointed look. "I watched the patio feed around the time of the shooting. I think you're right to be concerned the shot might have been meant for you."

Jax scratched his jaw. "I have a number of cases that are open right now, and the most notable one is the search for *El Caminante*. But my supervisor is about take me off that one, as there have been no new leads in months. Not sure why he would come after me now when the trail is practically frozen over it's so cold."

Kenna would like to see that footage. Even though she'd been sitting across the table from Jax, she wanted to get a look at everyone else. See if there was another person on the patio who might've been aware what was about to happen.

Did another one of Carlos' buddies take a job to end the life of an FBI special agent?

It was unlikely they would be able to track down the shooter if that was the case. And then, they also needed to be worried that another might show up at any moment to finish the job.

Kenna turned to Antonio. "Any word on Mr. Lightwood and how he's doing in the hospital?"

He smirked. "Because he's a friend of yours?"

She shot him a look.

Sheriff Bracken said, "If it wasn't a sniper, I'd be inclined to think it connected to my other case today. No gun crimes reported in eight months, and suddenly there are two shootings in one day? But I highly doubt this connects to a regular ole murder-suicide." She appeared fatigued for the first time since Kenna shook her hand.

"Would it be okay if I took a look at that case?" Kenna offered.

"I have deputies," the sheriff said, tilting her head to the side. "And I'm not in the market for a new best friend."

Kenna stared at her. Antonio seemed to think the comment was hilarious, and maybe it wasn't entirely uncalled for considering Kenna's track record with local sheriffs. Getting killed, getting fired. Maybe Bracken had done her research. Because Kenna knew she hadn't ever been in this area, and neither had her father. So this woman didn't know her personally.

"Also, there's another reason you aren't going to be looking into the case." The sheriff shifted her weight from one foot to the other but didn't remove her elbow from the top of the file cabinet. "A neighbor described a couple who left the house earlier this morning as matching a description eerily similar to the two of you. Does either of you know anything about who might've spoken to Esme and Carlos?"

Kenna's chest felt like steel bands had tightened around it. As if she'd been captured, and not because she was guilty of anything. "We can tell you where we were earlier today. It certainly won't match up with the timeline of any murders."

"The neighbor heard two shots," Bracken said. "One each? Or the same gun?"

Antonio chuckled. "You should haul them to your station and question them."

Because that would get them out of his way?

Kenna glanced at him. "What do you have going on that you need us elsewhere?" The accusation might offend her if it wasn't something that had been said regularly to her, and if every part of it didn't smell like these two were taking orders from Cecelia Warren. Or at least, Antonio probably was.

"They were alive when we left the house," Jax said. "Which you can prove if the neighbor confirms that we spoke with Esmeralda on the front walk of her property, and then she returned alive into the house and we never went back inside."

She hated that either of them even had to explain away the accusation that they had committed murder. The fact the investigators would find her business card in the house didn't sit right. It was entirely too reminiscent of the case where Kenna and Jax first met in Salt Lake City.

Felt like a lifetime ago, and yet now it seemed like history was repeating itself.

"We asked if they needed help," Kenna said.

Bracken's expression remained impassive. Unlike Antonio. "I'm guessing they did," she said, "considering what happened after you left. Now tell me what you're into before more people end up dead."

"You might want not want to know, *considering*." Kenna shrugged.

The sheriff pulled a paper from her pocket and unfolded it, a printout of a grainy camera feed. A man wearing the uniform of a utility worker, repair man, or cable guy passing a car parked on the driveway. "Who is this?"

Kenna took the photo and looked at it. "Walker?"

Jax leaned in. "I'm thinking it looks more like your friend."

Ramon? He was supposed to be nearby, but she didn't know how into this thing he was yet.

Bracken cleared her throat. "I got a tip that this guy, who I'm supposed to believe is the shooter, is some guy who used to be a fed." She shot a look at Jax. "Some turncoat who worked for a cartel in Mexico. Now he's up here taking out vengeance on people who wronged him. Like that's a normal thing to do. Maybe you came across him, and he decided to add you to his hit list?"

Kenna didn't want to believe Ramon was the shooter. He might be lethal, but she highly doubted he would take out a couple that potentially had information on how to get up the chain to Cecelia.

"Did you ID both of the victims?" Jax asked.

Bracken frowned, as if that was significant but she hadn't planned to mention it. "Just the woman, Esmeralda Juarez. Why, who is the guy?"

"Probably just some local lowlife." Antonio grunted.

Which was why his brother was a police lieutenant and he was only head of security at a fancy resort where not much crime happened and he would need to do little investigation. Except he apparently didn't like what was happening here, and tried to get his cousin to help him...what? Take down these people?

Seemed like Antonio might have let a lot of things slide just to keep his job.

Or was he being threatened?

"Sure, you could call him a lowlife. Until you run his tattoos, and his contacts." Kenna shifted in her seat, wondering when they could get out of here to go check on Lightwood. She felt his life expectancy may not be too long and that it was worth advising him to take precautions to ensure his safety.

Which she also needed to do with Jax.

It hit her like a wave, a rush of feeling that crested and then crashed down on her. Tears burned in her eyes. The loss of life she had witnessed in the last few days. First Noelle. And now Esmeralda was dead as well? No one else was going to die.

But she couldn't even make that promise to herself. She had no power here to ensure everyone else connected to this remained alive until they got all the way to Cecelia.

"I'll be sure to do that." Sheriff Bracken nodded. "I'm guessing it will lead me down a rabbit trail, and I might not like what I find."

"That's a fair assessment," Kenna said.

Jax stood. "If there are no more questions, Kenna and I are going to get back to our relaxing vacation."

She had to choke back the need to laugh, just a nervous reaction to everything. He was far better at schooling his features and keeping his emotions to himself than she was. Unless faced with a serial killer. Though, she didn't feel like testing that theory anytime soon.

He took her hand, and they made their way down the hall back to the lobby and outside. Kenna looked at the blue sky and blinked back tears.

Jax squeezed the back of her neck. "Come on. Let's go."

She wanted to make a joke about his desire to ride in the truck as much as possible, but just couldn't manage to fight her way through the sadness over yet another death. He started the engine and turned the music low, even though Kenna stayed silent for the drive to the hospital.

Had she told him where she wanted to go?

Jax pulled into a parking space at the wide two-story medical center that looked more like a little school in a midsize town. He shoved the truck into Park and turned in his seat to face her, apparently not intending to go anywhere for the moment, even if he had unclicked his seatbelt.

She hit the button on hers, adjusting her position on the seat and having to bite back a groan when all her aches made themselves known.

"You're not okay."

Kenna shrugged. "When is that ever a factor in what I do on a given day?"

He frowned.

"We aren't going to bring down Cecelia by taking naps on our vacation. Our cover has been blown. Our shot at information is dead, and there's no way to figure out who these military guys are getting orders from. We basically have nothing." Except a photo of a child and whatever corporation owned land around Pahrump, Nevada. "We've been scrambling this whole time, reacting to whatever Cecelia is doing to head us off."

"So it's time to turn the tables on her. Hit back."

"You can't do that without getting fired or winding up in prison."

Jax squeezed her hand. "I'm not going to let you take it on alone."

If she knew where Ramon was and what he was up to, she could argue she wasn't alone. The truth was, she'd rather do this with Jax than anyone else, even by herself. Ramon might prove helpful, but she knew who she preferred.

Kenna shifted to grab the door handle. "We need to go check on Preston. Make sure he hasn't been killed like everyone else."

She felt like she had lost her hope that this case would ever be over or that Cecelia would ever be brought to justice. She wanted Jax to see her strong and full of the drive to take this on, even though it seemed to be next to impossible. She was supposed to be a better Christian than this after so many months of learning and growing.

Maybe there was something wrong with her. She'd missed some key components, like the fact this work had nothing to do with people getting saved. Preaching the gospel—telling people about Jesus—didn't have anything to do with bringing down killers and dirty FBI agents. It was something she hadn't wanted to admit she was worried over.

After all, they could be on their own and she just hadn't realized it.

"Wanna talk about it?"

She sighed and hopped out. "Later. First we need to try and save someone's life."

Chapter Twenty-Two

"I can't believe he told me to get lost so he could talk to you alone." Jax clicked the locks on the truck as they approached it.

Kenna had the same reaction when Preston said that to them almost as soon as they entered his hospital room. However, considering she hadn't let it happen, there wasn't much for Jax to grumble about. "Just as long as he does what he said and hires a company that will protect him even if it's just in case, I'm not going to worry about the rest of it."

Jax's phone started to ring, cutting off whatever he had been about to say. "It's my sister. I sent her a text about the Willowbrooke Resort and the time we spent there when we were kids."

Kenna nodded, wondering if she should offer to take a wander and maybe make a call of her own while he spoke to his sister. She was curious enough about Lainey to want to listen in and definitely meet the woman someday, but the fact his family came in a package deal that involved his parents made Kenna hesitate.

Not that she thought there was something wrong with

them. More that it was wrong with her. She had no idea how to navigate family life. Once they broke the seal on making it official with his extended family, she'd be all in—no going back. Not just the two of them, but also holidays like Thanksgiving and Christmas with his relatives.

Things she had little experience with, and a whole lot of anxiety. Kenna wasn't sure she wanted to think about the fact it was easier for her to go up against a deadly serial killer than it was to bite the bullet and meet Jax's mother. Probably she'd simply left it too long, built it up as too big now and should've done it months ago.

Jax shifted the phone away from his mouth. "Are you getting in, Kenna?"

She held the door open and climbed into the passenger seat.

"That's what I thought," Jax said. He started the car and the call connected to the car Bluetooth, Lainey's response coming through the speakers now.

"You don't remember anything about that trip?"

Jax pulled out, driving away from the medical center. Kenna didn't know where they were going, and maybe he didn't even have a plan of what they should do next. She decided to be content spending time with him and having not much purpose in mind—except for the fact that there was a case to work.

"Isn't that where we played in the gravel?" Jax said. "I remember a lake, and the waiter gave us Jell-O."

Lainey was quiet for a few moments. Then she said, "That's it?"

"What else am I supposed to remember?"

"I've always wondered why you never said anything to me. The research I've done says it's a trauma reaction, where you block out something horrific because your mind doesn't know how to process it."

"Lainey, what are you talking about?"

Kenna glanced at him. He genuinely seemed confused, making her wonder over the answer to his question.

"It's a good thing you blocked it out," his sister said. "And sometimes I wish I could. But the truth is, I'm not ever going to forget what happened." She paused. "I don't even know what her name was. Dad screamed at me the one time I asked him about it. I wasn't ever supposed to talk about what happened."

Jax shook his head, pulling into the parking lot of a chain pharmacy. "What am I supposed to remember that I don't?"

"You were four and I was seven. I told you to hide, and I looked myself. Someone must've bashed her head in because I remember all the blood and the mark on her face. The police never talked to us. We left the resort later that day and never spoke of it. And we never went back. But I've always wondered if it was the reason you became an agent. The mystery. Needing to resolve things with answers. With the truth."

Jax's hands shook as he shifted to Park. "We saw a dead girl?"

"A few years ago, I was talking to Chad about it. He told me to hire a private investigator and find out who she was." Lainey sighed. "I was going to talk to Kenna about it when we finally meet."

Her stomach flipped over. Did she want to take on a case so close to the personal life she had been scared to embrace? Maybe solving this mystery for Lainey and Jax would help her find her footing in the family dynamic.

Or it could turn half the family against her for dragging it all back out.

Jax breathed hard, sucking in great gulping breaths. "How can I possibly not remember?"

Before Kenna could answer, Lainey said, "You were four."

Kenna reached over and laid her hand on his. He squeezed it hard for a second, then let go. Right now, he didn't need physical contact. He wanted to get a handle on what was going on by himself. If that was what he needed, then she should be the one to give him space. Let him process this with his sister.

"I know why I became an FBI agent," Jax said.

Lainey replied with, "You always said it was to tick off Dad, but I've never been convinced that's the full reason. You're not the vindictive one, bro."

He said nothing.

Kenna's phone started to vibrate in her pocket. She slid it out and saw Maizie was calling.

Jax glanced at her and lifted his chin. A signal to answer it? She would need to get out of the car in order to not disturb his conversation with his sister, but she could get a good look at the area around them if she did that. Make sure no one was going to take a shot at Jax. Again.

He mouthed, *I'm okay.*

Kenna wasn't entirely sure that was true and would definitely be looking into Lainey's story. But for now, she would honor what he wanted.

Kenna cracked the door and climbed out, closing it behind her. She swiped the screen and put the phone to her ear. "Hey, Maze."

"If you're not sitting down when I tell you this, you're going to wish you were."

Kenna wandered around the truck, looking everywhere. At the cross streets, stretching in all directions. Other cars.

People going in and out of storefronts on this busy intersection. "What's going on?"

"I think I figured it out. At least, it makes a lot of sense."

"Before you tell me, have you heard from Ramon?"

"No," Maizie said. "I'm still waiting for him to reply."

Kenna didn't like the sound of that. "What about Bart? Did Stairns get what he needed to exonerate the guy?"

"He's boots on the ground and working on it."

There was at least one thing Kenna didn't have to worry about, even if she didn't like the situation in the first place. Too many innocent people had been dragged into this situation already. "Okay, fill me in on what you have."

"I've been digging into the Rosenbergs and that girl Sarah who supposedly drowned, right?"

Kenna figured that meant she hadn't made much progress on the military angle and decided to change directions to give herself a break. "What did you find?"

"Super old money. Like they've owned certain pieces of land since the very beginning. Like when-America-became-a-country beginning."

Kenna lifted her brows, even though no one could see her who'd recognize her. "Just passing the land down from generation to generation?"

"That's exactly it. And building financial investments and starting companies. Buying and selling other companies. They've got foundations inside foundations inside corporations, all of which is nestled in some other kind of trust or hedge fund. It's a complicated mess that is going to take an accounting expert to dig through. Which was why I focused on the family tree instead. Hard to hide a person in an offshore bank account, although apparently it's not super difficult."

Kenna frowned. "Skeletons in their closet?" Or perhaps Maizie was referencing her upbringing.

"Edward Rosenberg is Sarah's father," the teen said. "He seems to be the patriarch, and the one who holds all the strings as head of every board. At the time of Sarah's death, his sister Georgia was living on the property with her two children, Celeste and Walter. Right after Sarah's death, there's a newspaper article with some very veiled references to it being suspicious. The reporter was killed in a car accident a few months later. But not before they wrote this article and published it before the Rosenbergs could squash it."

"Possible foul play?" Kenna turned slightly, keeping the phone angled away from a delivery truck that passed her.

"Mm-hmm. I guess the reporter got the coroner, who was his brother-in-law, to show him the body. Cause of death was listed as an accidental drowning, but the article suggests that the reporter saw evidence of blunt force trauma to the back of the head. And alluded to the fact that the coroner was forced to rule the death accidental."

"And then later he dies?" Kenna said. "What happened to the coroner?"

"He was promoted to the state medical examiner's office, and now he runs it."

Kenna wondered if it was worth making a trip to Massachusetts just to talk to the man.

Maizie continued, "Right after the funeral, Walter is shipped off to military school and his sister, Celeste, and her mother moved to Pennsylvania, where she was enrolled in private school."

"They were around the same age as Sarah when she died?"

"Yes. From the birth records, Walter and Celeste are ten months apart. But half-siblings."

And when tragedy struck, Mom and her children were torn apart and sent in different directions. "Is the mother still alive, this Georgia Rosenberg?"

"I'll find out." Maizie paused. "Check your messages. I'm sending you a picture of Walter from his entrance to military school, and one of Celeste from her high school cheerleading team."

Kenna's phone buzzed in her hand, and she lowered it to look at the photos. Grainy, not the best quality. And children who would be adults now. How much did a person's appearance change over a decade or two?

But she could see the resemblance.

Enough that everything in her understanding seemed to eclipse, and her mind seemed to skitter to a stop as her thoughts crashed into each other. "Celeste and Walter."

"I know," Maizie said. "Cecelia and Walker, much?"

And with Cecelia throwing out the name of the dead girl in deals. Her only shot at being associated with that family, probably. Because she needed people to believe she was one of them? A powerful old American family with their position of influence in the country spanning generations as they built an empire.

Using off-book army units comprised of men who were supposedly deceased. All to do their bidding killing off people who might compromise their hold on power.

What an utterly terrifying thought.

Jax got out on his side and rounded the bed of the truck, coming toward her. Still looking shaken by what his sister had told him. She wanted to ask Maizie to look into the victim Laney and Jax had found at the resort, but didn't want to do it only so that they could rule out its connection to this case.

Jax took a look at her and shook his head. "What is it?"

She explained what Maizie had just told her and showed him the photos, letting him talk to the teen while she paced a little and figured out what they should do next. The reporter had visited the coroner's office and dug into the deaths on his own.

Esme and Carlos were deceased—and all they had to go on was the word of a sheriff Kenna wasn't sure she trusted.

"Okay, sounds good." Jax ended the call and handed back her phone. "I'm about ready to pummel somebody. If Walker isn't going to show up, maybe Ramon could, and he and I could take out some frustration on each other." He rolled his shoulders, curling his fingers into fists and then stretching them out again.

Kenna wasn't sure she would offer to be his sparring partner even if her arms were fully functional. Unless they were talking about wrestling, in which case she was pretty sure she could pin him with her legs.

"They must have buried it seriously deep for no one to realize they're siblings."

"Half-siblings," Kenna said. "But the question is, which one of them killed Sarah?"

"And why would Edward let it slide rather than getting rid of them with the conviction of life in prison?"

"They must have believed they got away with what they did. I just can't tell if they're part of the family now in some way, or maybe even trying to get back in the fold after all these years." She shook her head. "I think we should go to the coroner here in town and ask to see the victims of that murder-suicide the sheriff mentioned."

"And if it really is Esmeralda and Carlos...?" Jax pulled open her door and held it for her.

She wouldn't waste time worrying about whether they

were safe if they were, in fact, deceased. Instead, she would be grieving for them. Knowing there was nothing she could do to help them now.

Kenna motioned Jax toward her with a wave of her fingers. When he closed in, she settled her knees on either side of him and touched his cheek. "Are you okay?"

He seemed relieved that she asked. "It's hard to worry about what you can't even remember. I just don't like the idea that Laney took something like that on board and I can't help her."

"Nobody in the world would put that much pressure on a four-year-old. You couldn't have known."

He nodded. "I know." He leaned in and touched his lips to hers, both of them taking solace in the soft moment. As long as they weren't going to get hit by sniper fire while distracted.

A few minutes later, he slid in the drivers' side and drove them to the coroner's office, letting GPS direct him. The sound of the turn instructions was the only conversation in the car, both of them deep in their own thoughts.

Jax dug his FBI badge out of his backpack. "I guess I'll have to tell them you're my assistant, or consulting on this case."

"Maybe you're *my* assistant." She hopped out of the truck.

Jax called out, "You wish," right before she shut the door. And they met at the front of the truck.

"Partners will probably always be a better idea."

He looked like he wanted to kiss her again, and she wondered if he was thinking about that trip to the courthouse he had mentioned.

Kenna pulled open the front door to the county coroner's office and found an older lady on the front desk, white hair cut short in a bob and a blue dress on. The only vehicle in the parking lot was a red pickup truck. This classy lady drove a truck to work?

Kenna smiled. "Good..." She checked the clock on the wall. "Afternoon."

The lady smiled at her, then looked at Jax, and her eyes flared.

Girl, I know what you mean.

He explained who he was, dropping all the pretense of why they'd checked into the resort. The sheriff would no doubt learn about them coming here and asking after the victims, but that was a problem for tomorrow or another day. This was bigger than Sheriff Bracken and whatever she had going on with Antonio and the resort.

The older woman frowned. "I don't recall anything like that coming in." She clicked her long manicured nails on the keyboard. "Since you're FBI and all, we had a guy who suffered a heart attack even last night. Nothing this morning. Certainly not a murder-suicide."

Kenna said, "Can you look up the name Esmeralda Juarez?"

"Sure thing, hon." She tapped the keys again and had Kenna spell the name a couple of different ways. "Nothing here. Maybe the sheriff's office knows what happened?"

"Thanks for your time." Jax stepped back from the counter.

"Sorry I couldn't help you," the lady replied.

Kenna pushed out the door first, trying to figure this out. The sheriff had said explicitly there was a murder-suicide that morning. "Did we get the wrong address or something? Maybe it was a different county and she just didn't give us a clear idea of where to look."

Jax frowned, standing by her on the sidewalk. "I guess we should head to her office and ask her."

Why did Kenna feel like they'd gotten valuable information—and been sent on a wild goose chase—all at the same time?

Definitely a case of one step forward, two steps back.

When would the dance finally stop?

Chapter Twenty-Three

Jax went first down the hall to their room. Kenna was busy enjoying the view from a couple of steps behind him when he stiffened.

"What is it?"

He slowed and she caught up.

No sign of activity at the door to their room. No noise.

"It's slightly open." Jax slid his gun from the holster at the back of his belt, under the tail of his shirt.

She tugged her weapon from the holster under her shoulder. There were two ways they could do this: using the shock factor of a rushed entry or making a methodical assessment before they went in. "Fast or slow?"

Another couple of steps, and Ozzy yapped. That must've been what Jax heard.

She stopped by the door, her shoulder to the wall.

"I'll go first," he said. "You come in behind and cover me."

She nodded once.

Jax pushed the door open fast and entered almost silently on the entry tile. Kenna hooked around the door, kicked away the shoe that had been wedged in the door to keep it open, and covered one direction as he swept with his gun in the other. Between the two of them, they had the entire main living area of the suite covered.

"Breaking and entering," Jax said. "Interesting."

Antonio strode out of the bedroom, saw them, and let out a curse word. Jax shifted the aim of his gun to the head of security. Sheriff Bracken crouched by Jax's open suitcase, rifling through his belongings.

Kenna didn't lower her gun either. "Looking for something?" If Antonio had touched all her things... Her stomach flipped over.

Antonio smirked. "What are you gonna do, arrest us?"

Jax crossed the entryway and stood by the couch, gun pointed at Antonio, still by the bedroom door.

Kenna approached the TV and told Bracken, "Back up and stand. Hands where I can see them, or I'll be explaining to the Arizona State Police why you're dead in my hotel room."

Ozzy started barking in earnest, loudly protesting this invasion of his personal space—or his quiet time. The door had clicked shut, so Kenna backed up and flipped the latch on the crate where they'd left him snoozing. Ozzy rushed out, going to Bracken first, where he sniffed her shoes. Then, he raced around to see who the other intruder was.

Kenna kept her focus on Bracken. "Start talking."

Antonio made a scoffing sound. Apparently, he at least thought they were above the law in this situation. Which only made Kenna wonder how many times they'd cut corners and then covered up questionable actions.

They probably worked for Cecelia.

Here to gather intel or shut down Kenna and Jax's investigation.

"And while you're explaining why you broke into our

suite," Kenna added, "you can tell us why Esme and Carlos weren't at the coroner's office."

Bracken flinched. "You went there?"

"We sure did. So tell me why the victims of a murder-suicide weren't with the coroner. Did you use a different county or have them cremated astonishingly fast?" Kenna smirked to give Bracken the impression that she'd consider whatever the sheriff said next a lie.

The other woman worked her mouth around, apparently trying to figure out how to spin this one.

Ozzy finished his zoomies around the room and came back over to her. Kenna was about to have a problem holding her gun up, and her arms would start shaking, so she lowered it and bent to pick up the dog. She scooped the Shih Tzu up with one hand and tucked him against her shoulder. "Hi, buddy."

Ozzy licked her neck, his collar jingling.

"Thanks for that." Kenna chuckled, which served to lighten some of the tension in the room.

"Start talking," Jax ordered. "Now."

"Just figuring out what your true motives are." Antonio shrugged, but he didn't move much with a gun pointed at him.

The sheriff shifted a little, but didn't reach for the gun on her belt—a good thing considering Kenna didn't want to shoot her. "Right. What he said."

"What are you looking for?" Kenna asked.

"Something that will tell us why you're really here," Bracken replied.

She'd kept Ryson—her Ryson—in the dark. He didn't need her to put his family in danger by over sharing and getting them on some bad guy's radar. "Are Esme and Carlos dead?"

"No." Bracken shook her hand. "But you'll never find them, so there's no point looking."

"Are they safe?"

Bracken flinched. "Of course. You think I'm new at this?"

Maybe not, but she certainly hadn't thought Kenna was after their safety.

"You helped them get away?" Jax sidestepped toward Kenna, enough Antonio could've made a run for the door.

Thankfully he didn't, but neither of them would've chased him. If the guy wanted to be a coward, he could go somewhere else.

Their job here wasn't for the faint of heart.

Bracken glanced at Jax, then at Kenna. "They were in danger, and he was hurt. So I set them up with a way to stay under the radar."

"And no one can ask you where they are because you have no idea." Which was exactly what Kenna had done with a young couple she'd met who were in danger.

Maybe she and Bracken were more alike than either of them had thought.

The sheriff nodded. "They're long gone."

"Good."

Bracken frowned.

She didn't think Kenna wanted them safe? "I'm guessing you and I have a lot to talk about."

Antonio snorted. "We don't need help. We're doing just fine."

"By snooping in our stuff? As if we'd leave sensitive information where you can find it?" Jax huffed a laugh that held no trace of humor. "Good luck with that."

Kenna kept her attention on Bracken. "You got them safe?"

Bracken nodded.

"What are you looking for?"

"Maybe put that gun down, and we can have a real conversation."

Maybe…

Kenna had to shift the dog to put her weapon back in the holster. Her gaze snagged on his collar, but she didn't need to worry about what caught her attention. "What's your goal here?"

Bracken moved far enough she could pull out the wooden chair at the desk and sat on the edge. Hands pressed together between her knees. "Other than saving lives? At least as much as I can to prevent their loss."

Kenna got the distinct feeling they were on the same side of this. Not just in the sense they both wanted justice, but maybe also an end to Cecelia.

She moved to the window and tugged back the sheer curtain that hung from the ceiling to the floor along the wall of glass. The balcony. The French doors. She surveyed outside, looking for a convenient place a shooter might be holed up.

All she saw were the grounds of the resort. People wandering around outside, and the golf course with a few groups here and there. Someone rounded the corner to the right, driving a golf cart that read SECURITY across the hood.

She let the curtain go and stayed by it, her back to the wall. Jax should get out of the line of fire as well, plus the sheriff and her buddy Antonio. She turned to her attention back to Bracken. "How long have you been doing that?"

"I've been the sheriff of this county for twelve years. I did a few years in the army, like my brother and my dad, and then I got on the ballot at home. So I could fight a different kind of war on the home front."

Kenna was still stuck on the military connection. "That's why you didn't arrest Carlos?"

"What would I have charged him with?" Sheriff Bracken shook her head, an innocent expression on her face before she schooled her features.

Antonio had stuck his hands in his pockets, leaning his shoulder on the bedroom doorframe.

Jax had his gun still in one hand, but down by his side.

Things in the room were still a little tense. One split second could turn it into a firefight, and Kenna and Jax might not be in the right when it all shook out, considering the sheriff's ability to write whatever report she wanted. Assuming she was alive.

Kenna didn't want to kill anyone if she didn't have to, even in self-defense. What a waste of life.

"Standard procedure dictates you investigate a shooting," Jax told the sheriff. "How'd you know he was holed up in his house with Esme?"

Bracken glanced at him. "She invited me over."

Had Esme told the sheriff more than she'd given to Kenna and Jax?

Kenna said, "What were you looking for here?" figuring it was about finding out where their loyalties lie.

"Your business card was among her things. I have it, by the way, just in case anyone broke into their townhouse later and thought you were complicit in their disappearance."

"Kind of you." Kenna didn't think it was completely altruistic, however. More like a bargaining chip to be used later. "Why break in?"

Bracken looked at Antonio, then at her. "We had to know if we could trust you."

"And...?"

Ozzy started wriggling so she set him down. He probably needed to go outside to take care of business. Hopefully, he didn't do it in the room before they made it to some grass—or a tree.

"Can you?" Kenna asked.

"Esme told me that Noelle had information she kept hidden," Bracken replied. "A tiny SD card with evidence on it that I'd be able to use to...continue my investigation."

Jax's turn. "Did you know Carlos was in the service?"

The sheriff shook her head.

"But you're inclined to help military servicemen and women like anyone would or should be. More so with your personal connection."

Bracken shrugged.

Kenna looked at Antonio. "And you?"

"I'm in it for me."

"What are you getting out of this?" She wasn't going to let him skate over this and just brush it off like nothing. "Why team up? Or did you just let her into a guest's room without their consent to perform an illegal search?"

Antonio lifted his chin. "Try proving it. Besides, it's not like the manager ever calls the police. They deal with everything in house. It's why the staff are terrified of crossing a guest."

Kenna hadn't had enough interaction with any of them to ascertain that. She looked at Bracken. "What did Esme say Noelle was hiding?"

The sheriff swallowed. "You might even overlook it the thing is so tiny."

"Shame you didn't find it in time to get out of here before we showed back up."

A muscle flexed in Bracken's jaw.

"Otherwise, you might've gained valuable intel." Kenna folded her arms loosely across her chest, wishing she'd brought something other than socialite-flavored business casual clothes. She'd feel much better in jeans, a T-shirt, and Converse.

She didn't glance at Ozzy, sniffing around the hem of the couch, but she thought about his collar. Noelle had stuffed the letters in the dog bed. Maybe it was a GPS tracker, or something else on him—tucked in the folds of that material with the clip around his neck. Or it was more than that.

Valuable intel.

Jax walked around the couch and approached Antonio. "Do you know this woman?"

He looked at the screen of Jax's phone. "Should I?"

"You know her." Jax had to have a better read than Kenna did because he'd surely seen it on Antonio's face to make that kind of a comment. "How about this guy?"

Antonio shook his head.

"That one I believe," Jax said. "But you know who the woman is."

"So what?" Antonio scoffed. "I meet a lot of people working here."

"Then she's been a guest at one time. Or she's a regular?"

Bracken shrugged it off. "Why are you asking about some woman?"

Jax moved to her and showed her the phone.

She stiffened.

"Did Carlos tell you who he works for?" Kenna asked. "Who gives the orders to him, or anyone he works with?" If they had a witness testimony, that would help. But it meant Carlos had to go on record—something that could greatly increase his chances of being the victim of a paid hit. Possibly even by someone he had worked with in the army.

"He chose freedom and a future," Bracken replied. "But Esme told us Noelle had kept records of communications. Orders her husband received. The things he was supposed to do, and the accompanying payment. Esme wanted him to have a future even though this situation killed Noelle."

"We looked him up. He's dead." Kenna wasn't so sure now. Carlos had been legally dead as well. "Where is he?"

"Hiding would be my guess, which is why I need to find him. Someone has to be willing to pass over evidence." Bracken shook her head. "Carlos just wanted to get out."

"I want to talk to Noelle's husband or boyfriend or whatever he is to her. Or *was*," Kenna said. "We need intel. Evidence. The same stuff you're looking for. Which means we're working toward the same end."

Why not work together?

Did Kenna really have what Noelle had hidden? There hadn't been an SD card among the letters, but then she hadn't dug around the whole inside of the dog bed. When she'd pulled out the papers, that was all she was looking for.

Kenna continued, "Who is behind these military guys that are all supposedly dead but still very much alive? And how many of them are there?" She wanted to know what Antonio got out of the deal if they succeeded in taking down Cecelia. Something to do with the resort or a more personal angle?

Maybe it was just about being wherever Sheriff Bracken was. Did Antonio have a thing for her, or were they together?

Antonio said nothing. If he had an answer, he would no doubt rub it in their faces.

"It's supposed to be on the SD card," Bracken said. "Everything Noelle compiled for her and her boyfriend to get free of this. Expose it all."

Kenna frowned. "You really have no idea where he is?"

"I guess we need to find that evidence." Bracken stood, tension in every line of her body. "Maybe you left it behind at Noelle's house."

There it was. Accusation even though they were on the same side.

Kenna's phone buzzed in her pocket, but she ignored it. She glanced at Jax, who said, "We'll be sure and let you know if we find it."

Antonio huffed and headed for the door.

"You do that." Sheriff Bracken shot Kenna a look on her way to the door.

"We should work together." It was worth a try.

"Good luck." Bracken grabbed the door. "We're all gonna need it." The door clicked shut with a heavy thud.

Kenna tugged out her phone. "Ramon sent me a text. Will you check Ozzy's collar?" She should be checking the room for bugs, considering Antonio and Bracken could have absolutely planted listening devices around the place.

"Check Ozzy's collar for what?" Jax asked.

"A microSD card."

"Huh." He moved, and she caught it out of the corner of her eye.

Kenna thumbed up on the screen and read the text. "This is a video. Why did he send me—?" She tapped Play and it loaded.

Ramon sat tied to a chair, hands behind his back. A gag over his mouth. Sweat and blood running from his left temple.

Her eyes filled with tears that stung and burned, making her nose hurt.

"You found something." Jax moved through the suite. "Kenna, what?"

A tear rolled down her cheek. She tilted the screen so he

could see and he leaned against her shoulder. Jax slid an arm around her waist, holding the SD card in his other hand.

"I have your friend." A voice off camera spoke—a man, and his tone sounded dead. Walker? "If you want him back, you'll meet me when and where I specify. And you won't bring any of your cop friends." The video ended.

Kenna gasped back the threatening tears.

She scrubbed at her face, but that didn't make her nose feel better. She let out a frustrated sound. "You found it?"

Jax didn't take the bait of changing the subject. "Did he tell you when and where?"

"Not yet." She shifted her weight, hands by her sides. One fisted, and the other was holding her phone. "We need to get Maizie whatever is on that storage device."

"How did you know it was on Ozzy's collar?"

"I spotted it when I picked him up. I doubt I'd have found it other than someone mentioning it was here." Kenna's phone buzzed and she started. "I can't believe Antonio and Bracken were just searching the place."

"What does it say?"

She read off the text. "Just an address. Eleven thirty tonight."

"I'm coming with you."

Kenna nodded. That was a non-negotiable for her. "We need backup."

Jax frowned. "Even though he said no police?"

She scrolled and found Bracken's number. If they really were on the same side, it was time for the sheriff to prove it.

"Are you going to tell her we found the SD card?"

Kenna shook her head, about to speak when the other woman answered.

"Sheriff Bracken."

"It's Kenna. How would you like a shot at bringing in a serial killer the FBI can't seem to find?"

Jax frowned at her, a little bit of humor in his eyes.

She waved her brows, even though her heart still squeezed in her chest over Ramon. *Lord, keep him safe.* "Jax and I need your help."

Chapter Twenty-Four

"Are you sure this is a good idea?"

Kenna, sitting in the passenger seat of the truck, didn't respond to Jax's question right away. She just transferred the laptop from its position on her knees to the center console so he could see the screen.

Maizie was working on hacking the SD card encryption. Considering it belonged to a bank teller, it shouldn't be that hard to break. But then again, the boyfriend had been into black ops, super top secret, off-book stuff—or he *was* into it because he was very much alive.

"Of course it isn't a good idea." That's why Kenna grabbed the new bulletproof vest from the back seat and slipped it over her T-shirt. No way was she going into this in fancy clothes. She already had her black Converse on. "That's why you're here, and Antonio and the sheriff are on the other side of the block. So you guys can be my backup if anything goes wrong."

"Pfft," Jax said. "As if I'm going to trust them to cover you."

"You don't?"

He made a noise in his throat. "Yeah, right. They were searching our things and they *knew* I'm FBI."

"Maybe they think you work for Cecelia and I've been blinded by your charm and your good looks." She leaned over, ignoring the laptop between them. "Which, of course, I have been."

He didn't smile. "Fine."

"Thank you, though." She did appreciate the fact he wouldn't take any chances. He considered it up to him to watch her back and make sure they all came out of this safe. "I'd like to think Ramon would do the same for me if I was captured."

"He wouldn't need to." As in, Jax would already have taken care of it?

"That's why I'm not so worried about going up against a serial killer," Kenna said. "Not this time."

Even if it was epically triggering, she'd lived a lot of life since that nightmare—the day Bradley died. These days she had more hope than she knew what to do with, and people in her life she cared about like family. She had Jax.

But it wasn't the only reason.

"There's just something off about him." She shook her head. "He doesn't fit any serial killer profiles I know. He sent Stan Tilley after me. What kind of serial killer does that? It seems more like he is a hired gun like the rest of these army guys."

"But he's even more of a ghost than they are."

"We need to find actual physical evidence he's connected to Cecelia now, not just back then. Stairstep our way to taking her down." If this was her empire, things were far worse than one FBI agent on the take.

The radio on the dash crackled. The time on the clock was 10:56.

Sheriff Bracken's voice came over the radio. "In position. No sign of Walker yet."

They'd explained Jax had been on the case finding him in San Diego, and that the investigation had been shelved in favor of active cases, as well as Kenna's involvement. It had been a long story that took them all to Mexico and back, at least in reflection.

Jax gripped the radio. "Copy that."

"Almost time to go."

He looked at Kenna. "You're nervous."

"Of course I'm nervous! I'd be crazy not to be, alone and up against Walker." She needed to walk a little, stomp off some of the adrenaline buildup making her antsy with anticipation. "I should go."

"For the record, I don't like you going in alone."

But she wasn't alone. "Are you going to let anything happen to me?"

"No."

"That's why I can do this." She leaned far enough to touch her lips to his, her fingertips dragging over the stubble on his chin. "Let's get Ramon back."

She hoped.

Kenna jumped out of the truck, armed without a holstered gun on her belt or under her shoulder but with several weapons out of sight. If it came down to it, she could protect herself.

Can I ask that it doesn't though?

It seemed more natural these days to pray like that, in snippets of conversation throughout the day. Keeping a running dialogue with God.

Help me get Ramon back. Show me how.

That was the only way she'd say the right words. Or see a

double cross coming. Much better odds than without God, worrying that she couldn't save a life.

Maizie would get the information from that SD card, which would give them a new lead. Kenna's job was going face-to-face with Walker. Finding out what he wanted in exchange for Ramon. What Jax didn't know was that if Walker asked her to trade herself for the man's freedom, she'd do it.

Then again, maybe he did know.

She shouldn't kid herself that Jax knew exactly the kind of person she was, and how far she would go to save the life of someone she cared about. Or any victim ever, innocent and captured.

She walked as quietly as she could down the side of an old abandoned building. Whatever business had been here decades ago was gone now. All that was left was an empty warehouse probably infested with rats.

She pushed the earbud farther in. "Mic check."

Jax came back first. "Loud and clear."

"Same here," Sheriff Bracken said.

"I've got you both." She rolled her shoulders. They would be moving in as she did, getting into position where they'd be able to see everything.

Walker couldn't possibly cover all conceivable angles. He was one guy. He wouldn't know if she brought backup unless he had a team of his own. It would be the only shot any of them had of getting out alive if this ended in a firefight.

Kenna found a door, no handle. No lock. All she'd have to do is push it open. "Going in."

"Copy that," Jax replied, his voice low in her ear. "In position on the south side."

Kenna tuned out what the others said, getting the lay of the land inside as she entered the expansive space. Just a short hallway from outside, and she pushed through to the massive warehouse. This had to be some kind of side entrance, the only one left open.

Walker had followed up with instructions that she was to move to the middle of the room and turn around, showing him her belt. Since that wasn't where she had hidden any weapons, it worked out fine.

Kenna scanned the periphery, even if only with her hearing. There were so many dark shadows in here, and then a few splits of moonlight coming through gaps in the roof where it had caved in. Not such a good sign, or particularly reassuring, given the chance that more ceiling could fall on her. Any high position would result in a massive crash, and Jax, or one of the others, would come tumbling to the concrete floor.

She pushed aside the worry and walked to the middle of the open room, where grooves in the floor indicated heavy machinery had once sat in here. Probably sold off and hauled out when the business fell apart. A place like this could make or break the economy of a small town. No doubt they'd taken a hit but likely had the resort—or whoever was supposedly buying up land in Pahrump—behind its survival.

Maybe they were one and the same.

A powerful force behind it all.

That had to mean Sheriff Bracken lived under their thumb. No one trying to operate with impunity in a small town like this would keep a do-gooder sheriff around. Not without pressuring her to cave and look the other way, at least on occasion.

Could be exactly the reason Bracken was working this with Antonio, along with the military connection she had giving her a soft spot for army guys forced to work for some off-book group. Maybe the military didn't even know they were alive.

As she approached the center, Kenna found a flip phone on the floor. The old-school kind she'd been eyeing since she didn't do social media. Why did she need a "smart" phone anyway, even if she considered it a way to make everyone dumber?

She turned around, looking at the entire room as she rotated on the spot. Watching dark corners wondering when Walker would jump out. Where was Ramon? He had to have brought her friend here if they really were going to trade, or did he have someone else ready to release the guy if she complied?

Kenna didn't like this.

The phone rang.

She started a little, spun around, and crouched. The screen displayed *Unknown Number*.

Kenna snatched up the phone and flipped it open. She hit the button to answer the call and put it to her ear. "You aren't even here?"

He had to know if that was the case, she wasn't going to be amenable to much. He'd already proven she couldn't trust him. Apart from the whole killer thing, of course.

She never would—but he didn't have to know that.

"But you are," Walker said. "And now we know you're capable of following basic instructions. That's good."

He thought he was in charge. "Where is Ramon? I want proof of life."

Walker chuckled. The sound of his voice was probably not loud enough to be heard through the radio, even if she switched it to that ear. After a few quiet seconds, right when she was about to ask again, she heard a gasp.

Ramon.

"Kenna, don't do what he asks," Ramon pleaded. "Don't come for—"

"There." Walker paused. "Your proof of life."

"Great. I'll be hanging up now." She even lowered the phone, just in case he was watching.

"You want him to die?"

Her stomach clenched. Kenna put the phone to her ear. "You're not here, and neither is he. That just means I have to look harder."

Walker chuckled. "I knew I liked you."

Great. A fan. "You called me. What do you want?"

"So impatient. Tsk-tsk."

"Get to the point." She could play it as if she believed Ramon could take care of himself, and if he died it wouldn't be that big of a deal. She would much rather save him, but Walker thought he had all the power because he held her friend's life in his hands.

"You want your friend back? I want something in return."

She crossed herself off the list. After all, if this was a straight trade—her for Ramon—Walker would be here to capture her. Or he'd have tried before now. "What could you possibly want that you can't get for yourself?"

"That's the point." He sounded frustrated now, which was interesting. He might be a cold-blooded killer, but he wasn't a psychopath with no conscience and no emotions if he was irritated. "I can't get to her."

Kenna kept quiet.

"Cecelia has her locked down. I can't get her back."

"Who?"

"My daughter." Walker blew out a breath that crackled across the phone line. "Get her back for me, and I'll give you Ramon."

Kenna's brows lifted. "Who..." The little girl in the safety deposit box. "The bank. Those photos? That's her?"

"Cecelia has us all in a chokehold."

"And you expect me to believe that things are suddenly different? You want out, and you want me to make a way for you." He likely wouldn't believe that she didn't care about an innocent child caught in the middle of things. "Tell me. Is she your half-sister?"

"She's a lot of things," Walker said. "Now do you want your friend back or not?"

What did that mean, *a lot of things*? Kenna wasn't sure she wanted to ask. She just knew that if he'd wanted absolute cooperation from her, he should've taken Jax. The old her would've thought that might be tempting fate, but life didn't work like that. "Do you even know where your daughter is?"

There was no way for her to find Ramon. All she had was a shot at new leads with the SD card and this. A way to trap Walker. Not that she wanted a kid in the middle, but it was worth a try if she could keep the girl safe.

If there really was a child trapped and in danger, there wasn't much Kenna would not do to rescue her.

"I know where she is," he finally said.

"So get her back yourself," she said.

"They'll see me coming. I'd never get in and out alone. And I have no one to help me. That's why you're doing it."

"What makes you think I'd succeed?"

"To save a child and get your friend back, I think you'll figure it out."

"Send me the information. I'll see what I can do." Kenna had to at least try to get more. "If you want out from under Cecelia's thumb, you know what you have to do."

"You think I haven't tried to kill her before?"

Kenna hadn't exactly been thinking that. "Then how about trying a statement. Testifying against her. Giving the FBI the evidence to take her down."

Walker laughed. "You think I'd survive even with a deal

that gets me in WITSEC? I already know how to live under the radar."

So he was going to take his daughter and disappear? "Is that the kind of life a kid needs?"

"Doesn't matter. Cecelia won't find us. There will be nothing she can do about it."

"All you want is to win?" She could understand that but didn't think it was nearly that simple. What she needed was to keep him talking so he would hopefully say more than he intended.

"You have no idea what I want."

"I want my friend back," Kenna said. Just so he was clear on what she was after. Which he knew, considering he was the one who'd grabbed Ramon and was currently holding him hostage. If Kenna didn't deliver what he wanted, Walker would likely kill him and then tell Cecelia he did it for her. She would never know he'd contacted Kenna and tried to make another deal.

"Then get me my daughter." Walker hung up.

Kenna snapped the phone shut. "Did you guys get that?"

"Most of it," Jax said. He sounded like he was moving. "Meet me at the side door."

She tugged the comms earbud out and headed that way, bringing the phone with her. Presumably, Walker would send her the location of the child she needed to save. And given the age of the phone, he might not be able to use it to track her. "Did Maizie get anything?"

"That's what I need to talk to you about."

Whatever it was, it didn't sound good.

Chapter Twenty-Five

Antonio folded his arms across his chest. "How long did he say you had?"

"Twenty-four hours. So midnight tomorrow." Kenna would rather be talking to Jax about what Maizie had discovered on the SD card, but as soon as she stepped outside the door to meet him, Antonio and Sheriff Bracken had both shown up.

After Walker sent the text with the deadline to the flip phone, they went back to Jax's truck to regroup. The address was a huge house in a swanky neighborhood in Scottsdale, only a forty-minute drive away. She had no idea if the child was actually Walker's, and the idea of handing over an innocent life to a man who had committed multiple murders didn't sit right. Not exactly father material, but if the child was in danger, Kenna would be rescuing her tonight.

Bracken said, "And you're going now?"

Kenna shrugged. "There's no sense waiting."

Overhead, something black and about the size of a bird flew between two buildings. She didn't want to know what lurked in the shadows. Even if it turned out to be a harmless animal.

There was also no sense in taking law enforcement officers with her in order to break into someone's house and steal an already kidnapped child. Sure, she had the choice not to rescue Ramon. But now another life was at stake.

Kenna didn't want to rely on Antonio, and figured she could keep Jax reasonably out of it unless things went sideways. "If I don't do this, we don't have anything to go on." She hadn't told them that she and Jax had the SD card. "So I'm going to go in there and get that child out."

Give or take any variables Kenna couldn't control.

"You guys go home," she continued. "I'll take care of this. Both of you have jobs you need to be alert for tomorrow." About the only card Kenna had to play, and she laid it down. "Jax can come with me. I'll text you guys later and let you know what happened. You don't want to get on Walker's radar if you can help it."

None of them had even mentioned Cecelia. When Kenna had shown Bracken the picture of the dirty FBI agent, Bracken had pretended she didn't know who it was. Which could be true—if Cecelia was some kind of mid-level player in all this. An entire conspiracy involving black ops soldiers co-opted into working for someone completely off book.

Bracken said, "I don't like it."

Jax was the one who responded. "You don't have to like it. You know it's the right call, and you get to keep your nose clean."

"If they call a break-in, I'll make sure it's me who responds."

Kenna nodded. She had no idea the house was in Bracken's jurisdiction, but maybe people around here were accustomed to passing things off and taking favors. "Thanks."

She and Jax headed for the truck and climbed in.

As soon as he pulled out, she said, "That was harder than I thought."

"Are you seriously good with going in and getting this kid out when we have no idea who she is?"

"I could say that I don't have a choice, but that's not true. There's always a choice, even when your back is to the wall. I want to save Ramon. He deserves a shot at a future, the same as all of us. Cecelia might be determined to destroy him, and I figure Walker will at best use him as leverage. Now there's an innocent kid caught in the middle?"

"I know." Jax reached over and squeezed her knee. "But we have no idea who these people are or what the situation is inside. We'll be going in blind."

Kenna wasn't going to explain right now that he wouldn't be going in at all. "What did Maizie find on the SD card?"

"Right," Jax said. "She found files. Three guys who are currently hiding under fake names in the penal system. Like they created their own witness protection and are biding their time in a prison cell."

Kenna shook her head. "Who would choose to do that voluntarily?"

"Guys who know they would be hunted if they were out and free." Jax gripped the wheel and turned the corner, bumping them up onto the blacktop street, almost deserted this time of night. "Or they would be used to do jobs." He shook his head. "This is shaking out like a full-blown conspiracy. Maizie put it all in an email. One guy was killed two weeks ago. One is up in Alaska, about as off grid as a person can possibly get. The other is Noelle's husband."

Kenna blinked. "Where is he?" Did the guy even know that his wife was dead? Perhaps if they could tell him that, he'd be willing to speak up and do something about the people responsible for his wife's death.

"He's local. According to the SD card, the deal is that they bide their time and then come out and testify when it's all exposed."

"Who put them there?" Kenna paused. "There has to be someone who is part of the system that is the one who arrested them under fake names, and got them entered in." They wouldn't necessarily have to go through any kind of trial, or even a court hearing. If the person on the inside faked paperwork and was able to alter database records, they could simply show up with a prisoner transfer no one was expecting and get the person added to the roster of the facility. Blame it all on some kind of glitch that meant no one was aware they were coming.

"They were all signed off on by Sheriff Bracken."

Kenna shifted in her chair to face him. "And you just let me send her on her way?"

Jax shook his head. "We have a job to do tonight. Tomorrow, we can track her down and find out what else she knows that she hasn't told us."

"And she pretended she didn't know where Noelle's husband was." Kenna scoffed. "She's been holding out on us."

"You mean the same way you've been holding out on her?"

Kenna waved a hand at that. "It's not the same thing."

"Seems like we've gone from no leads to more leads than we have time to run down."

"True," Kenna said. "Let's just focus on this tonight. Then we can get Ramon back and will have more people working the case. Especially if we can get Bracken to be truthful with us. Maybe Antonio is even on our side."

Jax let out a tiny huff that sounded like a laugh. He

didn't think it was that likely Antonio was on the up and up even if he might want out of the situation he'd gotten himself into. Though, given the way Javier had acted when he called her, maybe he already knew his cousin wasn't lily white. After all, he'd told her not to get mixed up with Antonio.

She figured it was probably easier to keep the guy close but withhold information. That way they'd know his true motives at some point. When he eventually gave himself away.

Jax said, "I feel like I need three hours to go through all the information on the SD card."

Kenna nodded. "I know what you mean. Do we know whose house this is where we're going?" The maps at street view hadn't given them a clue as to who owned the mansion. Just the fact it looked like an expensive place that could be hard to sneak into.

Of course, she couldn't exactly walk up and knock on the front door. Ask them why they were holding a child where the parent couldn't reach them. See if they'd possibly hand her over, so Kenna could exchange the kid for her friend, handing her over to a known serial murderer.

She frowned.

"Maizie was running it down," Jax said.

She checked her phone. "She sent some information." Kenna thumbed through to it and blinked at the text on the screen. "That address? The house is owned by Georgia Rosenberg."

"I know that name. Which one of them is it?"

Maizie had provided the information along with the rest. "She's Walter and Celeste's mother."

"And we're assuming Walker and Cecelia are siblings. So this kid is living with Grandma?"

Kenna blew out a breath. "I already knew this was possibly going to be a mistake."

"I don't like the idea of being in the middle of a family squabble. Probably not any more than you do."

"At least you can flash your federal agent badge if things go sideways." She glanced at him. "You did bring it, didn't you?"

"You want to go in by yourself at first, don't you?"

"Yes."

Jax sighed but didn't say anything. Better than lying—or pretending things were fine when they weren't.

"You'll be on hand in case it goes sideways?" Kenna studied him.

"You really think I wouldn't be?" Before she could answer that non-question, he said, "Keep the earpiece. That way I'll be able to hear what's happening, and you can alert me if you need assistance."

"Sounds like a good plan."

"Except that it's nowhere near a good plan."

"I've been flying by the seat of my pants for so long this actually feels like an okay kind of plan."

Jax sighed. "Good to know this is what I have to look forward to."

When he quit the FBI and came to work with her, or when they were married? Now, she was thinking about the courthouse again, and wondering what the plan would be otherwise. She wasn't sure how to ask what his intentions were, or whatever, and it for sure right now wasn't the right time.

"House is up there." He pulled over. "I hope for your sake they don't have trained guard dogs."

"Me, too." Kenna checked the map on her phone and climbed out of the truck. Jax switched off the dome light in the cab and stared at her from the driver seat, as if there were plenty of things he wanted to say. She didn't blame him. "Later?"

He gave her a tight nod. "Don't get killed. Or kill anyone and wind up getting arrested." He sucked in a breath, then shook his head. "I'll stop there because it's a pretty long list after that."

"I'll do some recon and let you know what I find. After that, we can figure out what to do next."

"Be careful."

Kenna closed the truck door. Bulletproof vest on, weapons in various holsters in different places. Visible and concealed. If something happened, she hoped it would be Sheriff Bracken who responded. After all, any other cop would simply arrest her for what she was about to do without asking her any questions.

Kenna found the corner of the property, where a split rail fence ended and an adobe wall began. As if the property owner here couldn't possibly allow passersby to see onto their land. They wanted total seclusion, or the illusion of being in the middle of nowhere in charge of their domain with no possible intrusion.

There were no good spots in the wall to stick a foot and heft herself up, and her arms wouldn't carry the weight of the rest of her to pull her over the top. She found a unit at the corner, one of those locked cabinets where utility workers hooked up phone and cable. She climbed on it and jumped at the wall, scraping her forearms before she managed to get one leg over.

She looked around first, trying to find the best spot for cover in the backyard.

"Honestly, that looked like it hurt."

She wanted to smile but didn't. "I'm okay."

"Glad to hear it."

She pushed the earpiece a little farther in and kept scanning the grounds.

Plenty of trees circled the yard, tall spindly stick-looking things that pointed straight up in the air and were barely as wide as Kenna. Probably kept alive by intense use of sprinklers. Huge boulders that were supposed to look natural peppered the planters around the edges inside the wall, along with bark because the trees pretty much killed the grass when their needles dropped and smothered the ground.

She spotted tennis courts on one side of the yard, and a pool between her and the house.

An expanse of grass that would expose her as soon as she decided to run toward the house stretched between her and the single-story structure with multiple wings. Clay tiled roof. A couple of chimneys, and a stone pizza oven on the back patio.

Kenna skirted the edge of the yard, following the tree line around to the tennis courts.

There were no outbuildings, pool house, or any kind of shed. So that was out as far as a spot where somebody might be keeping a child captive.

Any number of people could be inside the structure, and she could run into one of them in a split second and have to decide what to do next. Like Jax had said, it was best not to end any lives here tonight.

"I'm heading for the house."

It would be a pretty good tactic to start with peering into windows and getting the lay of the land. Unless these people had a security system and ended up triggering some kind of alarm. Kenna shook her head and kept going, trying not to think about all the things that could go wrong.

But then she realized she hadn't actually prayed and

asked God if this was a good idea. She had only gone with her gut instinct and done what she always did—whatever it took to save the life of the child.

Was this the one time it would snap back on her and she would end up in trouble?

Hopefully not.

She peered in a window on the east side of the house but couldn't see anything through opaque blinds. Her toe caught on another of those decorative rocks, and she landed on one knee.

"You okay?"

"Yeah, it's just dark out here." Snooping was a whole lot easier with a flashlight. She made her way to a side door, probably an entryway from the drive that stretched back here from the circular entry at the front of the house, with the wide fountain in the center.

She heard a rustle as a cat crossed the drive.

Kenna paused to watch it, hoping it didn't spot her and come over. "Maybe they don't have motion sensors." That, or they were calibrated to account for the cat. She wouldn't put it past the owner of a multimillion-dollar property like this to have a security guard on duty.

She took another step.

The door on the side of the house swung open, creaking as it widened. She expected someone to step out, but no one did. No one stood in the doorway.

What on earth?

Chapter Twenty-Six

"Come in, Ms. Banbury."

Kenna stayed right where she was outside, in the shadows on the side of the house. An impressive array of stars outside was only slightly marred by light pollution from whatever city or town was beyond the horizon. She could sneak off. Pretend she was never here. Or she could go in and find out what this woman—judging by the voice—wanted.

In her ear, Jax said, "What's going on?"

"I'm going in the house." She nearly added, *If I'm not out in fifteen minutes, dial 9-1-1.* But didn't because he already knew the drill. Jax would do something if she didn't emerge unscathed, or relatively that way, shortly.

"Be careful." He sounded mad.

Kenna figured he was probably right to be worried, but she was still going in. If he'd fallen in love with her, then it was with who she was—not some ideal of who she should be. Or whoever she now turned into in order to alleviate his fears to keep him from worrying about her.

She would change. She hoped between now and the end of her life she would grow and hopefully become a better person than she was now. Healthier. More whole, at peace with her life.

But she wasn't going to change to fit a person's idea of who she should be. That would only result in her twisting herself in knots, trying to be someone she wasn't.

He could be mad—but he also needed to be realistic.

Kenna stepped into the house wearing her vest and armed in more ways than most people would ever know. Which is why it worked for her.

Until she spotted two suited men at opposite ends of an expansive room—part open kitchen, part living area with vaulted ceiling.

A fire roared in a gas fireplace, even though it was warm outside. The AC had been cranked to a nice chill so the fire could be appreciated.

Kenna didn't really get it, but that's as much as she could figure out.

A slender lady with salt-and-pepper hair, presumably the one who had told Kenna to come in, entered the room. She settled into a cushy dark tan with a furry kind of accent fringe that worked in a kind of Old-English-castle way. Not Kenna's style, but then she hadn't ever chosen décor or furniture for herself. She picked RVs and Class C motorhomes based on fuel efficiency, function, and amenities—like being able to stand fully upright in the shower. Not interior design.

The lady wore a tailored black dress one might wear to a business meeting, and a suit jacket over it, plus she hadn't removed her leather pumps when she came in. Kenna didn't walk around the RV in her shoes. She kicked them off and didn't track dirt, or blood—let's be honest—in her home.

Maybe this lady had a housekeeper.

And someone to do her hair and makeup for her, given the unfocused and cloudy gaze of her eyes. She didn't look at

Kenna. She swirled a wine glass and took a sip, finishing the drink. Her face turned in the direction of the fire to the right.

To the left, under the window, custom-built shelves displayed books and antiques. On the interior wall at the end of the hall, a huge glass window offered a view into a massive room filled with rows and rows of wine bottles all tucked into their little slots. So during a dinner party, the hostess could show off her wine collection to make her friends and acquaintances quite jealous.

Or so Kenna figured. Honestly, it was exhausting absorbing all of it. Maybe this woman or either of the two men, probably bodyguards or hired security, could tell her they were going to shoot her. She could run or fight it out, and either way it would be over with.

Then it occurred to her. The vibe in here...

Not unlike that house she'd walked through in Vegas. The one where Maizie had been held, tortured for years mentally and physically. Is that what was happening to the little girl in this house? Her stomach clenched, and she strode forward.

One of the men, the one closest to her, reacted. But he didn't grab her or throw her to the floor as she passed him and went to stand by the fire. Where she could see this woman's face. A woman who couldn't see her.

Because she was blind.

"Georgia Rosenberg."

She touched the coffee table with one hand, then set her glass beside her fingers. "Georgia is fine."

"I'm guessing you know who I am."

"We endeavor to keep tabs."

"So you know why I'm here?"

Georgia sat with her back straight, perched on the edge of the couch. "I assume it's to offer me some kind of deal."

"Actually, if you've read up on me at all, you'll know I don't stand by while a child is in danger."

"And which child would that be?" She barely reacted, but maybe Georgia had spent a lifetime training herself to restrain her emotions.

"I think you know." It was an easy way to try and get information, and sometimes it worked.

Georgia sighed.

Kenna wasn't sure if she was going to tell Georgia that she knew Walter and Celeste, her children, were now Walker and Cecelia. The whole thing seemed like a messed-up situation at best. Maybe she was smack in the middle, and maybe she wasn't.

Kenna wanted to move a step or two away from the warmth of the fire, but that would put one of the guards out of her periphery. She needed to keep them in sight and not get distracted. Just in case.

"Last year I rescued a girl. A teen." Kenna paused. "She'd been captive for years, abused in ways...most of us can't even imagine. And if we can, we wish we couldn't. Now she's thriving. She's safe, and she lives a life she loves. But it's still there, the fear. I worry she'll get hurt, and there's no way she needs to go through that again. I worry that someone who knew her back then will find her now. That no matter what I do I won't be able to keep her safe forever."

Kenna let that hang in the air for a second, hoping Georgia heard the absolute truth in her tone.

"She isn't my daughter," Georgia added, "but that doesn't stop me from worrying like a mom. Hoping for the best for her."

Kenna wondered how far to go, edging around to the topic of this woman's children.

Georgia shifted slightly, probably wishing she had some

more of that wine. Enough to flush her cheeks and allow her to let go of a little of what had her buttoned up so tightly. She wrestled with it visibly, her body language shifting with a subtle move of her fingers. A tiny inhale through her nose.

"It's hard to let go."

Georgia nodded, doing just that—almost as if Kenna had suggested it. "You want the best for them. Or you want them to not burn down everything you've spent a lifetime building."

"But we can't control them. Sometimes we have to let go and allow them to make their own mistakes."

Georgia made a *huh* sound, sort of like a laugh. Nothing funny about what Walker and Cecelia were doing, though.

"She uses Sarah's name," Kenna said. "Tells people she's Sarah Rosenberg."

Georgia gasped and let out a shuddering breath.

"She destroys people. Using her power to ruin reputations, make herself look better." Or their family. Who knew why Cecelia did most of what she did. Simply because she could? Someone at the FBI should've noticed she was a psychopath. Kenna should've caught on. They'd shared a room at Quantico. Cecelia was a master manipulator.

But Kenna still should have *seen.*

"Cecelia needs to be stopped." Kenna paused. "Before she ruins everything *you've* built."

Georgia's expression shifted in a split second. From that of a woman whose worst fears had come true...to completely impassive. "You think I'm worried? She can't touch me and what I've built."

Not good.

"Cecelia is still a liability," Kenna said. "As is her brother."

Georgia's lips curled up. "I spent years hoping they would kill each other. Sadly, the opposite happened. In every way you can imagine."

Kenna didn't want to know what that meant.

"They killed Sarah. *My* Sarah."

Their cousin. "Your niece?"

"She was my sister."

Kenna couldn't totally wrap her mind around that, but figured Georgia's children were similar in age to her own sister. The rest she didn't want to think about. Abuse, probably. Incest, likely. All of it was a horrible pile of things Maizie didn't need to know about. And things Kenna didn't want in her own head for the rest of her life.

Kenna bit the inside of her lip. "How did they kill her?"

"A shove. Who knows? She hit her head on a rock on the bank of the lake. Which one of them did it, I never could tell. Daddy found Walter by her body and assumed it was him. He beat Walter half to death." Georgia said it all with zero inflection as if reciting a passage from a medical textbook. "He almost didn't survive. Celeste spent all her time in the garden. Heaven knows what she was doing out there. Torturing more squirrels, probably. When Walter walked out of the house for the first time after Sarah's funeral, she took one look at him and asked him to make her a sandwich."

"And the child that is supposed to be here now...?" Kenna didn't even know what the little girl's name was. "I had a picture. It was being kept in a safety deposit box in Nevada, in a small town."

"Ah, Pahrump no doubt. Daddy always did like that part of the country."

"Not exactly picturesque, but I guess it doesn't have to be for someone to call it home." What did this woman know about the bank robbery, or whoever was buying up land? "Have you been there?"

Georgia chuckled, a thin high sound like broken glass. "Of course not, dear. I don't leave this house."

"Can't make the family look bad, I guess."

"That's not it."

Kenna wondered if it was more because she was a shut-in. Agoraphobic. "Do they come to visit you...and the child?"

"I haven't seen either of my children in decades. Be sure and note that down in your records when you pass everything to the FBI."

So she knew about the investigation, or that they were close to finding evidence? That would be problematic unless she was prepared to add her statement. Or proof.

Kenna said, "I will. Thank you."

"You won't get much else from me, I'm afraid. Anything I know is ancient history by now. But I have people to keep me apprised of what's happening."

"What *is* happening?" Kenna asked. "Because as far as I can tell, this thing is a giant web of shadowy activity. Or a powder keg about to blow up."

"Both are true, I suppose."

Kenna shifted her weight from one side to the other.

Georgia tilted her head a fraction, leading Kenna to believe she might be able to see a little of something rather than nothing but black. The idea of being that vulnerable made Kenna's shoulder blades itch.

"Is there a child living in this house?"

"You mean...am I keeping her prisoner?"

"Pretend I'm a social worker conducting a home visit," Kenna said. "I'll leave you alone to live your lives if I'm satisfied with the situation. But I *will* take action if a child in this residence is in danger."

Georgia gave her a slow nod. "Very well." She unfolded herself from the couch, rising from the seat like a queen surveying her domain. She led Kenna down the hall in the same manner, almost silent in her steps even with shoes and stone floor.

A learned skill—the ability to be so silent. Whether by necessity or because she wanted to go unnoticed was another question.

Kenna said, "It can't have been easy growing up in a big house, with a powerful family, and being..."

"Disfigured?" Georgia finished. "Or perhaps inferior?"

Kenna needed her to keep talking, so she asked, "Is that how they saw you?" Just because she had children didn't mean this woman had ever been in love, or even dated.

"My life is not for you to pass judgment on."

"Like you did mine? I mean, you didn't even offer me a drink. Probably because, to you, I'm more like the hired help. Someone you pay to make problems disappear. Or blackmail into rescuing a child who's allegedly being held against her will."

"Ah." Georgia stopped before an interior door. "That's what she told you?"

"It was Walker—Walter."

Georgia nodded, her expression blank. "They've always been close."

"Um...excuse me?"

"They have a *special* bond." She typed a code into a keypad on the wall, and the door unlocked. "It's always been that way. My family is unique like that. We have never been who society insists that we are."

Kenna bit the inside of her lip again. Was Jax hearing this?

"The child belongs to Walter and Celeste?" She could barely get the question out, her mind reeling. They were half-siblings, both the child of this woman. Or had she missed something along the way?

"Most likely, though no one gave me the particulars. Celeste—whom you know as Cecelia—took some time off and retreated to one of our family's estates. Up in Canada, I believe. She returned to work only weeks later. But the baby arrived here days after her birth, all pink and squalling. She was adorable."

"Your granddaughter."

Georgia nodded, a flash of something endearing on her face. Would a woman who cared like that about her grand-child keep her captive? Hurt her?

Maizie's captor had been disturbed to say the least.

"Is this where she is?" Kenna pointed down the hall. Either that, or she was leading Kenna to a spot they had prepared where they would kill her and no one would ever find her body. "Down this hall?"

Jax would bust in.

Could he get here in time to save her?

Kenna slid two fingers into her pocket, ready to drag out her knife.

"See for yourself." Georgia waved down the hall, lit from the right by a sterile white glow. A window on the right-hand side that illuminated the dark wood paneling on the wall. Ornate, but also sterile. A back hall that didn't need deco-rating because not many ever saw it.

Kenna moved down the hall a few steps, wondering precisely what she would find here.

And how she would save Ramon.

Chapter Twenty-Seven

Kenna looked through the glass, a single-paned window on the other side of which a room had been set up like a child's bedroom. Twin bed, pink sheets. A huge LED screen on one wall portrayed pictures of tropical beaches and landscapes from mountain valleys, each image fading into the next after a few seconds. An expanse of bare floor had been covered with a rug under the bed and another under the table and chairs set up currently with a tea party.

A little girl in a white dress sat at the table, surrounded by various stuffed animals seated in their own chairs. Considering the late hour it currently was outside, she'd have thought the child would be asleep in bed. However, it appeared to be a time of activity and socialization.

Her life was sparse and neat, tidy almost to the point of surgically clean.

The girl had gorgeous long dark hair and a pale face—unsurprising given the way she lived. She said something to one of her stuffed animals and swiped her hand, spilling a cup of clear liquid onto the table. Intentionally or accidentally wasn't clear. Water ran along the surface and dripped onto the floor.

The little girl gasped and leaned across the table. "Look at what you did, Isabelle." She grasped a stuffed ragdoll that was at least half her height and whipped it out of the chair. "Naughty girls are punished."

She never looked at Kenna. And given the glass and the audio situation between what was likely a hermetically sealed room and the hallway on the other side of the window, she heard the conversation only in a low volume—as if from far away.

The girl moved to a counter that had been set up with drawers below and cupboards above. A stepstool on the left side went unnoticed as she rummaged in a drawer and produced a huge pair of fabric shears.

Kenna turned away from whatever that was and looked at Georgia. Did she even know what was going on in there? She would have to have someone describe the situation to her, unable to discern it visually for herself. Was that person even telling her the truth?

"You disapprove." Georgia's expression shifted, incorporating something that looked a lot like malice.

"She has lived her whole life in this terrarium?"

"Interesting choice of words," Georgia said. "Lydia Rosenberg has the finest nanny, tutors in every subject, music teachers, and healthcare providers. The best that money can buy."

"But does she go outside?"

"Four hours every day." Georgia lifted her chin. "She rides horses. Practices violin. Reads far above her grade level and has a rudimentary grasp of two ancient languages. She's also fluent in conversational French. And last week, she and her nanny successfully made soufflé."

Kenna blinked. "How old is she?"

"Lydia will be eight years old in a couple of months."

"My advice would be to steer clear of crème brûlée." Kenna figured no one needed that child having access to even a kitchen blowtorch. Her instincts were confirmed when she looked back through the window. The child had cut off both the fabric doll's hands and was currently sowing the ends closed so the stuffing didn't come out. "If I don't leave with her, Walter is going to kill my friend."

Georgia pinned her with a steady stare. "War has casualties, my dear."

"So I'm just supposed to accept the fact that my friend will die so that your family can continue?" Not to mention the fact that Kenna had zero idea how to start establishing the kind of long-term care this child would need.

As much as she wanted to believe this could be another Maizie situation, the truth was that mental health treatment existed for a reason—even with all its failures, it was better than the alternative. This child might need to be in a facility for the rest of her life. Or she might need the chance to experience functioning as a member of society. If only to prove to everyone whether she could do it or not.

Either way, discerning that was above Kenna's pay grade.

"So now you understand my dilemma." Georgia lifted her chin. "You know my secret, and why I would hesitate to allow you to leave this house." Before Kenna could explain that Jax would come in if he even got an inkling she wasn't safe, Georgia continued, "Don't worry. I know all about your FBI friend outside."

"Then you understand why I will be leaving this house in the same condition in which I entered it. Regardless of what you want, or what your two guards and whoever else is hiding around this house intends to do to me."

Georgia stepped back from the doorway, moving partially out of sight.

Kenna didn't want to leave the child. However, she also wasn't equipped to handle the girl's needs or the trauma she would experience suddenly being removed from everything she'd ever known. She followed Georgia, who closed the heavy wooden door behind them. The lock clicked, echoing in the empty hallway with its high ceiling.

Designed to be visually appealing more than functional. And yet underneath was only shadows and dark secrets.

Kenna needed to sleep in her RV tonight.

But then, she also needed to get Ramon back from Walker. She had no idea how to explain to him that he wasn't getting his daughter back. Cecelia's daughter. Kenna didn't even want to think about a relationship like that, other than to simply conclude they were both mentally disturbed. It certainly was easier to brush across them with a label that neatly tied their situation in a bow. As with most human relationships, the mentally disturbed she had experienced in her life as an investigator, and the aftermath of trauma and codependency, reality was far more complicated than a simple label or diagnosis.

Walker had only told her half the story.

Georgia walked down the hall, not touching the wall or using any markers to guide her. She knew this house and every inch of it. Even with little to no sight, she could move through it comfortably. "Come and sit with me in the study. I have an offer I'd like to explain to you."

Kenna glanced back at the front door. One of the suited security guys stood there, hands folded across his chest.

In her ear, she heard Jax say, "Do you want me to hold off?"

Out loud, Kenna said, "That sounds good," figuring it was enough to answer both of them.

Georgia led the way to a study featuring a huge wooden desk she didn't sit behind. Instead, she moved to a chaise lounge covered with striped fabric. She waved a hand at another chair, one with wood arms and velvet on the seat. "Sit, please."

"And if I decide to stand?" Kenna said.

"Do as you wish." Georgia waved a hand. "But it's been a long day for me."

Kenna scanned the room while Georgia collected her thoughts, catching the shelves of old books that were probably so expensive she'd be scared to touch them. No framed photos, or other personal items that would have sentimental value. Only a huge portrait painting above the fireplace, featuring a gray-haired man staring down at those below him. Lording it over them in his dark-colored wool coat with a white shirt, high collar, and lace between the lapels. He had a long face and white hair that had been curled above his ears.

Probably some patriarch from the Rosenberg family. The first in a long line of ironfisted rulers who chose to steer society in whichever way they deemed it should go.

Of course, that was a serious presumption on her part. But Kenna and her people weren't exactly the highbrow type. What was she supposed to think about the tiny percentage of über-rich who viewed themselves as above the law, and in control of everything?

How was one person supposed to fight against that much power and influence?

Georgia cleared her throat. "If you are open to listening, I have a favor I would like to discuss with you. An exchange if you will."

"You wanna make a bargain with me?" Kenna let a thick

tone creep into her voice, heavy on the accent of an everyday blue-collar American. Someone who hadn't been born into a house like this and fed with silver spoons.

She'd have to be careful not to let prejudice affect her, considering Jax had been brought up in a wealthy family. He didn't need to believe she resented him for the way he had been brought up. Something he had had no choice over.

Georgia's lips twitched. "My daughter is becoming a liability. You and your FBI agent friend have breached entirely too close to the life of this family. Closer than anyone has in a long time."

"In that case, I'm surprised I'm not dead already."

Georgia made a *hmm* sound in her throat. "We would like Cecelia Warren to be shut down in order that she no longer presents a direct threat to the sanctity of this family."

"You are cut loose, and you want me to do it?" Kenna studied her. Evidently, Cecelia drawing even just Kenna's attention was enough to get her carved out of the Rosenberg family—a family Cecelia seemed so desperate to be part of. Using the name of a person she had possibly murdered, a child whose accidental death she was responsible for, in order to associate with the family that had raised her and at the same time mentally destroyed her.

Cecelia would always be impressive, though. She had thoroughly duped anyone who met her into believing she was stable and responsible. The extent of what she's hiding would to some people seem unbelievable.

Georgia said, "We will turn over all the evidence you require. Once the FBI brings down Cecelia, your special agent friend Oliver Jaxton will then be promoted to Phoenix Assistant Special Agent in Charge. It would be good, after all, for him to get his supervisor position back."

That was the deal they were offering Kenna?

Apparently, they hadn't done *all* of their homework if they just knew not to offer her money, or much else. It was the people she cared about that they wanted to do a favor for. Earning them Kenna's goodwill.

As long as none of them even understood that Maizie existed—or where to find her.

If they went after the teen in order to retaliate against her, Kenna would burn the Rosenberg family to the ground.

"This is what...your family task?" Kenna said. "You make deals and orchestrate things like people's lives are just chess pieces and you're in charge of the game."

"That's the way the world works, dear. You are either the lion, or you're the prey."

"Maybe the world *you* live in."

"We all live in the same world. It's just that some of us understand the rules better than others."

Kenna wanted all the evidence these people had against Cecelia, but not if they thought that she had accepted their deal.

"If you refuse, your boyfriend will be summarily discharged from his position at the FBI. Or possibly even jailed for his"—Georgia made air quotes—"actions."

"Don't threaten me. Or people that I care about."

Georgia chuckled, a high-pitched, hollow sound. "We want the same things, Kenna Banbury."

"I highly doubt that's true."

"Do you want the information against Cecelia or not?"

"First, you can answer some questions about a group of soldiers who are supposedly dead, yet somehow seem to be taking secret missions. Most of which involve murder." Kenna paused. "Does your family have its very own personal hit squad?"

Georgia smiled. "Wouldn't that be a thing?"

"So they don't read you in on every part of family business?"

"That's how the Rosenbergs work. It's why we've managed to maintain the sanctity of family business for so long."

"Because the right hand doesn't know what the left hand is doing." She'd read that in the Bible and didn't think it exactly fit in this context. Hopefully, Georgia would understand what she was talking about.

"I'm starting to like you, Kenna Banbury."

Kenna wasn't sure that would still be true after she started a one-woman crusade to take down the entire Rosenberg family. Assuming they didn't have her murdered by an army hit squad before she could accomplish that mission.

"It can't *just* be Cecelia," Kenna said. "It also has to be about shutting down Walker, and everything he's been doing."

At this point, she still didn't know for sure if he was one of those black ops soldiers, or just had been co-opted into doing similar jobs because of his connection to the Rosenbergs. For all she knew, he was some kind of leader of the group. Or the enforcer Carlos had mentioned that kept them all in line. A bogeyman for the kind of elite soldier who took any kind of dangerous job.

"Your son is under investigation as a serial murderer." Kenna folded her arms loosely. "I need to be able to find him so that the FBI can bring him to justice."

"As long as you understand that the second he reaches prison, he will suffer the kind of unfortunate accident that ends his life."

The brazen way she stated that told Kenna a little more about who she was dealing with. The kind of person who would order a hit. Murder undertaken deliberately. And she would do it even in a situation where she was possibly being recorded.

These people were unbelievable. Yet, she had the distinct feeling that this woman sitting on the chair across from her was just the tip of the iceberg.

"Nonetheless," Kenna continued, "I'd like the means to close more than one case. And in exchange, you have two of your problems solved, not just one."

Georgia shook her head. "If that is the road you wish to walk, then so be it. I will ensure all the necessary evidence is sent to your email." She crossed to the desk, felt in the top drawer, and pulled out a small pad and pen. She wrote something on the pad, tore off the paper, and held it out. "This code will allow you access to the encrypted file."

Kenna took the paper.

"I trust you will never again return to my home in order to take my grandchild from me."

Kenna, personally? Definitely not.

Local sheriff's department plus the Arizona Department of Child Safety? Well, it wasn't like Kenna could control them. As if the world was simply a chessboard and she got to move around whatever pieces she wanted.

Kenna slipped the paper into her pocket. "You have a good night."

Chapter Twenty-Eight

Kenna spotted the truck. No Jax.

Her inhale was the only thing she could hear, just that rush of air in her ears while her head spun with everything she'd just learned—and the need to be aware of her surroundings.

A figure stepped out from between two trees. *Jax.* She picked up her pace, heading for him. Needing to be beside him after all that, to find solace in his arms. Not that she wouldn't survive on her own, standing alone. The point was that she didn't need to. She got to rely on him and draw strength from him. Maybe one day she would repay the favor.

Tonight, she needed someone to hold her up.

Jax opened his arms. She slammed into him so hard he rocked back a step. "Whoa." His arms wound around her and she did the same, holding on to his waist while he ran a hand up and down the back of the bulletproof vest.

They had enough weapons between them to start a war.

But still, in the quiet and the dark of this Scottsdale residential street, it was more about finding peace with each other than fighting a war side by side.

She closed her eyes, her cheek against his vest. All she could see in her mind was that little girl playing dolls in the middle of the night. Cutting and sewing her "friends" when they were bad.

Kenna shuddered.

"Seems like you came to some kind of arrangement," Jax remarked.

She nodded. "That house was epically creeptastic."

Jax chuckled, but there was no sound. Just a shake of his chest under her cheek. "Wanna get out of here?"

"Yes." She gave his waist a squeeze and pulled away.

"For the record, I'm available for hugs anytime, anywhere."

And boy, could that get both of them in trouble. "Noted."

He rounded the hood of the truck. "Personally, I think hugs are underrated by most people."

After they got in and buckled up, Kenna said, "I wouldn't know, I only hug *you.*"

Physical touch couldn't be something she needed because it wasn't part of her life on a regular basis. Her dad hadn't been a hugger, though he would occasionally pat her shoulder with that heavy hand of his. She'd just never required it or really craved it.

She glanced at Jax.

Until now.

He looked at her. "What?"

"Nothing." Kenna shook her head and checked her phone. "It remains to be seen when Georgia is going to send that information. Or if she will."

"She knows you could expose her if she doesn't."

Kenna wasn't so sure about that. "I was thinking I'd send Bracken and the Department of Child Safety, but what's the likelihood they'd let them see the child? More like when they knock on the door, Georgia or the kid, or both of them, will be long gone."

She would put money on the Rosenberg family having means to make someone disappear like that. There were likely no records anywhere for the child to prove she even existed. Let alone means to find her, or trace whether she was being well cared for or not.

"So you think you'll get nothing?" Jax asked.

"If she wants Cecelia taken down, which she claims to, then she'll send it. Your career skyrockets or implodes depending on what I do with it."

He reached over and squeezed her hand. "Don't worry about me."

Yeah, right.

She must've made a noise because he said, "I'm serious, Kenna. I can handle whatever the Rosenbergs throw at me. I'm not going to let corruption continue because I don't have the stomach to stand up against it."

He might be able to handle it, but if he was ruined because of her, she probably wouldn't be able to stomach what happened. "She said you'd go to jail for murder."

"Guess you'll have to visit me in federal prison and help me plan my escape."

"That isn't funny." She folded her arms, but it was uncomfortable, so she wiggled down her seatbelt and took the vest off. He took a turn, and she realized they were headed back to the resort. Why did it hit her like the need to stand up against his direction? "I don't want to go back to that hotel and pretend everything is fine when it isn't."

He took his foot off the gas. Thankfully, there were few cars on the road in this part of town. "Then where do you wanna go?"

"I want to sleep in my bed in the RV, but we have to take care of Ozzy."

"So we're going to the resort?"

Kenna figured they'd end up sleeping there just for convenience's sake.

"You're just ready for this to be done," Jax said. "You're exhausted."

She would probably slap his hand away if he tried to squeeze her hand again. Good thing he didn't because she wouldn't have liked acting like that.

"Or you need a heavy bag so you can punch out some of this frustration in a workout."

She fisted her hands on her thighs, felt the slice of pain flexing her forearms, then let the tension go. "Is that what works for you?"

"Sometimes."

"What else works?"

"Seeing you." He grinned.

Kenna pouted. "I'm being a baby."

"You left a child in captivity."

"It might be the best place for her." Kenna winced. "And I might be hunting her in ten years because she's killed six people in horrible ways and I could've stopped it before it happened but I didn't. I left her there. I let them win."

"Is that what you think?"

"It doesn't matter what I think." She glanced out the side window just as he pulled onto the freeway and hit the gas to merge into the sparse flow of traffic. There were no stars, just the glow of humanity and all the materialism people needed to live comfortably. Next up, she wanted wide open space, like Wyoming or Colorado. Or a beach in the middle of nowhere. She'd be able to watch the waves and not have to contend with anyone.

She could pretend there weren't children in danger across the world. That there was no crime to solve and no corruption in the government. Just freedom and goodwill.

"I want to call Bracken before we get in the room." Jax tapped the dash screen.

Kenna closed her eyes, her head leaned back against the seat. Her nose ached, and she needed sleep.

"Sheriff Bracken." She didn't exactly sound like she'd been woken up from deep sleep, but she'd definitely been dosing.

"It's Jax. Kenna is here, too."

Bracken said, "It's them," in a muffled voice.

"Antonio?" Jax asked.

"We're both here," she said.

Kenna thought that was interesting—the two of them together overnight. Collaborating on the sheriff's attempts to save these military guys. Did it connect to the resort? The Rosenbergs might use the place for...whatever they needed. Maybe they both got something out of working together.

Jax said, "Kenna met with Georgia Rosenberg. We should be getting the evidence we need to take down Cecelia Warren shortly, enough to shut her down."

"That's good news."

Kenna wasn't so sure, considering it didn't solve all their problems. It wasn't that it was a convenient solution. More that it was the right thing but for the wrong reasons. They would only get a win because Georgia and her family wanted Cecelia shut down.

If that was the case, they should just send a shooter to put a bullet between her eyes.

Why have Kenna and Jax make it official?

Unless it was because they needed it to be above board. Official so Cecelia knew she was done, rather than just ending her life. Being disgraced could be worse than being dead. Kenna had lived that, and she could see why it might destroy Cecelia far more than just solving the family's issue by killing her quickly.

Plus, no one could trace it back to them. A shooter could testify.

Kenna and Jax, if he got promoted and she got some kind of kickback, became liable in any fallout that occurred if Cecelia fought back. They would be complicit because they had knowingly accepted evidence. Falsified or not.

Jax said, "Now, tell us how it was you who signed off on a number of prisoner transfers of these army guys hiding in state facilities. Because it's not just Noelle's husband, is it?"

"You found the SD card." Her voice sounded tight.

"Do you know you lost one a couple of weeks ago? That wasn't on the storage device, but we discovered one of them was killed recently in an incident."

"We need to warn the others in case someone ordered it. They could be picked off and we don't know until a report is filed."

"How can you do that?"

Bracken was quiet for a few seconds. "I'll figure it out." She sighed. "It would be easier if we had someone on the inside looking out for them."

Kenna figured Antonio should volunteer, but that he likely wouldn't. "Call the warden at each facility. Tell them you have a CI that passed you a tip they were in danger."

"It doesn't work if I'm making contact. That's how they get found."

Jax said, "They might have already been discovered."

Kenna ran her hands down her face. This whole situation had turned into a complicated mess. She needed to call Maizie, so she sent a text first.

You awake?

Jax pulled into the resort. "I've got to let you go. See what you can do or make a plan. Call me first thing."

Kenna heard something in his tone. She put her cell face-down on her leg and when the call had ended said, "What are you thinking?"

His nose crinkled. Kind of a mini shrug. "I'm just puzzling it out. It's not ideal, but I've done some undercover work and I could go in. Bracken could 'transfer' me in like the others and I could make contact with Noelle's husband."

Kenna turned in her seat to face him. "Send Antonio. Not you."

"Do you trust him to do that?"

She pressed her lips together.

"Me either."

"You're not going to prison." Her phone buzzed. Maizie was awake.

"We might not have any other options." Jax pulled up in front of the valet, who popped out of his chair—probably snoozing—and came over to open her door. She hopped out and strode to the door.

The doors slid apart before she even got there, and Kenna made a beeline for the elevator. The lobby lights might be down low, but it wasn't empty. A couple occupied two armchairs on one side by the fire. Two employees stood behind the desk on the left. Cookies had been left out on an entry table.

Avery intercepted her halfway, dressed in black slacks and flats with a sweater over a buttoned shirt. Dark circles under her eyes that her makeup couldn't quite disguise.

Kenna said, "You were waiting for me?" She should have given the woman her number.

Avery didn't stand still. She shifted her weight from foot to foot. "Preston checked out of the hospital and the resort in the same day. He left town. He's gone."

And she'd wanted answers from him. "You didn't get a chance to talk to him?"

"Not after you warned him I was after the truth." Avery lifted her hands, then let them fall back to her sides. "That's why he left, right? Because he knows I'm onto him and he has something to hide. Why else would he run?"

"I can understand wanting answers about how your mother died. Trust me, I understand." Kenna needed this young woman to grasp that letting it eat at her would destroy her life from the inside out. "I'm in the middle of something right now, and it's blowing up, but I want to help."

Before she even finished, Avery was shaking her head. "You know what, don't worry about it."

Kenna reached for her with the intention of offering that comforting hand, just not as heavy as her father.

Avery shifted, her arm whipped in an arc, and she slapped away Kenna's hand with the back of hers. In a split second, her hand was back by her side. She took a step back, her eyes wide.

Kenna didn't move. Someone trained her to defend herself.

"I'll figure something out myself." Avery took another step back.

"Avery—"

"It was probably stupid to want answers anyway." She turned and walked fast to the stairs.

Kenna watched her go.

"What was that?" Jax moved to stand beside her.

Kenna shook her head. "I wish I knew."

"Come on." He slid a hand up her back to the back of her neck and gently squeezed.

Checking how tense she was? Kenna figured it wasn't good back there and took his hand, holding it until they were at the room. "Door closed?"

"Yep. You can stand down." Jax pulled out his key. "Time for sleep."

She shook her head. "Gotta call Maizie and..." The words dissolved into a yawn.

"You're worse than the instructors at the academy." He pushed the door open and did a quick look around. "I'll take Ozzy outside for a minute. You call her."

Kenna unlaced her Converse and toed them off in the entry, nodding. "Be careful."

"Don't worry." Jax kissed her cheek. "Ozzy will protect me."

Kenna peeled off her clothes, setting all her weapons on top of the dresser except one knife. She pulled on shorts and an oversize T-shirt and flopped onto the bed, letting out a loud sigh. Two seconds and she would be asleep.

She slid the knife under her pillow and used the one on the other side to prop her up while she listened to the phone ring on speaker. Elbows to the bed, pillow in front of her so she could just turn her head to the side and...

"Hey."

Kenna blinked. "Hey, back at you."

"How bad was it?"

She winced, grateful she didn't have to school her expression on a video call. "Bad. Superbad. Might not be bad later, but it could be epically bad as in I'll be hunting that kid down and locking her up ten years from now."

"I have no idea how to decipher what that means." Maizie chuckled. "You sound tired."

"Then I'll close my eyes, and you tell me what you've got." Kenna shifted her face against the pillow and closed her eyes, feeling her body let go of a lot of the tension.

"I've been going through the files on the SD card, tracing these military guys."

Kenna wondered, was she going to dream about being trapped in a white room? Or about Maizie growing up like Lydia Rosenberg? She shivered.

"Trying to figure out if they joined at the same time or served together on the same team..." Maizie's voice drifted away.

Kenna fell asleep.

Chapter Twenty-Nine

Someone shook Kenna's shoulder. She moaned and swatted away the hand.

"Careful you'll spill the—"

She jerked her head off the pillow, blinking. "Coffee?"

Jax stood beside the bed, holding a steaming mug. "I went to the breakfast buffet and got a few things."

"My hero." She twisted and sat up enough to get her back against the headboard. She curled up her legs, her skin cold. She'd slept all night on top of the comforter. She eased her legs under the sheets and accepted the mug.

He sat on top of the covers on the other side, looking far too good in sweats and a sleeveless shirt. A sheen of sweat on his skin. A little red on his cheeks.

"Did you go for a run without me?" She eyed him and took a sip of her coffee.

He grabbed his own mug from the side table. "I hit the gym since you were unconscious."

Probably a better plan than waking her up. Except he had, as soon as he returned. "What time is it?"

"After nine. Maizie called me since she couldn't reach you." Jax held his mug with one hand and lifted over her laptop, also from the side table. "She says you got the packet about four this morning, and she needs the code to get in."

Kenna took another mouthful of the coffee, set it on the nightstand, and reluctantly left the warmth of the bed. She snagged her jeans from last night and handed over the paper folded in the pocket. Leggings. Bathroom. A little freshen up —hello, ice-cold water—and she was back in the room. She got back under the covers, still chilly.

Coffee.

She held it to her lips, letting the mug warm her hands. "Tell me when she opens it."

"Maybe you two should get a room."

Her and the coffee? Kenna smirked. "We already did, it's just that you're here, too."

Jax chuckled. "Sleep okay?"

She didn't answer, not wanting to lie about her dreams. Nightmares really, but what else was new? "Did you?" She studied his face, seeing what she needed to in his expression. He'd been wrestling with something all night. Hopefully, that was how to contact Noelle's husband *without* getting put in prison under a fake name.

"We can talk about it later."

Uh-oh.

Before she could ask, he said, "Can you hear me?"

"I can hear you." Maizie's voice came through the laptop speakers. "Can you hear me okay?"

"Yep. Kenna is here, too." Jax turned the laptop so she was on camera, and Kenna let go of the mug long enough to wave at the teen. Quick visual assessment.

Hair braided back from her face. No dark circles under

her eyes, unlike what Kenna had looked like in the bathroom a second ago. She looked healthy. At peace.

Which eased some of the undercurrent of tension Kenna lived with.

"I'm in." Maizie's gaze shifted side to side. Looking at the contents of the packet of information Georgia had sent.

"Part of me can't believe she really followed through." Kenna bent her knees, angling her body toward the laptop. "Though it's completely self-serving."

Jax said, "You don't like the idea of doing what the Rosenbergs want. On principle."

She nodded. "I'd rather say no, but the problem is, the world is a better place with Cecelia shut down."

"The enemy of your enemy is your friend?"

"Unless I go after them next." But Kenna wasn't sure that was a good idea. She didn't want to think what would happen if the Rosenbergs thought she was a threat. "They've brought me into the fold. Which means if I try to go up against them, it'll be the end of me. They'll produce something that gets me discredited or even jailed." Just like they'd threatened to do with Jax.

"So we play along?" Jax suggested. "It's a means to an end. We aren't going to let this go."

She agreed with that. "But I don't know if I have war with a powerful family in me." Maybe a few years ago when it didn't matter the cost because it was only her. "I've got too much to lose these days. Too many people I care about who could be caught up in the fallout as soon as they realize I'm moving against them."

Jax glanced at her.

She had to turn her head painfully to the side to see his face, but the soft expression there was worth it.

He thought she was sweet. "For the record, if you think it's worth the fight, then I'm in. If you go after them, I'll go with you."

"Me, too. If we're all throwing down," Maizie said. "I know enough about these people to know they're the kind I don't like."

Not exactly surprising. "They're powerful."

The teen said, "We've been up against powerful people before, and we survived. We get stronger every time."

Kenna sipped her coffee. Sentiment was fine and dandy, but it didn't keep you out of a lifetime prison sentence when someone presented proof no one was able to argue with. If either of these two wound up like that, she would never forgive herself. And to live knowing she couldn't do anything about it?

The thought of it was enough to make her want to pack her bags and leave.

Finish it herself with no help, go up against the Rosenbergs solo. No weaknesses. No family to make her vulnerable. Take all the risk herself and keep them safe in the process.

Once it was over, she could see if they'd accept her back.

"You need us." Jax sounded a little too much like he was trying to persuade her rather than simply speaking a fact. "You know you do."

Whether she *wanted* to need them was a different story. "I need a way to get Ramon back when I have nothing to trade for him with Walter." *Walker.* Whatever his name was. "What's on the drive, Maze?"

"They sent a whole packet, a folder of documents and images. Financial records, phone records. Transcripts of conversations. Looks like everything we'd need to take down Cecelia. Assuming it all points to a specific crime the FBI can pin on her."

"Uh," Jax said, "I think you mean file charges. If it's not true, we won't be pursuing a conviction."

Maizie blinked. "Right. Honor, integrity. All that jazz."

Kenna smirked around the rim of her mug. "I nearly need a refill."

"This should wake you up," Maizie said. "I have my computer doing a search of this folder and there's nothing in here about the military guys. No mention of Cecelia running any black ops team, special forces, special ops, or army anything. Nothing."

"We have Noelle's information," Jax said. "Anything in there to connect that to Cecelia?"

Maizie shook her head. "I'll double-check, but at face value no."

Kenna wasn't interested in taking her down if they found nothing about who controlled these army guys. She'd assumed they worked for Cecelia. But it could be that she'd assumed wrong and the Rosenbergs were the ones who sent them to the bank to kill Noelle and take the contents of the box. To protect Lydia's identity—that made sense.

Cecelia ordered Officer Paige to kill Kenna. They sent Carlos to shoot him.

Might be that they would back off now, considering they thought Kenna would do her dirty work. "It isn't enough that Cecelia goes down. We need Walker behind bars. And we need those army guys free to live their lives, not hiding in prisons or being ordered to kill people. Like ghosts who do this family's dirty work."

Maybe right now she didn't need to bite off the whole piece. Could she peel back those three layers, and then tackle the family itself later?

"There's a subfolder of images in here," Maizie continued, sounding distracted. "I'll share my screen." A second later, a list of files popped up. The first was a street, where Cecelia sat at a coffee shop table outside.

"They had her under surveillance?" Jax said.

"Makes sense." Or so Kenna figured. "Then they have weight to pressure her with. An idea what she's up to. And now a noose to hang her with."

Maizie said, "So-o-o creepy."

Kenna shared a smile with Jax, pretty sure the teen couldn't see them. He leaned down and kissed her gently on the lips. Because they were raising this girl, right? *As it were*, at least. Neither of them spent much time with her in person, but they both cared a whole lot about her future and her needing to feel safe as much as she was safe.

Neither of them would like it if Kenna did what she had to do. But the bottom line was that she didn't risk other people if she could take all the risk herself.

That's just how she was wired.

One day, she might be able to let go of it, but that wasn't going to be today.

"Huh."

Kenna looked at the screen. "Is that Ramon?"

Jax said, "We know she was his handler before he went to work for that cartel in Mexico."

The photo showed the two of them—Cecelia and Ramon—sitting in a car. Her in the driver's seat, him on the passenger side. It looked like nighttime, but there were no landmarks or any view of the place they'd parked. Could even be a traffic camera, but Kenna didn't think so. They were talking, and neither looked particularly happy about being there.

Kenna didn't think it was suspicious. "We already knew they know each other."

"This photo is timestamped," Maizie said. "It's from April

this year, which means the image was taken just a few months ago."

Kenna frowned. "After Wisconsin?" She'd told him how his sister was killed and worked to take down the person responsible. Nearly losing her life in the process—not to mention Jax. "How is that possible?"

"Did he tell you he hasn't seen her?" Jax asked her.

"Why would he have seen her? He hates her. He's working with me trying to take her down." She'd wondered why he didn't just try to kill her, given how angry he had to be about being betrayed. "This doesn't make any sense."

"It does if he's been playing you this whole time."

She didn't like how easily Jax said that. If it was true, it meant Ramon had duped her into believing something that wasn't true. He'd lied, and she fell for it.

She pressed her lips together.

"We'll figure it out." Jax squeezed her knee.

"We have to find him first. Then we can beat him for the truth."

Maizie said, "You'd do that?"

"Can't." Kenna sighed. "I don't have the arm strength to go more than one round."

Jax glanced at her, one brow raised. "That's the only reason?"

"When I've only had one cup of coffee?" Kenna couldn't possibly be expected to act like a reasonable human being yet. Of course, she was going to take that betrayal and hit back with the full force of her anger. That was why she usually read her Bible while she drank it.

She reached into the top drawer of the bedside table and pulled out the Bible she'd found in her father's things. She used an app with different versions when the old English didn't make sense to her, but she liked reading the same words her father had.

"Right. I forgot it takes at least three cups to tamp down the violence."

Kenna felt the corner of her mouth curl up as she located the verse in Psalms she'd read a few days ago. "And of thy mercy cut off mine enemies and destroy all them that afflict my soul: for I am thy servant."

"Interesting perspective."

"You don't get that verse of the day?"

Jax chuckled. "You're going to hear him out before you kill him, right?"

Kenna said, "It's generally how you get the truth."

There would be a reckoning. Somewhere in the mess of taking down Cecelia and Walker, dealing with Bracken and Antonio and figuring out the mess of a hit squad of military trained guys...

She would have it out with Ramon.

"I'll listen to what he has to say." Kenna unfolded herself off the bed so she could pace...and let Ozzy in. The dog wandered around, and thankfully didn't decide to relieve himself on any furniture. "Then I'll figure out what to do with him."

"I was starting to like that guy." Maizie sounded disappointed.

Kenna looked at Jax and mouthed, *Me, too.*

He nodded at her, then said, "We'll figure out why he was meeting with Cecelia. If there's something going on, or he's been lying to us, then we'll deal with it. Together."

She liked the idea of that.

"Okay." Maizie nodded.

"Kenna?"

She frowned at him. Of course, he was going to put her on

the spot. She couldn't very well take off on her own and do this solo if he made her agree they would continue to be a team. The guy was crafty and he knew it, given the smirk on that face.

Maizie said, "Where did she go?"

"She's still here." Jax stared at her, a distinct *for now, at least* in his tone.

"I'm here, Maizie." Kenna bit the bullet and said, "I'm not going anywhere."

"We're doing this together," Jax added.

"I'll keep digging and let you know what I find." Maizie must've ended the video call because Kenna heard the chime from the laptop.

Jax closed the lid and set it aside, sitting forward on the bed with his elbows on his knees. "You're not going to take off and do this alone."

She folded her arms. "Then you can't get put in prison just to talk to a guy. Go as your special agent self and just visit him like it's for a case."

"Fine."

"Fine." She stared at him, only slightly aware of Ozzy wandering into the bathroom.

The spark of attraction crackled between them like electricity. She could feel it in the air. Tingling the skin of her arms.

She could stay right here and never move, just drinking him in from across the room.

The fact they weren't even touching each other and it felt like this nearly buckled her knees.

Jax broke the stare. He cleared his throat, getting up and taking his mug. "I'll get out of here and let you get ready for the day."

I'll be taking a cold shower if you need me.

He wandered around the bed, over toward her. About to pass her...

She should've headed for the bathroom.

"Told you we should've gone to the courthouse." Jax shut the door behind him.

Kenna rolled her eyes, a smile stretching her lips wide. "Don't tempt me."

Chapter Thirty

"Are you sure about this?"

Maizie's voice came through the car speakers. Kenna had borrowed the vehicle and connected her phone so she could make the call and drive.

Kenna stared out at the dark sky through the windshield, navigating traffic on this street in the center of town closest to the ranch. The mountains east of Phoenix were shrouded in night, and the light of the city to the west, on Kenna's left as she drove north, made the road a kind of natural divide. East versus west. Good versus evil, not that it was tied to geography.

Two opposing forces.

Which side was Ramon on?

"Kenna?"

"I'm here." She heard a slight noise from the back seat but ignored it. "Yes, I'm sure of this. Walker needs to be brought in. Regardless of what side of the line Ramon is determined to be on, I need to know the truth and justice will be served where it's needed."

Maizie sighed. "You could've waited for Jax."

"He needs to talk to Noelle's husband. The only time he could get into the prison to see the guy without it going on paperwork"—something she now owed the warden a sum of money for—"during normal hours." They'd talked it all through before he left. She'd ensured precautions were taken so she wouldn't be going in alone. It was never foolproof, but she'd done what she could.

"When Walker sees you don't have the kid, he'll kill Ramon."

"He'll see two people in the car."

"But—"

"Maze," Kenna said, cutting her off. "Don't worry so much."

"I like it better when you guys work something together."

"Life isn't always as neat and tidy as that. We do what we can, we flex when we need to, and we make the best of it."

Jax felt that he needed to have that conversation. To dig with the Rosenbergs and find out from Noelle's husband anything he could to take them down. Kenna wanted to tackle things in order.

Ramon. Walker.

Then Cecelia. After that, she would see about the Rosenbergs.

Things could go sideways if Georgia, or whoever else at the family, noticed they weren't doing what they thought Kenna agreed to—taking down Cecelia. Only her, or her first. Kenna wasn't sure. It wouldn't likely be a one-and-done thing. Probably more like an ongoing "arrangement" whereby Kenna kept doing favors for her and they kept threatening Jax's job if she didn't.

"Are you guys fighting or something?" Maizie asked.

Kenna rolled her eyes. "Jax and I are fine."

If anything, it was the opposite. And taking some time

apart, even if it was only a few hours, would be good for both of them. Things had sparked like crazy between them back in the hotel. Enough she wouldn't be surprised if Jax slept somewhere else tonight.

"Fine." Maizie dragged the word out in full teenage mode.

The times when she sounded or acted like a normal young woman her age were bittersweet but only in the sense that they'd have to contend with the normal "teenage" stuff.

"I'll call you later," Kenna said.

"You should hang on the line so I can hear if things go sideways and alert local whoever to come and help you."

"I have help on hand."

Maizie sighed and hung up.

The music came back on in the speakers, and Kenna turned it down. From the back seat, Sheriff Bracken said, "How old is she?"

"Seventeen." *Or thereabouts.* Kenna wasn't about to explain that they didn't exactly know how old the girl was, and they'd let her pick her own date of birth.

"Sounds like a smart kid," Bracken said. "They're always the most precocious."

Kenna smiled. "I'm getting that." Before Bracken could ask why it was slow going, Kenna said, "How about you? Any kids?"

"My ex-husband didn't want kids. He also wanted to be the one in the relationship with the gun and the authority to detain the other." An edge crept into her voice. "I divorced him two years ago."

"And Antonio?" Kenna glanced in the rearview mirror at the car behind them—where Antonio was following behind, though not close enough anyone would realize they were sticking together.

Bracken shifted. "I don't know if he wants kids. Right now, it's just about letting off steam."

"I know his brother. He's a PD lieutenant in Salt Lake City."

"Yeah, he mentioned he has family all over."

Kenna couldn't put her finger on it, but there was something off about the guy. "Javier has a wife and kids. They're the best people I know aside from Jax."

"Antonio is..." Bracken paused. "Don't worry about him. He'll do the right thing in the end."

Kenna wanted to ask if it had to do with the resort, or the Rosenbergs. Maybe he felt trapped working there and wanted out but couldn't see how to do it. She didn't need another case to work—another person to save. Especially not when she needed to have a serious talk with Ramon about lying to her.

That is, if Walker didn't kill him tonight when she showed up without Lydia.

She wasn't sure this was even about Walker wanting the girl. She doubted he really, deep down, wanted to raise her himself. Far more likely, this whole thing was a power play. Lydia was only a bargaining chip to ensure he'd be the one calling the shots. With the family. With Cecelia.

The poor kid was probably nothing but leverage to every adult in her life.

Meanwhile, was she really getting the care she needed?

"We're here." Kenna pulled into the parking lot at the edge of a twenty-acre city park. Center of town. Public place. Not much of a crowd at this time of night.

She could walk to the designated tree and wait for Walker to show.

There were no other cars in the lot.

Antonio didn't pull in behind her, but kept going. He'd go to the next street and then double back on foot.

Kenna sent Walker a text.

I'm here.

Then twisted toward the back seat. "Do you have everything on hand?"

Bracken sounded like she was moving around back there. "Looks like it. You?"

Kenna patted the vest. Both thigh pockets. Checked her boot holsters. "Aside from showing up like I'm geared up to go stop a riot, I'm good to go."

Bracken huffed. "Can't believe this is *El Caminante*."

"I never quite believed that he was your run-of-the-mill serial killer." Kenna watched the grassy expanse, the trees around the perimeter. The playground and single building with bathrooms. "It just didn't fit when he had no conceivable MO that he did what he wanted."

"So you think he was just like the other guys, ex-military. Co-opted into carrying out the Rosenbergs' orders."

"If they show up to take him out tonight, there won't be much we can do." If Ramon died, she would never get the truth, and she doubted the Rosenbergs would care enough to let any of them live. Unless they thought Kenna could still be useful to them. "We'll have to keep our eyes open."

"As long as this ends with Walker in my cuffs, the rest we can handle. Right?"

Kenna liked the sound of that much certainty, but she didn't exactly feel it. "Tell me when Antonio is in position."

"He's moving over this way," Bracken said. "GPS has him at the alley between two houses. Neighborhood access to the park by a path. He'll be on the green in a minute."

Kenna never saw him emerge. She didn't study the end of

the path for long, in case Walker was watching her and saw where she paid attention.

She kept scanning the whole park.

Her phone buzzed.

> Your two o'clock. Bring the kid.

"Showtime." Kenna climbed out of the car and shut the door. She walked solo to the tree line at her two o'clock. Heading with slow, measured steps in the direction he'd told her. Gun close to her open hand. As much protection as she could have on her. Ready to face down a serial killer.

Get Ramon back.

Maybe she should just let Walker kill him. But that couldn't be the punishment for deception. It smacked more of revenge than justice.

She spread out her hands. "I'm alone."

"Where's the kid?" The baritone voice came from behind her.

"In the car." Kenna turned to face him. "Where's Ramon?" She lowered her hands so her gun was in reach, just in case.

Antonio was covering her, but she didn't completely trust him to watch her back. No one would do it the way Jax would if he were here. Tonight was a night to work this from two angles. She had to rely on herself, Ramon if he was trustworthy, and locals—the sheriff and resort head of security. People who all had a stake in this.

Even if it was only about bringing down a deadly serial murderer. That would be a good boost to Bracken's resume if she went on official record as the one who arrested him.

"Close by," Walker said.

"This is supposed to be a trade."

"I'll show you mine if you show me yours."

As she opened her mouth to respond to that, which he wouldn't have appreciated, a gunshot echoed across the open field. Walker grunted, ducked, and started to run.

Kenna flinched, landed on one knee, and drew her weapon.

She tracked Walker as he ran, then got up and followed him into the trees. She pumped her arms and legs as hard as she could after him, determined not to let him go. She and Jax had agreed to come back together later with news, and she wanted hers to be about success. That way he wouldn't worry so much about her when she was somewhere else, working.

The way she did when he was.

They had to trust each other's abilities.

Like the sense that Walker had ducked behind cover and intended to turn the tables on her. Kenna slowed her pace and listened for where he'd gone. Bracken and Antonio both raced behind her, crashing through the tree line with both of them breathing hard.

"Where did he go?" Bracken asked.

"That's what I'm trying to find out." She should buy herself some night vision goggles, or something with heat sensors. "Spread out and check everywhere. He can't have gotten far."

Wherever Ramon was, Walker now knew she didn't have Lydia—at least, most likely not—and he could be rushing back to where he'd stashed the guy and murdering him out of revenge.

"Walter!" Kenna wanted to use his given name so she could keep him off balance. She took a couple of steps and called out, "Let's talk about this!"

Antonio grunted, and she heard a thud. A gun went off, the flash enough to illuminate the dark and the sound of a crack like a firework. Kenna winced and ran for the spot, ducking around a tree. Praying none of them got hit by a bullet.

Antonio wrestled with Walker, both of them rolling across the ground as if neither was willing to let go. Kenna held aim on them. Bracken showed up on her left and clicked her flashlight on.

A knife glinted in the dark.

"Watch—"

Walker drove it into Antonio's side.

Kenna said, "Hold your fire," to Bracken and rushed over. She kicked out before Walker could swing the knife around at her. A reflex after her shout and him finding her running toward him. She caught his head.

He swung with the knife.

She felt fire across the inside edge of her calf and went down on one knee again. Bracken got closer. "Drop the weapon."

Walker launched off Antonio. Kenna palmed her stun gun and jabbed at him with it, her thumb on the trigger.

Walker's body stiffened. The sound of crackling electricity filled the area around him. He jerked a few times. Bracken stepped back, and Walker slumped to the ground.

"Thanks for not shooting him," Kenna managed to say.

"I was about to."

"I know."

Bracken pulled handcuffs from her belt and gave them to Kenna. "Secure him. I'll call for an ambulance." She knelt by Ryson's cousin. "Antonio, you with me?"

He groaned. "You should've killed him."

Kenna knelt, dragging Walker's hands behind his back. "We need information. Killing him will also kill our ability to find out what he knows about all of this." She slid the cuffs around his wrists and tightened them beyond where regulation dictated, listening to Bracken call for an ambulance and tell them to hurry because they had an officer down.

Given he'd been hurt trying to help them detain a wanted man who'd killed multiple people, Kenna figured that was about right.

Antonio would go down a hero.

She decided while cuffing him that Walker needed to be uncomfortable, and she'd done well with the cuffs even if it had been a while.

Kenna tapped the light on her phone and shined it at his face. Out cold. "We cannot underestimate him. Or his family's need to take him out before he can make a statement that buries them along with his freedom."

"As long as you don't give him a deal." Antonio directed that at Bracken.

"I just want the credit," the sheriff said. "But now I also want to hear what he had to say."

"Would've been satisfying to shoot him, though. Right?"

Bracken snorted. "Sure, babe. I'd have been defending your honor."

Antonio grunted.

A few minutes later, during which she'd texted Maizie and Jax but only heard back from the teen, a sheriff's department cruiser pulled into the parking lot. Followed by an ambulance shortly after. Kenna was in the middle of patting down Walker, pulling everything out of his pockets, which only turned out to be a set of car keys.

The deputy jogged over. "What have we got?"

"Do you guys have this?" Kenna looked up. "I need to go find my friend."

Bracken nodded. "I've got this." She turned to the deputy,

an older guy who looked fit and experienced. "Deputy Camery, watch over the suspect."

"Yes, Sheriff." The guy took Kenna's spot.

She holstered her gun and knelt on the other side of Antonio. "You good?" Blood covered his side, and his breathing seemed labored.

"Never better."

Kenna patted his shoulder. "Injured taking down a dangerous killer. Sounds like a headline about a hero."

Antonio huffed.

"Hang in there." She passed the EMTs hustling over and tried to figure where Walker had come from.

She hit the button on the keys and heard a car honk.

Chapter Thirty-One

K enna walked out of the park to a side street. She clicked the locks again. This time the beep was louder, a quick unlock-then-lock just in case Ramon made a run for it.

The stillness of the night wasn't entirely unwelcome. She didn't want to distract herself with a phone call that meant she might miss something that came at her out of the shadows. Walker was in custody. Antonio had been injured, but he would hopefully get patched up and recover. She prayed Jax had success and said a sincere thank you for what they'd achieved here tonight.

El Caminante was off the streets.

If they did this right, they should be able to get testimony on both Cecelia and the Rosenberg family from Walker. Make him some kind of deal that reduced his sentence and gained them intel they could use to bring the whole clan down.

She spotted the car on a side street, a residential area. People who used the park for recreation rather than clandestine meetings with serial killers.

In the front window of one house, light from a TV flashed between the curtains.

Probably not the only person awake this time of night.

Kenna turned on her phone camera flashlight and shined it into the car. No Ramon in the front or on the back seat.

She went around to face the trunk and hit the button to open the lid.

It flipped up.

Ramon lay across the trunk, hands and feet tied. A gag tied around his mouth. He sucked in harsh breaths, his eyes wide while he stared at her. Bruises on his face. Blood around the gag. Sweat and tears dampened his hair, and he reeked.

Kenna slammed the trunk closed again.

He yelled at her from inside the trunk, but she ignored it and climbed in. Drove away from this spot, where cops and other first responders were all going to gather to see the arrest of a dangerous serial killer. She didn't want state police to catch her interrogating a man wanted by the FBI on the street in the middle of the night.

Ramon continued to yell and make a fuss as she drove.

Kenna flipped on the radio and turned it up loud, tapping her index finger on the steering wheel to the rhythm of a classic rock song.

She found an industrial area, scouted for security cameras, and found a spot she could park and she could hopefully be less visible. It was that or get a room at a no-tell motel, where no one would think twice about her marching a bound, yelling man into a room.

Kenna backed up to the side of a building in an out of the way corner of the parking lot. It didn't look like the blind store warehouse had people who worked overnight, but she wasn't going to rule out security.

She shut the car off, climbed out, and made a phone call.

Maizie picked up two rings later. "How did it go?"

"Everyone is alive. Walker is in cuffs. Antonio got stabbed, but he was conscious, and he'll be on his way to the hospital soon enough."

"And Ramon?"

"I'm about to talk to him." Kenna leaned back against the car and looked around. "Anything from Jax?"

No one could take a phone or any weapons into a prison, not even an FBI agent and not even for a clandestine meeting with a man who wanted to be anonymous and hidden so badly that he'd chosen solitary confinement. Biding his time until he could expose the people who had taken away his freedom first—before he chose to give it up for the greater good.

"I'm listening to local dispatch, but there haven't been any callouts to the prison." Maizie paused. "They did bring in one of their medical staff, a doctor who was an ER attendant for years. He came in after hours, but that doesn't mean it has anything to with Jax or Noelle's husband."

"Hack their system. Then you'll know what's happening in real time." Kenna stomped her feet, trying to get her energy level back up.

"Can't," Maizie said. "Prisons have closed systems for security and things like door controls. They can't be hacked from the outside because they aren't connected to the outside world—not like the regular office staff computers."

"What about the warden's computer? He's got to have email."

"Hmm." Maizie paused. "I'll poke around."

The cell phone screen was warm against Kenna's cheek. "Let me know. Just in case."

She figured neither of them wanted to hear that something had happened to Jax after the fact. Kenna planned to be ready to rush to that prison just in case.

"Call me if you get something." Kenna hung up.

She repeated the same process of opening the trunk, right as she realized she'd have to go back to the park for the truck Jax borrowed from some guy he knew. Oops. If it got scratched—or stolen—they were going to have to replace it.

Ramon stared up at her.

She flipped out her knife and cut his feet free, then pulled down the gag from his mouth, working it over his chin so it hung around his neck. "Climb out." She needed to gauge how ambulatory he was. Then they could have their conversation about the fact he'd met with Cecelia after his return from Mexico and neglected to tell her.

Ramon grabbed the edge of the trunk. "Cut my hands free."

"In a minute. Climb out first, then we can talk about the rest."

"Where's Walker?" He worked his way to sitting, and she catalogued a couple of aches and pains—or stiffness from being cooped up—in his movements.

If the kidnapping had been fake, they'd done a convincing job of making it look real.

She stepped back, hand close to her holstered weapon. Phone in her free hand. Kenna watched him climb from the trunk and gain his feet. Then she moved in and shoved a hand at his chest so that he stumbled back and sat on the edge of the open trunk. His head whipped back farther than she'd meant it to and bumped the open lid.

He cried out.

"I can't tell if you and Walter are friends."

Ramon flinched. "So you figured out who they are. That doesn't mean anything to me!"

"So you say." She kept the hand pushed against his chest.

Ramon lifted his bound hands and only nudged hers away from him. "Get off."

She let her hand go but said, "No, I don't think I will. Jax is at a jail talking to someone who might be helpful while I'm out here cleaning up *your* mess. What is going on, Ramon?"

"What are you talking about? Where is Walker? I thought you were going to arrest him!" Ramon flushed. "Don't tell me he got away."

"If he did, would you call your friend Cecelia and inform her?" Maybe that was it. He was feeding her updates on the situation so she could stay a step ahead of everything Kenna and Jax were doing.

Kenna would guess she didn't know about the packet Georgia had sent.

At least, not yet.

"What are you talking about?"

Kenna stared at him. "You knew they're siblings."

His jaw flexed. Shoulders tense. "I'm not part of it."

That remained to be seen. "You met with Cecelia after you came back from Mexico. Don't lie and tell me you didn't. I've seen a surveillance photo."

Ramon worked his mouth around.

The question foremost on her mind was, *Why didn't you tell me?* But that was an emotional reaction to what was going on. And for Ramon this might be anything but emotional. "Start talking."

He scrunched his nose in an expression she couldn't really decipher.

She waited. Aware of the condensation trails of an airplane streaking across the sky. People going somewhere for work or business. A vehicle on the road too far away for her to see, but which she could hear heading away from them. No birds. No people. No sense they were being watched, which had happened a lot the past few weeks.

Because of this man.

The gun holstered on her hip. A warm cell phone in her back pocket. Her vest constricting every breath with its weight, but for which she was grateful enough she'd wear it anyway. After all, it saved her life in Pahrump.

"How did you learn his name?" Ramon finally said.

"*Both* of their names."

He winced.

"When did you figure it out?" She could give him the benefit of the doubt. "Or are you one of them...another illegitimate Rosenberg?"

"I'm not one of them." He sniffed. "But I grew up with them."

Kenna stared at him.

"My father was their head gardener. We didn't live on the property, but we lived close by. Sometimes in the summer, I would help him, and I'd see Celeste and Walter playing."

"Did you know Sarah?"

Ramon flinched. "They killed her. Celeste told me, years later when she knew there was nothing I could do about it because I had no proof. I kept my mouth shut."

"And in return they got you and her both into the FBI." They'd been at Quantico at the same time, the training group Kenna had also been a part of.

"I've done a lot of things I'm not proud of. Working with you wasn't one of them."

"But you didn't tell me everything I needed to know."

Ramon said, "They—"

"Pressure people," Kenna finished. "Do whatever they want. Control everything. Take out anyone who steps out of line. Anything else I forgot?"

"Why do you think they burned me?"

"Feel free to explain that," Kenna said.

She'd been under the impression—like everyone else—that Cecelia's undercover agent had turned to the dark side. When she found Ramon in Mexico working for a cartel, she'd assumed it was all true. Until she heard him out.

In fact, there was far more to the story that he'd neglected to include.

Ramon looked aside, his gaze unfocused. "They wanted me to join the group. Like Walter. The rest of those army guys. Take jobs like Walter does, keeping the guys in line."

"So he's the guy who takes out the ones who want out."

Ramon nodded, but still didn't look at her. "I said no."

"Funny. Considering you're still alive." He'd even been there when Officer Paige was shot.

"Why did you go see her when you came back to the US?"

Ramon turned his head to look at her then, and she saw sorrow in his gaze she hadn't expected to see. "Why do you think? I figured if I could at least get her to believe I wanted back in she might trip up, show her hand, and get me—us—in far enough to take them all down."

"You should've told me that."

He shook his head. "It didn't work."

So he'd hidden his failure from her. Because he wanted her to see him as capable and not a guy who couldn't turn his life around? She could understand that, but withholding the truth wasn't much different from lying. "I have what we need to take down Cecelia. Walker has been arrested, he'll get booked, and he's never going to see the outside of a prison cell for the rest of his life."

"And the kid?"

"What do you know about her?" She didn't want to hand over *everything*.

"Lydia is..." Ramon winced. "I met her once. Swear she looked at me like she wanted to castrate me."

"She needs help."

"She'll get it with the Rosenbergs," Ramon said. "Problem is, they just might help her into being a killer for hire like everyone else on their payroll."

"Do you know how to find Cecelia?"

"She finds *you*," Ramon said.

"Not good enough. We might need to draw her out." Kenna for one was ready for a showdown. But she didn't want Georgia to think she'd done what the Rosenbergs wanted. As far as she was concerned, they'd done an end run. Beat Georgia at her own game and used the information she'd sent to start dismantling all of it. Every part of the empire they'd built.

"You can't go up against them."

"Don't tell me what I can or cannot do," Kenna said. "I don't respond well to threats like that."

"You'll get yourself killed."

He thought she should only be worried about herself? "I can take care of me." It was just that these days she had a lot more than nothing to lose. "Question is, are you going to start being straight with me so we can end this once and for all?"

Ramon stared silently at her for a few moments. Then he lifted his bound hands.

"I'm not giving you a weapon." Kenna flicked out her knife again and cut the zip ties.

He hissed and rubbed his wrists.

"What did Walker tell you? Why kidnap you, and leverage that for the kid?"

"He hates them," Ramon said. "He wants out, and he wanted to take Lydia with him."

"As if we'd let him go free?" More likely, he'd be hunted for the rest of his life. Especially if he kidnapped a child on the way. "He can't have believed we would exchange her for you, even if I wasn't aware you guys knew each other."

"He thinks you're his ticket out. You'll be so focused on everyone else no one will see him slip away."

"He hates them?" Kenna paused. "Wants out?"

Ramon nodded.

"Good. We can use that to flip him to testify against them." Kenna figured the family would try to shut it down. Do something like send a hitman to take him out in prison, or lean on a corrupt cop.

"I'm never gonna get my life back. You know that, right?" Ramon ran a hand through his military-short hair. "They won't let me have a life."

"I'm not going to let them kill you."

"I'll never be anything." Ramon spoke in a low tone. "They made sure of it."

"So be nobody with me." Kenna shrugged. "I'm just a PI. I've never hit their radar before, and these days I'm just a nuisance they can't get rid of. They're trying to deal with me like they deal with everything else. By making a trade. They think they can pressure me by leveraging Jax's career."

"What do they want?"

"Cecelia shut down," she said. "Everything else, status quo."

"I guess we're after the same thing, then."

"Except I'm going after all of them." Once she'd said it aloud, she realized it was true. Kenna wanted the family taken down, rendered inert. Exposed for the cancer they were in this country. She wanted to free all the people they had under their thumb and give them their lives back.

Even Ramon.

Chapter Thirty-Two

Kenna climbed out of the front seat of Walker's car, outside the sheriff's department where Bracken ran the show. A two-story building in the center of town. So close to the resort and everything else that had gone down lately.

Dawn had only just started to lighten the horizon, the slow creep of day showing up to wake the world.

After they'd talked, she'd taken Ramon to the resort and left him in her room. She'd told him he was in charge of Ozzy and to get some rest while they figured out what to do next.

Two spaces away, Jax climbed out of the front seat of a nondescript car, a compact he'd driven to the jail. The sight of him gave her a boost of energy rather than the fatigue she'd been feeling the last few hours. Even with the amount of coffee she'd drunk.

She met him at the sidewalk in front of the main door. He held his arms out, and she slammed into him, winding her arms around him as he did the same. Sinking into his embrace. "You're right," she said. "Hugs are definitely underrated."

Jax held on to her as if there was nowhere he'd rather be. "Turns out I'm right about a lot of things."

Kenna chuckled. "I'm too tired, I think everything's funny right now." She leaned back from the hug but didn't step away. "What happened with Noelle's husband?"

His expression took on a sad note. "I just had to tell a man who misses his wife that she's gone and he'll never see her again."

Kenna figured it was possible he might not even get out of prison soon enough to bury her. "Does he want Ozzy?"

Jax winced. "He did ask about the dog. We talked about a lot of things."

Kenna nodded. "Is he really hiding in prison, biding his time?"

"Pretty sure he's lost his grip on the plan. Told me to call him Steve, but I doubt that's his real name. It isn't even the name he was booked under."

"Sounds like a guy who has been undercover for too long. He's starting to lose his grip on who he is and why he's doing what he's doing."

"Exactly," Jax said. "He needs help, and I all but promised I'd give it to him. Though, I don't know what kind of help he wants."

"I don't like the idea of using any of these guys to further our own ends. Even if the cause is justice, and bringing down powerful people. Haven't these military guys given enough? They didn't ask to be stuck in the middle of it."

Unlike Ramon.

As far as Kenna was concerned, he'd kept himself in the middle of this when at any time he could've walked away. She figured that meant he wanted to be part of taking them down. It was just his motivation and his loyalty couldn't exactly be categorized in a neat box of good versus evil. Or right versus wrong. Ramon had always been a gray area.

Maybe he would always be that way, no matter what happened.

Or what he chose to do with his life.

Jax nodded. "Then we are on the same page. Though, that's not surprising."

"Go team?"

He shook his head, sort of rolling his eyes. Then he touched his lips to hers. "He's grieving. And I have to pray he doesn't do anything dumb in prison until we can figure out the next step."

"Did you tell him what he and Noelle did was key? She helped us, even though it cost her life. She gave us what we needed to bring them down."

"I doubt it will be much of a comfort to him, but I did tell him." Jax squeezed her gently with his arms, then dropped them to his sides. "I called my Assistant Special Agent in Charge on the way over here and woke him up to tell him that the serial killer we've been hunting for months is in custody. Thanks to a small-town Arizona sheriff."

That must've been an interesting conversation. "And you didn't have anything to do with it, but just happened to be precisely in the area at the time?"

"Exactly." Jax nodded. "I played it off like when we met up with local law enforcement to hang out, like dinner with someone in the same line of work. Maybe we got to talking about Walker a little too much and she started to do some digging. Realized he was close by and took him down."

"And did your job for you?"

"We aren't going to talk about that part."

"Of course, not. After all, the FBI doesn't need any help from outsiders." Kenna grinned. "Or so I've heard."

Jax chuckled. "He's coming here this morning. We need to transfer Walker back to California so he can be arraigned."

And that meant he was leaving town. "You have to go with them?"

"I should." He looked like he wanted to hug her again, but just stuck his hands in his pockets.

"Don't worry, I got this. I'll take down Cecelia with suspiciously obtained information that will lead to her being discredited and probably arrested. And then after that, I'll go up against the powerful family and expose their influence." She waved a hand. "No big deal."

"At least with Walker in custody, I'll probably get a commendation or something. It won't matter what the Rosenbergs want to do to propel my career along. I'll have to graciously turn down the promotion. After all, it was a small-town Arizona sheriff who brought in the deadly killer we hadn't located." He grinned.

"So gracious of you."

"We should go congratulate Bracken on the arrest of a dangerous killer."

"Assuming he hasn't been murdered already, or somehow escaped," Kenna said.

She didn't want to be pessimistic, but the life expectancy Walker was now facing didn't look good. The minute the family discovered he was in custody, they would no doubt take steps to shut him down.

As they walked into the sheriff's office, she wanted to hold Jax's hand. This was a work thing, not a vacation thing. Still, the solidarity of being side by side again wasn't lost on her. She preferred it to working alone. Especially considering the alternative was Ramon, who she trusted a whole lot less than she had yesterday.

Even so, while she might want him to work with her, she also didn't want him to throw away the career he had spent years building. Jax deserved a shot at what he'd originally gone into the FBI and set out to do.

Maybe when things calmed down, they could talk it over. She could ask him more about why he'd joined the FBI. Because she didn't think it was over a buried memory of a dead body he'd seen as a young child, back at that resort. There were likely multiple reasons, and nuances of things that drove him to join the FBI. To spend his life seeking justice.

Bracken walked out of her office, on one side of the room. Separated from the main area by a wall of glass windows from hip height to the ceiling.

A larger male in a deputy uniform, probably about late forties, glanced over from his seat behind a desk. "Busy night," he muttered, barely paying them any attention.

Jax went first to the area behind the counter, where four desks had been placed but only to seem to be occupied.

Kenna looked around for the coffee station.

"Everything good?" Jax said.

Bracken motioned. "See for yourself."

Kenna walked around the corner to go look. Over on the right-hand side of the room, toward the back, a wide barred cell had been tucked in an alcove. Out of sight of the front doors, but visible from the workstations of the cops who occupied this office.

Walker lay stretched out on a cot, his arms bent and his hands behind his head. Elbows splayed out. Staring at the ceiling.

"Hasn't made a peep," the deputy said. "Not one word. He just lays there and stares at the ceiling."

"Maybe you just haven't asked the right question."

Kenna noticed a tiny shift in Walker's mouth. Just a fraction of the curl of his lips. She called over to him, "Ramon is fine, in case you're curious. I got him out of the trunk."

Walker said nothing. He just kept staring at the ceiling.

"See?" The deputy wandered back to his desk and slumped into his chair.

Bracken stood by Jax. "I got all the paperwork drawn up," she said. "Am I signing it, or are you?"

Jax glanced at her. "You're the hero who caught him."

"That's not going to look good for you." Bracken winced. "Especially given how convenient this whole thing is."

"I'm going to guess," Jax said, "that given Kenna's proximity to this whole thing, my boss isn't going to be surprised at all that Walker is in custody now."

"Maybe she should sign it," Bracken suggested.

"Don't swear me in as a deputy." Kenna lifted her hands. "It never goes well."

Jax shot her a smile.

Kenna walked to the bars of the cell and stared at the suspect. A man who had killed and terrorized. Even if it was in the name of the Rosenbergs and their agenda, that didn't mean he wasn't the one who had taken lives. "They are going to take you back to California where you will stand trial for what you've done."

Walker only stared at the ceiling.

"Unless you think you won't make it that far. Will the Rosenbergs take you out?"

"Does it matter?" Jax said. "It's over."

"Thanks to Sheriff Bracken, yes." Kenna shifted her weight and leaned her elbows on the horizontal bar, her hands in the cell. "I'm not going to try and convince you that you have all the power here. But no one is ignorant to the fact you know a whole lot about these people. You lived under their thumb almost as long as anyone else, and when it comes to Cecelia, you just might be a linchpin."

Walker reacted to that, a visceral twisting of his expression.

"You're going to let her go free, while you spend your life behind bars. Forgotten. Not even important enough for them to send someone to shank you in the lunch line."

"You're the one who said I wouldn't make it that far."

"Meanwhile, Cecelia goes free."

Walker smacked his lips. "Far as I'm concerned, if I go down, everyone does."

His need to be vindictive was something they could all work with. "And if the FBI is prepared to offer you a nice deal in exchange for all the information you have about Cecelia, and the Rosenbergs? What do you say, Walter? Do you want to live to see their end?"

His stomach clenched under the T-shirt over his abdomen, and he started to laugh. "Yes," he said around the laugh. "I would like to see their end."

Jax shifted behind her, but not coming close enough to draw Walker's attention. "As soon as we get back to California, we can start talking about everything." He paused. "Anything you know can put you in a better position to ask for certain considerations. See if we can't make your future a little more comfortable than it would be otherwise."

"But I'm still spending the rest of my life in prison."

Kenna said, "You might have thought you had no choice, but you know the consequences of taking a life. Everyone who lives in a just society knows that."

This wasn't some disturbed individual with no conscience. Someone who understood that rules existed, but simply didn't believe they applied to him. This was a man who'd been backed into a corner and forced to work for his family. Coerced. Probably abused and twisted around. Given everything that came into play with Lydia's existence—if she really was the child of Walker and Cecelia—none of it had been good and there was some serious codependence going on between him and Cecelia. Or a mutual hatred that somehow translated itself into the means to make a life. A way to have yet more leverage to cause one another pain.

She couldn't even imagine what kind of life had forged a person like that.

But she would thank God daily for the rest of her life that she didn't know. That Maizie would never go that far, so twisted up she had no idea what the difference was between right and wrong.

"Just answer me one thing," Kenna said.

Walker turned his head, staring at her with eyes that had barely a flicker of life in them.

"Why do they want Cecelia shut down, and no one even mentioned you?"

The question might wreck everything Jax needed to do. All the goodwill they might have forged with the suspect. But if her instinct was right, it would solidify his need to see them taken down.

Either the Rosenbergs thought his shot at freedom was over, given the heat of an FBI investigation on him. Or they still had work for him to do and needed him to remain free. The investigation stalled and the FBI spinning their tails.

"Maybe they just don't think I'm a threat to them."

Kenna wasn't sure that's what it was. "Did they ask you to do something else?" Perhaps Walker's arrest had been part of the plan. A way to divide and conquer Kenna and her team and those invested in bringing him in from the inside.

"If they did, I guess it will only be a matter of time before you find out what it is." Walker shifted on the bed, turning away from them to lay with his back to them.

Jax touched her shoulder.

She turned away and went with him, trying to figure out all the variables of this. Soon enough, Jax would pack up everything and take Walker back to California. They were accustomed to goodbyes, but that didn't mean she had to look forward to it.

A trail of black SUVs slid into the parking lot and stopped, blocking everyone in their spaces.

Kenna guessed she was staying here until they all left. "Looks like the cavalry is here."

"Were you expecting an entire team?" Bracken walked to the front window and looked out. "There's like thirty of them."

Jax was about to answer when the door swung open and the group of FBI agents entered. Men and women all in suits, looking as if they'd rushed here from the local office. Not Jax's boss, who was on his way from California and wouldn't get here for several hours.

No, this was an entirely different group.

One with Cecelia Warren in the lead.

"I hear you finally caught *El Caminante.*"

Chapter Thirty-Three

Kenna stared at her, not quite sure whether to run or start shooting. Jax strode past her, his hand out to shake with Cecelia. "Yes, we did, ma'am. It's good to see you."

He didn't ask how the Phoenix office of the FBI even knew that Walker was in custody. Then again, maybe they shouldn't have been so surprised Cecelia heard about it quickly. Fast enough that she was able to rush over here.

The question was, what had she come for?

"Kenna Banbury." Cecelia pasted on a smile. Older than she'd looked the last time they saw each other, but that was hardly surprising given at least ten years had passed since they'd shared a dorm room at Quantico.

"Cecelia Warren." Kenna wasn't sure precisely what she was supposed to do next. Shooting this woman was still on the table, of course. She just wasn't sure she wanted to do it in front of Cecelia's colleagues, who would no doubt respond by returning fire. At Kenna.

That wouldn't do Jax's career any favors.

Cecelia's agents hung around, waiting for their cue from her. Something that told Kenna they followed orders well.

Probably why she kept this group close and had them on hand in case anything went down. Kenna wanted to talk to whoever worked at the Phoenix office that didn't get invited to the secret operations, or the last minute trips out of town with the boss. Anyone that always strived to follow the rules wouldn't work well with an Assistant Special Agent in Charge who was harboring a deadly secret. Even if it only manifested itself in workplace conflict.

Cecelia strode over, holding her arms out. Dressed in a gray pantsuit, a white shirt, and simple gold necklace. Her long hair hung over her shoulders. Styled but not enough that would tell anybody she had forewarning to prepare her appearance before she left the house in a hurry, determined to oversee the takedown of a dangerous suspect.

Kenna tried not to look freaked out while the FBI agent gave her an odd hug. Kind of creepy, actually. Thankfully, she was no longer wearing the bulletproof vest. That would have been an awkward embrace. However, she was packed with enough weapons that Cecelia had to have just discovered at least two of them.

She leaned back. "Kenna, so good to see you."

Kenna was about to throw up, but managed to say, "You, too. But I have to admit I'm surprised. I didn't know the Phoenix office was aware of what was going on here."

"Of course, I tried to keep apprised of everything important."

The question was precisely what she meant by that.

Before Kenna could ask, Jax folded his arms. "The Phoenix office isn't taking my collar from me. I've been tracking this killer for months now. He'll be returned to San Diego, where all the evidence and the entire case file are located."

Cecelia smirked, but it didn't seem devious. Just a professional squabble. "You can't blame me for jumping on the chance to see him behind bars."

And the fact it was her half-brother didn't play into it?

"Maybe you and I could talk privately?" Kenna suggested.

There had to be a conference room or break room they could go into where she could figure out how they were going to play this. Without everything she needed to bring down Cecelia on hand and a signed warrant from a federal judge—something Jax would have to coordinate—they couldn't exactly slap cuffs on her. And if they started questioning her in an interrogation room, Cecelia's people would realize something was up. They'd only be tipping off anyone and everyone —including Cecelia—to the fact she was now currently under investigation.

Even if any of her people were ready to testify against her, the fact they hadn't raised any concerns to date meant they weren't prepared to do the right thing. Not really.

They didn't have the motivation Kenna had.

Cecelia nodded. "Good idea. I could use a little catch up with you. Maybe some coffee."

Bracken gestured. "You can use that room." Then looked at Kenna as if there was something wrong with her to want to talk to this woman alone. "I'll make a fresh pot."

"Thanks." Kenna led Cecelia to a sparsely decorated conference room with furniture that had probably been here more than fifty years. Hearkening back to a vastly different era of policing. But one truth had withstood the test of time.

Policing had to be about justice—it had to be impartial. And there was no room for corruption in law enforcement.

Cecelia was the epitome of everything that needed to be routed out.

About the time Cecelia closed the door, Kenna had figured out how she was going to play this. She looked at her former roommate, bringing to the forefront an expression of sheer relief. "You won't believe everything that's happened the last few months."

She didn't need to bring up the fact that Walker had sent a hitman after Kenna. Another one of those military guys, but this one much older. Which just added another layer of complexity to this whole situation.

Cecelia shot back, "That's what happens when you try to fight for a guy who walked away from the FBI as a turncoat, knowing full well that he would never be able to come back."

"And yet," Kenna said, "it seems as if things are so much more complicated than just that one man." She looked at the floor and blanked her expression, then looked up at Cecelia. "I know about the Rosenbergs and how they have your child captive. They won't let you see her, right?"

That was something Kenna needed clarity on.

Cecelia nodded, soaking up the sympathy. "It's been... years." She even choked on the last word.

"I know you were raised as one of them, and I know that given your mother's choices, you would never be a full-blood member of the family. I can't even imagine everything you've been through." A pause. "Having them take her away from you and not knowing when you would ever see her again."

Let her think that Kenna was only in this for the sake of saving the life of a child. Something that was entirely on brand for her.

But this justice wasn't about freeing Lydia.

It was about bringing down all of them.

Cecelia let out a tight breath. "Let me guess, they probably asked you for a favor?"

"You must be causing them enough problems that you're hindering their plans. They want you shut down."

"What about Walker?"

So she figured that Kenna knew the man they had in custody was Cecelia's half-brother. Or at least that they were personally connected.

"Georgia didn't mention him," Kenna said. "The focus was taking you down. You're so much more of an integral part of what they have going on. Walker is more like a foot soldier type, right? As Assistant Special Agent in Charge, you have much more power. That makes you a bigger threat to them."

Cecelia turned and sat on the edge of the table, her body language closing in on itself. Trying to seem diminished instead of strong—the victim in this instead of the perpetrator. "I don't even know what I would say to her if I got her back. What must she think of me?" She glanced at Kenna, tears in her eyes.

"Why did you come here today?" Kenna asked. "It only puts you on their radar."

Maybe she planned to take Walker so that she could let him go somewhere else and tell everyone he escaped.

"I still care about him," Cecelia replied, "even after everything he's done. Justice needs to be served, but I wanted to make sure he's not mistreated."

Kenna nodded. "He hasn't told us anything. I don't know if he's even prepared to testify against the family. But I just can't allow people to continue holding a young girl captive and raising her in a cage." She hoped she didn't lay it on too thick, but Cecelia was enough of a narcissist she might not notice.

"You don't even know the half of what they are capable of." Cecelia sighed. "Or all the things they have going on."

But she wasn't going to share? That was a shame.

"Help me take them down," Kenna said. "Give me what I need to fracture their organization all the way to the center.

That way they'll never recover from the blow and you will be free. You'll know you were the one that hurt them."

Cecelia let out a long sigh as if thinking it over.

"They've been one step ahead of me this entire time," Kenna continued. "Sending their military guys to kill Noelle, and make that mess look like a bank robbery. Ordering Officer Paige to kill me and then taking him out when he failed to finish the job...and who-knows-what-else." Maybe Cecelia wanted to believe that Kenna thought she'd been feeding information. Helping Kenna out in her investigation. "I couldn't believe it when I saw the pictures of your little girl. She's beautiful, and the minute I saw those pictures, I knew I had to help her. I didn't even know she was yours."

"Now you know why I'm so motivated to ensure there is not so much fallout that we all go down along with them."

"You think they'll try to take us all with them?" Kenna asked.

Cecelia nodded, her dark expression earnest. As if she actually believed what she was saying. Maybe there was enough of a glimmer of truth in it that she could. "Definitely. None of us are safe if we start to make moves to shut them down. That's why they've been able to continue for so long. Acting without impunity. As if they were the ones with all the power."

As far as Kenna could see, Cecelia was the one who desperately wanted the power.

"We could work together," Kenna suggested. "Make sure they get shut down for good. Protect each other's backs so that neither of us is hit too hard by the backlash."

"Work together."

"There's no way I could do what they want when there is an innocent child in the mix. Lydia is the most important part of this." Kenna could say it because she honestly did believe that was true. It was just not the most pertinent thing right now. She didn't actually believe that Cecelia would team up and help her to take down the Rosenbergs, at least not without figuring out that Kenna would eventually do the same to take her down.

But she'd believe that Kenna might decide not to care about the consequences or the fallout for the sake of a child.

Kenna didn't like leveraging her care for an innocent life in this way. But faced with the overwhelming force of a toxic family and all the parts and pieces of what they had established over the years working outside the law, she was prepared to risk more than usual in order to end this.

"I'd like to talk to Walter."

Interesting that she used her brother's given name, not his alias. "Let's go see him."

Kenna led her out to the office again, and around the corner to where the cell was located. Jax came over while Cecelia closed the gap between her and her brother's cell. Kenna wouldn't be entirely surprised if the woman pulled out a gun and killed him. They just had to trust that wasn't her plan.

Jax said, "I convinced them all to go to breakfast while we sort out this turf war."

Kenna noticed that the FBI agents Cecelia brought with her were no longer in the room. "Bracken?"

"She's on the phone with my supervisor, confirming the transfer."

Kenna opened her mouth to respond, but a yell cut her off.

"Get out!" Walker was on his feet, close to the cell bars.

"I just want to talk to you." Cecelia even sounded sympathetic, upset that her brother was in this situation.

"They'll kill us both and keep her." Walker's voice rose to a roar. "You should never have come here."

Cecelia turned to Kenna, swiping a tear from under her eye. She said nothing, made her way through the office and out the door. As if she were too upset to speak to any of them after that. The insinuation their family would see them being in the same place at the same time as an opportunity to take them both out.

But with the way Cecelia left, she had no fear that a squad of army guys would show up with guns blazing, ready to take them all out.

A second later, her car peeled out of the parking lot.

Kenna turned to Jax and kept her voice low. "Guess that answers my question about sitting down and making a plan. Exchanging some more information."

"She agreed to that?"

Kenna tugged on his arm, leading him away from Walker just in case he could hear their conversation. "She's on board with helping me take the family down. As far as I know, she isn't aware we've been investigating her this whole time."

Jax looked relieved. "Is there a way to turn the tables on both and get this all done in one operation?"

"If we cut off the head, all those army guys will be scattered and we will never understand the extent of their reach. There might even be some who are still trapped and forced to work for them after the fact."

"You want to set them all free?"

He did as well. That wasn't what he was asking. "I want to draw them out and let them know that it's over. And I want to make it big and public."

"Doing it like that increases the risk that the Rosenbergs or Cecelia will be able to skate out from under this. Probably both of them will try to pin it all on the other."

Kenna folded her arms across her chest. "We can't let that happen."

"That just means the plan has to be solid."

"The list of people we can trust with this is short. But it's not just the two of us."

Jax nodded. "We need a place we can control, and a way to draw out Cecelia. You'll have to let Georgia know that we aren't going to take her out. Then they'll send a bunch of army guys to kill us all and Cecelia along with us."

"Walker needs to tell us how far their network spreads. How many military guys who are supposedly deceased or, in fact, still out there."

Once they knew that, they could get on with the plan.

Their best shot at finishing this.

Chapter Thirty-Four

"She's supposed to come out and meet you to talk about ending the family?"

Kenna had explained everything to Jax, but Sheriff Bracken evidently didn't feel like she was close enough in the loop to grasp what was going on. "Yes."

That and Kenna had made sure Georgia would find out they were now working together.

"Risky move."

Jax responded to Bracken's comment by saying, "You can't make an omelet without breaking some eggs."

Kenna snorted. "Isn't that from a movie?"

She moved from her spot looking out the window to the door, twisting the handle and stepping out onto a porch. One house in the long row. Half a dozen dilapidated structures, meant to appear as if they had been here for at least a hundred years. Maybe two at this point in history.

Remnants of some Old West town that had been turned into a tourist spot. One that was supposedly haunted. As if she believed in any of that enough to be suckered into it.

This was just a great out-of-the-way spot where they

could guarantee there would be no civilians at lunchtime on a weekday, when the attraction was closed to the public.

Cecelia hadn't come back to the sheriff's office since she left earlier that morning, supposedly so upset about what her brother had said that she couldn't face anyone. She played the part well.

When Kenna had explained the content of their conversation in the conference room, Jax had said the same about her. She didn't want to be in that league. Kenna would rather be honest and know she operated with integrity than come across as anything close to someone like Cecelia.

Even as a means to an end.

She looked around, but didn't spot Jax at his hiding spot in another of the buildings—a post office across the street. Bracken was at the far end, inside a clothing store. And they weren't the only ones here waiting for Cecelia.

Once they had passed on the information Georgia provided, which was turning out to be useful in opening all kinds of doors, maybe it shouldn't be so surprising how many honorable law enforcement officers showed up. As soon as they found out that Cecelia was in fact the pawn of a powerful family, people either wanted to help her or take her down. No one wanted to stand by and do nothing. Not while the status quo was maintained.

Kenna figured the fact at least some of them wanted to hear her out would mean she wasn't going to be immediately shot the second anything went down.

That was a better group of backup than she could have hoped for.

The only downside was that Sheriff Bracken had insisted she come along. Meanwhile, Walker was back at her department under guard by two deputies and three of Cecelia's agents. Where the others had gone after breakfast was anyone's guess.

But what mattered was that Cecelia had agreed to a meeting.

Kenna's cell phone buzzed. A message from Maizie.

> I should get myself a surveillance drone. I
> don't like being blind.

Kenna didn't blame the girl. Who would? But there was a reason she had to be out of this, apart from using her tech skills to accidentally—on purpose—alert Georgia to what was going on. All so that the Rosenbergs would send an army to take them out.

The last thing she wanted was for Maizie to get on their radar.

A girl with serious tech skills whose life was almost entirely off the grid, with little to no record she had ever really existed. Not to mention all the other things that had been done to her and what that might mean to people like the Rosenbergs. No way was Maizie getting anywhere near this with a live feed or more than one email—message board—or whatever it had been.

The incident commander, a state police captain who insisted on being the boss of this operation got on the radio. "Heads up. We've got one black SUV incoming."

Kenna listened to the radio chatter, but at the end of the day, she was the one who would go out to meet Cecelia on her own. What happened here depended on what Kenna said to her in order to stall her long enough for a team of black ops army guys to show up and try to kill them.

Or so Kenna hoped, anyway.

Cecelia's SUV pulled onto the street and drove slowly down the center lane. The spot where horse and carriage would have traveled years ago, if this were a real town and not just based on one.

Kenna waited by the porch steps, since it was the closest spot to the boardwalk that stretched up and down the row of storefronts on this side. If she had to, she could race away along the raised wooden walk all the way down to where it ended. There she would find cover in the mock cemetery or the church beyond it. Plenty of places to hide that weren't sparsely decorated buildings, some of which had no doors or rear wall.

The fact she was standing in a façade and currently undertaking a façade was not lost on her. There was a whole lot of make-believe going on right now.

The SUV stopped. Cecelia climbed out the passenger side, and two FBI agents exited as well. One from the driver's side and one behind Cecelia.

Kenna said, "Thanks for coming."

Cecelia stayed by the car. "I want them taken down as much as you do."

The two men took up positions, one at the front left corner of the SUV, so he could cover the entire street. The one by Cecelia stood closer, probably to tackle her to the ground as soon as bullets started flying. Did these men even know what all she had done in her career?

They might be complicit in her poison, and yet they might have no idea.

Only time would tell who Cecelia took down with her. After all, she'd learned from the best being raised by that family.

"I've been thinking about Georgia." Kenna didn't say *your mother* just in case Cecelia wanted that kept private from listening ears. "Do you think we could talk to her and perhaps suggest she turn on the rest of them?"

Kenna figured a woman who didn't seem to have entirely toed the line with the family couldn't possibly be one of the key players. Georgia was more like a mid-level associate, someone who would in the end prove to be expendable. But that was after she'd spent a lifetime trying to reinforce her loyalty to the family.

Cecelia shrugged. "It won't do any good coming from me. I've pleaded with her too many times to get away from them, but she never does."

"Is there anything you can think of in her past that would convince her they're only interested in what she can do for them?"

"She lives for what she can do for them." Cecelia ran her tongue across her bottom lip. "I doubt there's any point trying to reverse all the brainwashing."

Kenna hoped that was figurative and not literal. There was far too much about this that she didn't know, and Cecelia had her at a distinct disadvantage. "What about the rest of the family? How many people do we have to worry about, and how are we going to round them all up? Seems like this might be a job for more than just you and me. But who can we trust?"

"I have plenty of people I can trust," Cecelia said. "Like these agents. You just have to inspire loyalty."

Like the Rosenbergs had?

Kenna didn't want to know what narcissistic tricks Cecelia had played on the people who worked for her. She just wanted to get this woman out of the FBI so they could start going in a better direction.

"Maybe you could send me information on all of them," Kenna said. "The ones you know who are part of what they do."

Kenna's earpiece crackled. "Everyone look alive, we have incoming."

She tuned out the conversation from the people scattered around the area and listened to Cecelia instead, concentrating on her part of this operation. "...spread all over. We might even need a multiagency taskforce."

"That's going to be a problem," Kenna said to the cops. She needed some kind of self-serving facial expression. "Unless you can get me signed on as a consultant. Or somehow reinstate my FBI credentials. But I'm sure you could pull off something like that to get me onto the taskforce."

Cecelia smirked. "You let me worry about the details. You just worry about closing the case. That way when it all shakes out, every single one of us comes up smelling like roses. But you and I are going to go far. The president might even give us medals."

Kenna smiled. "I've always wanted to get a medal."

"I think we can work something out," Cecelia said, grinning.

Kenna tuned back in to the chatter in her ears, but it was too late. Vehicles pulled onto the street from both directions, guns already firing. Rifles held out the windows of the pickup trucks that came at them at high speed. She dove back toward the door, twisting and landing awkwardly with her neck at an angle and her elbow tucked under her so that her shoulder pulled too far.

Bullets peppered the side of the building above her.

Cecelia screamed, "Return fire!" and jumped back in the SUV. Which was evidently bulletproof given how she knew to take cover inside a vehicle. Rounds embedded themselves in the sides, front, and back of the SUV.

"Kenna, move."

She didn't think about Jax's order. She just got up and scrambled into the building, shoving the door closed behind her. She drew her weapon, breathing hard.

"All units, move in." The incident commander gave the signal for everyone to emerge from their covered positions and converge on the gunfight erupting in the middle of the street.

No one had so far come out to help the special agents fighting against an overwhelming force of firepower. All of the assailants had dark clothes and helmets, body armor, and high-powered rifles. Whoever set them up had some seriously deep pockets to provide them with this much funding. And then, they drove rusted-out pickup trucks—probably stolen.

Police officers emerged from every corner of the street. Snipers took their positions on upper floors, standing on the balconies holding their weapons aimed at the assailants.

One of the FBI agents was already dead, lying on the ground by the SUV. Cecelia had hunched over, her arms covering her head. The other fired at two assailants coming toward him, until his gun clicked empty.

Before the men could shoot him, the swarm of police officers surrounded everyone. Called for them all to lay down their weapons and raise their hands. The FBI agent never got the chance to reload and start trying to shoot again. The gunmen realized there was nowhere to go except to fight their way out against a force with twice their number.

And no one apparently wanted to die for the Rosenbergs.

It was a smart move, laying down their weapons. Each of them would have to explain their actions to police officers, lawyers, and a judge. Which meant they'd get the chance to tell their own story. Probably for the first time in forever.

Kenna stepped out onto the porch, her gun still in her hand. She held up the other with her palm out even though she had already met each of these officers. They knew not to shoot her. The FBI agent? She wasn't so sure about him.

The fed said, "What's going on?"

Kenna went to the passenger side door. "Maybe Cecelia can tell you."

She reached for the handle and realized too late Cecelia had slid over to the driver's side. The engine revved, and the Assistant Special Agent in Charge hit the gas. Her colleague didn't move out of the way fast enough. She clipped him with the front corner of the SUV as she picked up speed.

State police and gunmen dove out of the way, scrambling to keep from being another victim in her hit-and-run escapade.

Kenna watched her drive away, and several state police officers ran to their vehicles to follow, while the incident commander called out orders in her ear.

Jax stood on the other side of the street, now visible since the SUV sped off. He shook his head. "Are you okay?"

Kenna holstered her weapon. "Did she run because she thinks we're on to her?"

"It was a smart move. But only if she believes we have no shot at finding her."

"That means she has a plan in place to disappear."

Kenna's phone started to ring in her pocket. She slid it out and thumbed across the screen to answer the call. "Yeah, Maizie. What is it?"

"The land around Pahrump, Nevada." She sounded out of breath, almost desperate. "Maybe you could call NORAD. Is it possible to give them an anonymous tip? They can scramble some jets in time to—no, it's picking up speed."

"What are you talking about, Maze?"

Jax came closer, touching her elbow but not saying anything.

"You need to get out of there," Maizie said. "I was thinking about satellite surveillance and looking at the land around Pahrump, trying to distract myself. Trying to figure out if the Rosenbergs had something going on out there and —" She cut herself off. "You all need to start running."

"What's coming?" Kenna asked.

"A shipping container in the middle of nowhere just outside Pahrump suddenly opened and something drove out —like a cross between a truck and a tank. It's something called a precision strike missile? It was on the back. It launched and it's heading right for your location and moving fast. Go! It'll be there in seconds."

Kenna ended the call and turned to Jax. "The Rosenbergs are trying to take us all out. And Cecelia." She grabbed his hand, and they ran together to the incident commander.

"We have intel that a missile is heading our way," Jax said. "We need to clear the area."

The incident commander blinked, was silent for one second, then yelled, "Everyone move out!"

Each of the state police officers grabbed the gunmen and dragged them. Rushing to the vehicles they had parked behind a building on the far side. Or they'd get as close as possible before the missile reached its target.

Jax dragged her left instead of right with everyone else, and she didn't question why he felt the need to find shelter somewhere different. She just kept up with his punishing pace as they tore between buildings, down an alley, and out into the open land.

Seconds later, the missile hit the ground behind them.

Chapter Thirty-Five

Kenna coughed, which hurt. A lot. Then again, she had been shot in the chest—right in her bullet proof vest. Of course it hurt.

A heavy weight crushed her, and she had to get it off or she wasn't going to be able to breathe.

Jax.

She rolled over, still wedged under...a piece of a wall. Everything hurt. She got her knees up, set her feet against the underside of the wall, and kicked it off.

Blue sky glared down at her.

She shielded her face with her hand. Nothing changed. She could still see sky.

Panic raced through her. *My arms.* Kenna got her right hand on the dusty ground by her hip. The other...was pinned under another person.

Each breath came fast and hard, choking her with dust and debris.

Kenna pulled on her arm. Pain screamed through her shoulder and came out of her mouth in a sharp cry. *No, no, no.* Not good. What was—

He moved.

Kenna's eyes rolled back in her head. She slumped back on the ground, breathing hard.

Jax's face swam into view above her. "Kenna? Don't move." Blood ran down his temple, but those blue eyes didn't seem to care.

She wanted to say something, but all she could do was breathe through the pain.

"We need an ambulance." He set his hand on her hip while he looked around.

No. She didn't want to go to the...

Kenna blinked against the harsh light of the sun. No, not the sun. A light on the ceiling in... *a hospital.*

"Hey." He settled next to her, and she fought to focus on his dark features. The dark brown of his eyes. "Jax said you passed out."

Ramon. "Where is he?"

He made a face, mostly displeasure. "Figures you'd ask for him. I just wanted to come by and see if you were okay. He said you dislocated your shoulder, but they put it back in place and you'll heal up just fine. Except for this incurable infatuation for a certain blond special agent."

"Sorry."

His lips curled up. "Don't be. I'm not. It's nice."

"You're lying."

Ramon leaned down and kissed her forehead. "I'm glad you're all right." He got up from the side of her hospital bed and walked toward the door.

"Where are you going?" She craned her neck.

"To tell your hero you're awake."

Kenna didn't know what to say.

"I'm gonna go find Cecelia. Finish this." He grabbed the door handle. "Ozzy is with the spa staff again. Having the time of his life."

"Thanks."

Then he was gone, and the door stood wide open. Not for long, though. Jax came in, a bandage on the side of his face and dirt all over his clothes. But it looked like he'd unbuttoned his collar and washed up with a cloth. Cleaned his face and hands. He'd probably had coffee already.

His expression softened. "Hey."

She took a breath to speak, but had no energy. She could barely put a thought together. Tears stung her eyes, traitorous emotions she didn't want. Hadn't asked for.

Jax leaned over and touched her cheeks, rubbing the curve with his thumbs. "You're okay. Or you will be. We're okay."

She closed her eyes and just memorized the feel of his hands on her cheeks. *Thank You, Lord.*

After she'd absorbed enough of it she could remember it months from now, alone on the road. In the middle of a case. When the nightmares returned...

She opened her eyes. "Tell me what happened?"

Jax set one hand on the other side of her, so he leaned across her. Partially on her hip. Scanning her. With his other hand he touched her shoulder, more gentle than anything she'd ever felt. "How does this feel?"

"Like it should be in excruciating pain, but there's a curious lack of feeling."

"Yeah, it'll hurt later when the meds wear off and you refuse to take anything powerful enough to combat the pain." He gave her a smile that was only a tiny bit exasperated. "I explained your stance on narcotics."

She blinked. "I have a stance?"

"Um...yeah, you do."

Huh.

"You dislocated your shoulder," he said. "One of the state guys is a medic, so he popped it back in while you were out. Figured that was best since the ambulance—even the helicopter—was a half hour out. We had a couple of really badly hurt cops, and one bled out in the sand before the chopper showed up. They did everything they could."

Her heart squeezed in her chest, and she moved her right hand to cover his. "How many are gone?"

"Four, one from the army crew, both of Cecelia's FBI agents, and one state officer. Three more cops are injured."

A single tear escaped from the corner of her eye. "Thank you for staying with me."

He leaned down and kissed her. "Anytime."

Jax looked as reluctant as she was to go their separate ways again. It was only going to get more complicated after this.

"Don't worry about it." He squeezed her hand. "We'll figure it out."

"But first..."

"I know. Cecelia. And the Rosenbergs."

"Are the army guys that were taken into custody talking to the state police?"

He nodded. "Statements are being taken now. They're reluctant, but I explained a few things about you and what we're doing here."

"That we're gunning for all of the people who've kept them under their thumb all this time?"

He nodded again. "I can't believe they had military artillery in Nevada. Everyone watching thought it was a training operation, the chance to respond to suddenly seeing a projectile in the air. They were supposed to let it hit the ground though—and the area should've been deserted according to the military reports. Maizie is still flipping out about it, looking for anywhere else in the country they might be hiding another one of those things. It's insane just thinking about it."

"I need to get out of here." Kenna groaned.

"I know that as well. Just give it a few hours, get checked out one more time before you leave so we don't have to worry about anything else. Okay?"

Well, since he asked like that... "Fine."

He grinned. "That's my girl."

She stared at him, the warmth of that statement filling her in a way that was unexpected. Why did a relationship feel so brand-new when she'd been in a solid one years ago? It shouldn't be so surprising. It should feel familiar, but he put her so off balance she constantly had to struggle to keep a grasp on her equilibrium.

"I want to talk to Walker before my boss takes him back to San Diego." Kenna frowned, and he continued, "ASAC Clarke got here an hour ago. He's setting up the transport with Bracken, pretty sure he took one look at her and fell in love. Antonio might be history."

"Is he okay?" He'd been stabbed the last time she saw him.

"He's out of surgery and recovering. Sounds like Ryson might come down and pay him a visit."

Everything in her tensed. "After we take down the Rosenbergs."

"He knows the risk. He said he'll play it smart."

Whatever that meant. "Are you going with Clarke?"

He stared at her as if he'd heard it in her tone. The *I don't want you to go* mixed with *I don't want to get between you and your job.* "I told him I should stay here and finish this, because it's important to me. He told me not to mess with the Rosenbergs, but that he wasn't surprised to hear you were in the middle of a shot at bringing them down."

She wasn't sure what she had at this point. Fragments of a case she needed to stitch together. "Walker is probably our best shot. Cecelia ran off, right?"

Jax nodded. "Got in her SUV and took off."

Kenna's mind insisted on replaying images of her hitting a man with the vehicle as she sped away. "We need to find her."

"We will. *After* you're cleared to leave here."

Kenna pressed her lips together.

"Then it'll be nothin' but coffee and catching bad guys."

She smiled. "Go tell the doc I'm awake."

An excruciatingly long three hours later, they got to the sheriff's office, which had more cars parked outside than Kenna figured were even registered in this town. It seemed like half of law enforcement in the Southwest had converged on this tiny town.

Jax put the truck in Park. "We should hit the resort at some point. Grab our stuff and check out. No sense paying the bill if we're not even there."

"Even if we'd rather be."

Jax twisted in his seat. "Really?"

She didn't need to get into another conversation about the courthouse, but she was injured. "My arm is in a sling. I'm dragging, running on no sleep like you. Trying to puzzle this out when half my brain cells disappeared while I was unconscious."

"That's the beauty of backup. FBI. State police. Bracken and her people. It's not just you, or only us working this. It's a whole team." He squeezed her knee. "And when it's done, you can sleep for a whole day. Eat a cheeseburger. Drink a pot of coffee. Jump in your RV and hit the road."

"You make it sound like I'm boring. Or at least easy to figure out."

"Trust me." He leaned over. "There's nothing easy about you." He grabbed the handle on his side and pushed the door open. "Good thing I like a challenge."

Kenna didn't even know what to say to that. He was out of earshot anyway, rounding the hood of the fancy truck he wanted enough to borrow it from a friend. She used her good arm to open her door. The other was confined to a sling, which was a good idea. Keeping the weight off hurt less. She wanted to remember it was injured so she hadn't taken anything yet. But she would. She had a feeling her shoulder situation would quickly settle into *blinding* pain. She wouldn't be able to do anything but get horizontal and cry through it.

No, thanks.

Things to do. Cases to solve.

"You were supposed to let me open that."

Kenna turned on the seat. "I'd say you can help me down, but my legs work just fine." She grabbed the handle on the door and swung down. Her Converse hit the ground, and the impact jarred her shoulder. She groaned. "Great. It's great. Feels so good."

"I can see that."

She shot him a look. "Don't tell anyone I'm hurt."

"Pretty sure it's obvious from the sling."

"I sprained my wrist."

"I'm not going to lie."

"Then do me a favor and keep your mouth shut."

Jax pulled open the door, grinning.

"This isn't funny."

Bracken looked up from the front counter. "What isn't funny?" She took in Jax and Kenna. "Huh, you guys look like you got blown up. Or you walked through a dust storm."

Meanwhile, the sheriff appeared to have taken a shower and changed clothes. Because of the handsome older FBI agent who walked up behind her?

"Jaxton." ASAC Clarke nodded.

Jax nodded back. "Sir. This is Kenna Banbury."

Clarke looked at her. "You look like you need some coffee."

Jax barked a laugh.

Bart. Kenna turned to face Jax. "What happened to Stairns in Pahrump?"

"Let's find you a chair." He led her around the counter. "He told Maizie this morning he's pretty much proven it couldn't have been Bartholomew who shot Paige, so he'll be released once the judge signs off on it. After that, the cops can figure out who else to frame."

"Excuse me?" Bracken wheeled over a chair.

"Different town." Jax pulled out a chair for Kenna, who sat by an empty desk.

Clarke set a mug of coffee by her elbow. "The deputy is bringing out Walker."

"Thanks." Kenna grabbed the mug handle, taking a moment to assess Jax's boss. His supervisor. Not good-looking, but he dressed nicely. His dark-gray hair had a natural wave to it. Didn't look styled, it just lay that way. Kept himself in shape, but not obsessively, and he worked behind a desk.

Caved when leaned on, pressured by up high.

The three of them sat, Jax closest to her but back to professional distance. Clarke on the edge of a desk. Bracken in a chair with her iPad, tapping the screen. Walker was led into the main room by a different deputy, hands and feet cuffed with a chain linking them. He shuffled across the room, and the deputy found him a chair. No one offered to uncuff him.

"So they have missiles?" She sipped her coffee.

Walker stared at her. "What do I know? I'm a serial killer."

"Yeah, that never jived." And she wasn't leading this interview.

Jax cleared his throat. "You work for the Rosenbergs. Your family. You have this whole time, even when you were in Mexico with those guys."

"Only people I ever knew said no and lived." Walker sniffed.

"Because they fled south of the border?" Jax said.

"It's looking appealing as a tactic."

Kenna could see how that was true. She wouldn't mind a warm place and a nice beach right about now. "You want out."

Walker nodded.

Clarke said, "Then tell us what we need to know. Because some of the people here are crazy enough to go up against them."

Walker looked at her, and Jax. His face remained impassive. Even with the jumpsuit and the cuffs, he carried the same weighty presence as before. There was nothing diminished about him. He was a Rosenberg and he always would be, no matter what happened next.

Finally he said, "Lydia needs to be taken care of."

The way he said it, Kenna wasn't sure precisely what he meant by that. Whether he wanted her to get help, or if this was more of a *take care of her* mafia-style. Save everyone in the world the trauma of whatever Lydia Rosenberg did when she grew up.

As if Kenna would sanction the murder of a child. Even if she proved to be mentally disturbed enough that she'd likely grow up to be a killer. Kenna was in no way qualified to make that assessment. "I'll get her the help she needs."

That was all she was prepared to promise, and hopefully that was what he'd meant.

Walker nodded. "Fine." He looked at Clarke. "I'll tell you whatever you want to know."

Clarke got a voice recorder from the desk beside him. "Names. Dates. Things you've witnessed. Anything you can prove with evidence. Holdings. Land they own. Houses. Assets. People who do their dirty work. Sympathetic figures planted in key positions they lean on to get things done." He glanced at Kenna and Jax. "Anything I'm missing?"

She had her mug to her lips, so couldn't shake her head.

Jax said, "Just a focus on—"

The window across the room shattered. Walker's body jerked as a bullet entered his head. At the same moment a splash of coffee, hit Kenna's lap and she cried out. Then again when Jax dragged her to the floor and covered her with his body.

"One shot." She tried to think around the pain in her shoulder.

Clarke said, "Looks like someone is fighting the shooter," calling over to them from the other side of the room. Beside the window where he could see out. "It's clear."

Jax helped her up. It still hurt, but he was considerate about it. Kenna headed for the door and pushed all thought from her mind to keep from thinking about the pain. Outside. Way too warm, but her body was chilled. The warmth of the sun on her actually felt good. See—she needed a beach.

They walked around the building to the rear lot. The street behind the sheriff's department building had sparse traffic in both directions. Short trees that barely reached the first floor of the buildings. Storefronts. Independent small businesses, coffee shops, and gift stores. A little grocery probably struggling for business against the huge chain store a few miles away.

"There." Jax pointed to the roof of one of the buildings. "Stay here." He pulled his gun and ran into the street, weaving between cars.

She held her breath.

Someone honked.

Jax reached the sidewalk on the other side, and she let out the air she'd been holding. On the roof where he'd pointed, a man wrestling with a tall woman, both of them dark-haired. Fighting viciously for their lives.

Ramon and Cecelia.

But which one of them had been the shooter?

As Kenna watched, they grappled with each other. A rifle still sat perched on the edge of the roof. The origin of the shot that had taken Walker's life. Just like Paige. Another person cut short because someone else had been so determined to silence them.

Ramon turned to something out of sight.

Kenna raised her good hand and shielded her eyes from the sun. Cecelia took the opportunity and kicked his leg from behind. Ramon retaliated, shoving her away from him so that she stumbled backward.

And then disappeared out of sight.

Jax came into view, running to the spot where she disappeared. He looked down. Over the edge?

Cecelia had fallen.

Kenna hit the button for the crosswalk, then rushed to the other side the second it turned green. The corner of the building where Cecelia had perched to shoot her half-brother had a fire hydrant. A Closed For Business sign in the window —permanently closed, so it looked.

She sprinted around the corner, hugging her left arm to her body.

An alley stretched out in front of her. Couple overflowing trash dumps, bags on the ground and stacked to the lip of the dumpsters. Cecelia lay on the ground, unmoving.

Kenna strode slowly to her, just to be sure. But there was no mistaking this. For Cecelia, there would be no more chances. It was over.

Jax touched her hip, breathing hard from his sprint up to the roof and then back down.

Kenna swallowed. "She's gone."

Chapter Thirty-Six

"**Y**ou need to sit down."

Despite the fact Jax's words were true, she didn't want to agree with them. He pulled the door open for her, and she stepped back into the sheriff's office. As if being in here was any safer than being outside at this point.

Bracken stood up, pulling off plastic gloves. "He's dead."

"Sir," Jax told Clarke, "Cecelia Warren is dead in an alley across the street."

The sheriff glanced at Clarke, who straightened out of his crouch. "I'll go secure the scene."

Someone should help her. Clarke slumped into a chair. Maybe Jax would go with her, though he'd been more concerned with getting Kenna back here. Cecelia wasn't going to get any deader.

Where had Ramon gone? Kenna really did need that chair.

Clarke seemed to need a minute to absorb this information, and the latest turn of events. "You caught the shooter?"

"Yeah, they did."

Kenna and Jax both spun around. Ramon stood in the doorway, but he didn't look at them.

Instead, he said, "I'm turning myself in. I want to testify against all of them, and the Rosenbergs."

Clarke pulled his gun from the holster on his belt.

"He isn't dangerous, sir." Kenna didn't want to see another dead body today. There had been more than enough. It wasn't about Ramon possibly having a thread of good in him, along with a wash of bad, giving him that gray-area outlook he had on life.

She just wasn't sure if his life was a product of the outlook, or if he'd crafted the outlook after everything that'd happened in his life.

"That remains to be seen," Clarke said. "I know exactly who this is." He turned to Ramon. "Hands on your head."

Even Ramon didn't seem to agree with her assessment of him.

"Why come in now?" Kenna sank into a chair.

"I don't want Walker's death pinned on me when Cecelia is the one who shot him."

Jax eyed him. "Can anyone corroborate that?"

Ramon lifted his chin. "Left front pocket, there's a phone. It's clearly Cecelia's, and she uses it for more than just FBI business."

Clarke said, "Keep your hands where they are," and fished out the phone, which he tossed to Jax. "See what we can do with that. And make sure it's logged, whatever it is."

"Yes, sir." Jax hit the button on the side of the phone. "Sheriff Bracken probably has a setup here to access a phone admitted as evidence."

Kenna leaned her head back against the chair as Clarke patted Ramon down, making sure he had no weapons. Hand by hand, he got Ramon secured in the cuffs. All the while, the dark-haired man watched her.

His face impassive.

What are you doing?

He would never be off the Rosenbergs' radar doing this. They'd know where to find him any minute of any day, given the fact that as soon as Clarke got it all straightened out, Ramon would be hauled in front of a judge the first chance they got.

Ramon would be lucky if he didn't get life in prison.

The disgraced FBI agent finally caught, but only because he turned himself in. Charged with the murder of another FBI agent.

He couldn't have turned himself in because he felt bad for killing her, could he?

She didn't understand this guy at all. But then, she didn't need to. She'd done what she set out to do, and he now had the chance to tell his story. "Cecelia isn't going to be mourned as a hero. Too many people witnessed her actions in that ghost town, and many other times. There's no way they'll be able to sweep this under the rug."

"It's over." Ramon looked away.

"But it isn't when the Rosenbergs have access to military armaments they'll use whenever they want, and they think they can get away with it."

He didn't even shrug. "I say what I want to say. That's it."

"You think you have no choice but to give a statement, and whether anyone believes it or not doesn't matter. You think they'll come after you and put a bullet in your head?" Kenna said. "Those military guys are done. We have them all in custody, giving statements."

"You think the Rosenbergs can't take out a hit on someone because their special squad got decimated?"

"I think you're gambling too much on what you think is a certainty and not leaving room for any other options."

Ramon stared at her.

"There's hope. Even on the darkest night, in the worst situation." Even Clarke stared at her now. Jax, too, probably. But she couldn't see him without looking around and she needed Ramon to see the confidence she had. "There's *always* hope."

He knew what she'd been through. What she managed to survive. Now she had a different perspective on it all, but even back then, she'd had reason to live. Bradley had lost hope, which led to him losing his life.

Never say never, but she didn't believe Jax would ever let himself get to that point. He was a different guy than Bradley had been. Kenna would've lived her life happy with her choice, raising a family with her partner. But that dream all died in one night.

Now she had Jax, determined to stand by her side. Support her. What was it that the Bible said? *Dwell with her with understanding.* If anyone knew how to do that with her, it was Jax.

He just seemed to...get it.

She wanted to repay that favor more than anything. To always be there to stand by his side and fight whatever battle he thought was important enough to risk it all.

Ramon shrugged. "I guess we'll find out."

Kenna watched him, trying to figure out what to say. Her phone rang, the number for the resort. "Hello?"

"Mrs. Hawthorne? This is Brian from the Willowbrooke Resort and Spa. I'm sorry to inform you that we've had an incident with your dog. I'm so sorry..." He sniffed. "It seems as though someone has checked little Ozzy out of the spa. The staff were confused because Ozzy seemed so happy to see him. They let him take your dog, I'm afraid."

"Someone checked him out?"

"Our surveillance was down at the time," Brian said. "We're not sure why. It seems as if a nice young man collected Ozzy and then simply...disappeared. I'm so sorry that—"

"Thanks for letting me know," Kenna cut in. "I'll call you back, or I'll be there soon."

Brian sputtered. Kenna hung up on him.

"What was that?"

She turned her chair to face Jax, on a computer across the room. "Someone checked out Ozzy and took him."

Jax frowned for a second, and then said, "Ah."

"What?"

"I might know who that was." He winced. "But he's not supposed to be roaming around doing whatever he wants. The state police were supposed to pick up Noelle's husband and bring him to their office to take a statement. I'll call them, but I bet he gave them the slip."

"That doesn't sound good." Kenna frowned.

"The Staties in Alaska haven't even confirmed the guy up there exists."

"If I was a recently widowed guy just out of prison who loved my wife's dog, where would I go?" she wondered aloud.

"To get the dog," Jax said.

"But where would I go *after* that?" She stared at the door for a second.

He didn't walk in the way Ramon had and turn himself in, so staring didn't work. But it was worth a try.

She sidestepped her feet on the floor, turning to see Ramon and Clarke in the corner, talking. Clarke had an iPad, recording his words or typing the statement in. Walker's body lay on the floor between her and the window.

She kept turning, past the empty doorway.

Back to Jax.

Then she pulled her feet up to the chair, her knees bent in front of her. A second later, Kenna reached out and grabbed the desk phone. She dialed an internet-based number that no one would be able to trace. That number rerouted to another number, which rang on the landline phone beside Maizie's computer.

"If you're calling me, then you're not dead."

"I'm not," Kenna said. "But only just."

Maizie made a choking sound. "Who is?"

"Walker and Cecelia. Some cops. Gunmen. A couple of FBI agents." That probably wouldn't be all of it by the end of this.

"What do you need?" Maizie asked.

"A lead on where Noelle's husband might go?"

Jax called over from the other side of the room. "Could've just asked me."

"You missed me," Maizie said. "You didn't think I had anything for you."

Kenna sighed. "My shoulder hurts. I called so I can be irritated at you and not take it out only on Jax." He grinned but didn't take his focus from the computer screen. Did he have something from Cecelia's phone?

"Where's Ramon?" Maizie asked.

"Here. Helping." Kenna glanced over. "Better than being dead on the street. It's far more efficient to die in the proximity of law enforcement. Much less paperwork."

"Will Noelle's husband come after him?"

Kenna lowered the phone from her mouth and asked Jax, "Where's the rifle used to shoot Walker?"

"The deputy secured the scene."

Hopefully, if someone else showed up for a hit, he or

Bracken would notice and take care of it before it happened. Her instinct wasn't currently trying to tell her there was immediate danger. But given what had happened today, maybe that electrical impulse was fried right now. She'd have to rely on discernment from the Lord because she had nothing else to draw from.

Not a bad deal at all.

Maizie said, "We have everything on Cecelia, so people will know the truth. You just said Walker is dead, right? So the FBI doesn't have to worry about him. Georgia Rosenberg got what she wanted."

Kenna couldn't argue with any of that. "They'll rebuild. We put a dent in their operation at best."

A family like the Rosenbergs would have contingencies. Ways to bury even the most public scandals. She wouldn't be surprised if Georgia followed through with her threat and Jax got fired even after he solved several cases today and exposed the truth of Cecelia Warren's actions.

"Except for one teeny thing," Maizie said.

Kenna frowned. "What did you find?"

"Another container with a precision strike missile inside. I'm pretty sure. It's in South Dakota, on land they've owned as long as they've owned the acreage around Pahrump. Town under their thumb. The sheriff has been in that position for fifty years. Every year, he goes on a monthlong cruise with his wife, their kids, their families, and some friends. And not one of those cost-effective cruises in the Caribbean. I mean, the ones on the Mediterranean where it's like five grand a person."

Kenna whistled. "On the take much?"

"He's not even hiding it. Anyone runs against him, they suddenly change their mind before election day. Some of them even disappear."

"So what are we doing about it?" As much as she wanted to jump in her RV and go fight a new battle in South Dakota, she needed to sleep first. And let her shoulder heal.

"A strategic tip to the Army Corps of Engineers and the South Dakota National Guard with satellite photos showing specific materials under the surface," Maizie said. "Given the outlines, it's pretty obvious there's something down there. Where there definitely shouldn't be something."

"These people are unbelievable." Kenna shook her head. But she had to add, "Thanks for taking care of it."

"I also called some news outlets. No way will they be able to squash this."

"You're the best, Maze."

"I should get a pay raise."

Kenna smiled. "Deal."

"Wow, I wasn't sure that would work. It's just..." Maizie hesitated. "I think I'm gonna enroll in school. Online, of course. Get my GED and then a college degree."

"You're already smart enough. You don't need to prove it to anyone."

"But if I want to get a good job in a few years, I'll need qualifications."

"You're quitting?"

"No." Maizie chuckled. "I'm just thinking about the future, that's all."

Seemed like that was going around.

"I might want to leave this trailer at some point. Venture out into the world."

"I'm available if you need a bodyguard."

Maizie chuckled again. "I just might take you up on that."

Jax sat back in the chair. Kenna said, "Gotta go."

"Love you."

Kenna swallowed past the lump in her throat. "Love you

too, kiddo." She set the phone back on its cradle and asked Jax, "Got something?"

He nodded. "Cecelia has a back door into the whole Rosenberg operation."

Chapter Thirty-Seven

"In national news this week, headlines hit the world of a deep conspiracy embedded in the heart of US politics."

Kenna set the knife down and turned on the water, washing her hands while she listened to the unnecessarily good-looking talking head on the TV.

"We go now to Massachusetts to hear from our local correspondent on this breaking story."

The image switched to another good-looking woman, this one a brunette who stood in front of an expansive lawn. Behind her was a *Jane Austen*-worthy mansion, all brick and manicured landscaping.

"Thank you, Janice. I'm here in front of the Rosenberg family home just outside Shrewsbury, Massachusetts, where this week federal agents from several bureaus converged with search warrants on every property belonging to the family. For generations, the Rosenbergs have been at the heart of politics, with their foundation providing cookie-cutter bills to states and their influence in Washington, DC."

She turned slightly, motioning to the house. "Behind these upper-class doors, the Rosenbergs curried favors, made deals, and lived a life of privilege and debauchery. Their connection to the deceased Assistant Special Agent in Charge of the FBI's Phoenix office is said to have rocked the Department of Justice, many of whom were in talks to support Cecelia Warren for the position of head of the FBI's Washington D.C. office. The jump in position would have only increased the Rosenbergs' influence in areas of power throughout this country and overseas."

Kenna dumped the meat on the cutting board into a dog bowl, then poured herself more coffee. The clock on the microwave said it was barely past six in the morning.

The reporter continued, "Law enforcement has arrested several members of the family and seized all assets. It is my belief that the fallout of this investigation won't be truly understood for a long time. Perhaps even years to come."

On the TV, the feed switched back to the studio. The anchor said, "No doubt we will learn everything this family was involved with in time."

The on-scene reporter nodded. "So far, only some details have been released, but it's not looking good for them."

Kenna said, "No one likes corruption. Only those who have another way to get stuff done will let it be exposed." She might be cynical about this, but there would be a lot of unhappy people in the country now. The status quo had been upset. But somewhere, someone was entirely satisfied that things were going just as planned.

It remained to be seen who would seize the vacuum in power—and what they intended to do with that influence.

The news anchor said, "We go now to a live look at a press conference at the Phoenix office of the FBI."

Kenna said, "Here he is."

A scratch at the door to her RV drew her attention. She opened the door far enough Cabot could hop up into her rig. Kenna set the bowl of food on the floor and drank her coffee while the mutt ate breakfast.

"Thank you, ladies and gentlemen." It wasn't Jax. It was Clarke. "We appreciate your patience as we explain the enormity of this case and ask that you hold your questions." He paused a second. "For the last several months, the FBI has been investigating corruption in our own department. In our effort to root out what we consider a disgrace to the oath every one of our agents has sworn, we discovered that Cecelia Warren was in fact connected to a man we were also investigating. Both this dangerous killer and Ms. Warren were killed in the same day, and a formerly disgraced FBI agent has sworn a statement that righted an egregious wrong.

"As the FBI dug to the truth, it became clear that at the heart of this case was a powerful family who has been directing US politics and policy for some time. If not for generations. The use of munitions on US soil directed at law enforcement personnel was not taken lightly. I'll pass the mic to my colleague who spearheaded this investigation."

"Thank you, sir." Jax switched places with him. "The FBI's mission to protect the American people and uphold the Constitution meant that we could not stand idly by understanding there was a poison in our bureau, and a much greater one in this great nation. We appreciate everyone's patience while we thoroughly investigate the full extent of their network, and we will no doubt continue to bring charges against key players in the coming days. We would like to thank our agents who have proven themselves above and beyond, to the state police in Arizona, and our consultant, without whom this case would not have been solved."

The crowd of reporters erupted into questions.

Clarke moved back to stand by Jax again. "One more thing." He looked pleased with himself. "The FBI would like to announce the promotion of Special Agent Oliver Jaxton to the position of Special Agent in Charge of the Phoenix FBI office."

Everyone applauded.

Kenna smiled so wide her cheeks hurt. "Good for you. But that's a desk job." She chuckled to herself, alone in her RV except for Cabot now licking out her bowl.

The news report continued.

Kenna stepped outside, and Cabot hopped down after her, looking spry despite a hard life and getting up there in age. "Bodes well for the rest of us."

She let the door snap back on its hinges and looked at the mountains, great rich forest-green peaks that reached for the sky. Along the bottom hung a layer of mist, adding an eerie note to the early morning hour. A fire crackled and snapped in the pit in the center of a circle of chairs.

One occupant.

Maizie's Airstream to her left, set back farther than her RV. The main cabin where Stairns and his wife lived to the right. Cows on the neighbor's field.

A faint scent of smoke in the air.

She wandered to the chairs and kicked the back of the occupied one.

Ramon sputtered awake, shoving back the hood of his sweater. "What is it?"

"Coffee is done." She slid into a seat beside him. "Get it yourself." She saw a flash of teeth in his grin out the corner of her eye and sipped her coffee.

"Please tell me there's gonna be a case soon. I'm going crazy."

"You're resting. It's called a *vacation*." She motioned to him with her mug, careful not to spill it. "You should've taken that job at the FBI."

Ramon snorted. "And have to go through all the psych evals? No way." He lifted his hands to the heat of the fire. "I'm freelance."

"There's a terrifying thought."

"What?" he said. "It works for you."

"You want me to train you as a private investigator? Someone has to sign off on the hours." Might as well be her. Assuming if she decided it wasn't a good idea, he would listen and find something else to do.

"Maybe." He glanced around. "I see why you like it here."

"It's not just here. It's the whole world," Kenna said. "It just feels different when you're free."

The door to the Airstream swung open, and Maizie stuck her head out. "I figured you guys would be up." The teen probably hadn't slept yet.

"What have you got?" Kenna asked.

Ramon was about to jump out of his chair.

Maizie smiled. "I think I have a case."

Keep Reading For...

- Where to find more great Lisa Phillips books.

- How to sign up for Lisa's newsletter and get a FREE book.

- Where to find Lisa on social media.

About the Author

Find out more about Lisa Phillips at her website, where you'll discover more romantic suspense fan-favorite series and heart-pounding thriller novels.
https://authorlisaphillips.com/

If you loved this book, please consider sharing about it on social media. Or leave a review at your book retailer website, on Goodreads, or on Bookbub. Your review will help others find great books to entertain and encourage them!

For a FREE novel from Lisa Phillips, scan the QR code below to connect to Lisa's newsletter and be the first to hear about sales, new books, and recommendations for your TBR pile.

Find Lisa on Social Media!

facebook.com/authorlisaphillips

instagram.com/lisaphillipsbks

bookbub.com/authors/lisa-phillips

Also by Lisa Phillips

Find out more about Brand of Justice at my website:

https://authorlisaphillips.com/product-tag/brand-of-justice/

Book 1: Cold Dead Night

Book 2: Burn the Dawn

Book 3: Quick and Dead

Book 4: Over the Limit

Book 5: Skin and Bone

Book 6: Dust and Ashes

Book 7: Long Road Home

Book 8 : Dead to Rights

Book 9: Fear No Evil (November 2024)

———

Other series by Lisa:

Last Chance Downrange

Chevalier Protection Specialists

Last Chance County

Northwest Counter-Terrorism Taskforce

Double Down

WITSEC Town (Sanctuary)

Numerous other titles including several with *Love Inspired Suspense*, find the complete list here (or scan the QR code):

https://authorlisaphillips.com/all-books/